Sorrow Without End

Also by Priscilla J. Royal
Tyrant of the Mind
Wine of Violence

To receive a free catalog of Poisoned Pen Press titles, please contact us in one of the following ways:

Phone: 1-800-421-3976
Facsimile: 1-480-949-1707
E-mail: info@poisonedpenpress.com
Website: www.poisonedpenpress.com

Poisoned Pen Press
6962 E. First Ave. Ste. 103
Scottsdale, AZ 85251

Sorrow Without End

Priscilla J. Royal

Poisoned Pen Press

Copyright © 2006 by Priscilla J. Royal

First Trade Paperback Edition 2007

10 9 8 7 6 5 4 3 2 1

Library of Congress Catalog Card Number: 2005928746

ISBN: 978-1-59058-332-6

Poisoned Pen Press
6962 E. First Ave., Ste. 103
Scottsdale, AZ 85251
www.poisonedpenpress.com
info@poisonedpenpress.com

Printed in the United States of America

"Once to die is better than length of days
in sorrow without end."

Aeschylus, *Prometheus Bound*, 1.750-1
From Chambers *Dictionary of Quotations,*
translator unknown

To Katherine V. Forrest, Judy Greber (Gillian Roberts), Michael Nava, Katherine Neville, and Sarah Smith. Thank you for all you taught me in class and continue to teach me through your books.

Acknowledgments

California Writers Club, Bonnie DeClark, the staff of Poisoned Pen Press, Peter Goodhugh, Charles L. Juricek DVM, Ed Kaufman of M is for Mystery in San Mateo CA, Henie Lentz, Dianne Levy, Anne Maczulak, Barbara Peters of Poisoned Pen Bookstore in Scottsdale AZ, Sheldon Siegel, Luisa Smith at Book Passage in Corte Madera CA, Lyn and Michael Speakman, Meg Stiefvater, Janet Wallace.

Chapter One

Where was he? He rubbed his face, then stared at his hand. It was wet. Had he been weeping?

The man from Acre looked up, narrowing his eyes as the sky dissolved into a gray, pelting downpour. It must be God shedding the tears.

As he watched the dark trees, he shivered. Their branches bent like the bows of archers. This rain was unlike anything he remembered. The drops stung his face like grit from a dust storm in Outremer. Was England not a Christian land? He should not feel so much pain so close to home.

Just before he rounded a bend in the road, a gust of wind howled about his ears. Was that the cry of some hell-bound soul? He looked behind, then, seeing nothing, turned again. If that sound had risen from one soul in Satan's claws, perhaps another would soon be added.

The soldier was not far ahead of him, alone, walking slowly and hunched against the force of the blinding rain.

Had the time come at last? He swallowed, savoring the possibility. How often he had hoped for this moment from the day the soldier had decided to join the same large company travelling toward Norwich from the coast. Eventually, he knew that he and the man would have to take the same route homeward, even if few others were travelling in that direction. Thus he had not grown impatient, believing that either God or Satan would give the soldier into his hands when the time was right.

From the day he had boarded that ship from Acre, he had taken care never to let anyone see his features, wrapping a cloth around his face to hide all but his eyes. No one knew that he was the man who should have died in Outremer. Indeed, he looked much like an infidel, or even a leper not yet forced to carry the warning clapper. Many had avoided him out of fear. This had pleased him. He did not want their company.

By the time they had reached the village inn at Tyndal, the crowd of fellow travelers had thinned, many taking the road to Norwich and the shrine of Saint William. A few, the soldier and he among them, had stopped to rest a day or so. To avoid curious eyes, he had kept to his room, yet watched from his window lest the man leave without his notice.

He had followed him yesterday when, despite the chill squalls, the soldier had gone to the village market day. He knew the man would. With the bad weather, there were few customers and many merchants eager to sell at cost. Like any good predator, this soldier had always known when the prey was most vulnerable.

Having no desire to harm an innocent man, he had also wanted to make sure the soldier should be his target. Memory was ever a faithless whore, but he no longer had any doubt. Other crusaders might bear the red cross. No one else could have that face.

He had slipped from the inn to follow the soldier, taking some small pleasure in stalking him like he might a wild boar. He could see the man's brown teeth poking at odd angles through thin lips that could not quite close, his face framed by sparse, pale hair. As he stared at those close-set eyes and the flattened nose, he had begun to sweat despite the chilling dampness of the East Anglian autumn. He might have been the hunter in this mortal game, but he also felt the numbing terror of a condemned man facing the hangman.

As he stood on a small rise overlooking Tyndal's market booths, he had crossed himself. "Haven't I suffered enough for my sins?" he had whispered into the wind, but a heavy cloak of silence descended upon him. God, it seemed, had turned His back on his yelping prayers.

Even then he might have turned aside from his purpose, he thought. He could have left the man alone, hoping that someday God would kick this man's soul like a boy would a rock. He might have, that is, until the soldier laughed.

That laugh! He stopped suddenly, pressing his white-knuckled fists against his closed eyes until he saw sparks of sharp light. In dreams that sound had flowed over him, drenching him in burning sweat even on nights when the frosty air turned his eyebrows brittle white. Nor had he been safe from it when he had knelt, moaning to God for respite. Even then, the man's mocking laugh would besiege him like a flock of cawing ravens, leaving him to twitch on the ground, a lunatic in the full face of the cold moon.

He swallowed to keep from choking, then began walking once more against the wind while he clutched at the hilt of his knife. Perhaps he should no longer care why God had chosen, not to honor him for his acts of faith in Outremer, but to burn his soul into charcoal, shattering it into countless specks of dying ash. The only thing that mattered, after all, was what lay in those ashes with his soul.

Even with his eyes tightly shut, the vision was seared into the black curtain of his lids. The woman lay on her back, her naked body streaked with glittering dust from Acre's hot earth. Was he still looking down at her, her legs splayed obscenely as if begging a lover to pleasure her? When she had seen him, she had screamed and reached out, eyes black with animal fear. Coward that he was, he had stood as immobile as if chained with iron, at the edge of that circle of men.

Gall now burned in his mouth and he swallowed the searing acid. How could he have stood in silence that day as the soldier rose, adjusting the drawstring of his stained linen braies? Then it was that the soldier had laughed, picked up his sword and laughed, before slowly skewering the glistening blade into the softness between the woman's legs.

"This infidel whore gave little pleasure, my lord," the man had said to him with a grin, then spat on the twitching corpse. "Maybe Satan will teach her how to pleasure his minions in Hell."

Although he might now be standing in the middle of an English road, his eyes could only see the mutilated body of his wife, her staring, dead eyes cursing him for his cowardice and lies. He looked toward the streaming heavens and screamed at God like a man burning at the stake.

The soldier spun around.

The crusader drew his dagger and attacked.

Chapter Two

"Sheep! The future of England lies in sheep, my lady. So should Tyndal's." Brother Andrew, a short monk with head so bald there was no need for the tonsure, shrugged and shot a glance of weary appeal toward his prioress.

Brother Matthew, his body composed of an impressive variety of angles, waved one bony hand in a dismissive gesture. "Nay, good brother. I'll grant there is merit in wool, but I've been told that the beasts bearing it are prone to hoof rot. What Tyndal must have for an assured and profitable future is the odor of sanctity, not the stench of wet sheep." His nose wrinkled in disgust. "We should acquire the body of a saint, or some suitable part thereof. A relic would bring a stream of pilgrims eager to part with their coin…" He hesitated, then poked one long finger heavenward. "And a greater reputation for holiness."

Brother Andrew shook his head with patent disbelief.

"Consider but a moment, Brother! You are surely familiar with the popular shrine of Saint William of Norwich? Not only are Norwich inns quite dear, the number of miracles at the site has diminished. If we had our own relic, we would surely attract those thrifty pilgrims travelling some distance and keep the local ones as well. The coins they saved might well be left with us out of gratitude. So I do believe." In his enthusiasm, Brother Matthew danced from foot to foot with all the grace of a ghostly skeleton freed for All Hallows Eve.

Eleanor, the youthful prioress of this Fontevrauldine daughter house of Tyndal, took a sip from her cup of monastic ale. "Indeed, good brothers," she said at last, "you have both contributed praiseworthy ideas for increasing priory profits."

"And, my lady," Brother Matthew continued, his gaze charged with that focused look common to both cats and merchants about to pounce on a chosen victim, "I have just learned of a reliable source for the thigh bone, with kneecap attached, of a confirmed saint." He paused, then leaned forward, a swordsman delivering his coup. "The price is quite reasonable." Smiling with triumph, he stood back and folded his arms.

"And I am sure Brother Andrew can recommend a good sheep merchant as well." Eleanor rose from her chair, the signal for an end to further discussion. "We are not obliged to make a choice today. The election of our new prior will take place soon, and I do believe whoever is chosen should have his say in this vital decision." She hesitated briefly, then added, "After his selection has been confirmed by our abbess in Anjou, of course."

A wise proviso always, Eleanor thought. The delay would most certainly give her time to bend divergent opinions to whatever course she would prefer, but she was quite aware that no priory selection was ever guaranteed. In the summer of the year just passed, King Henry III had appointed her as prioress, overruling this priory's own elected choice. Few would have forgotten this recent proof that any priory's right to select its own leaders was honored only in the absence of the king's wish to choose otherwise.

"My lady, I abide by your will with joy as always." Brother Andrew's eyes twinkled, either with gratitude that she had put a stop to the seemingly endless discussion or else with amusement at her blunt silencing of his talkative fellow monk. Then he bowed, wincing as he did.

His old war wound must be troubling him in this damp chill, Eleanor thought as she watched him limp from her chambers. Not for the first time she admired how this former soldier turned monk bore his pain with patience and little complaint.

Brother Matthew chose not to follow his fellow monastic. Instead, he turned back to the prioress, raising his finger once more to command Heaven's attention. "The kneecap and thigh bone…"

Eleanor gestured toward her door with courteous but indisputable meaning. "Brother Matthew, I have heard your well-argued views on this matter. When more details are needed, I shall surely call on you."

"I…"

Eleanor walked to her chamber entrance. As she rested her hand on the rough wood of the open door, she looked up at the monk, and her eyes now matched the color of the gray storm clouds outside. "Please leave us, Brother. There is another matter that requires our immediate attention."

The tall monk bowed with grace enough, but each loud slap of his soft shoes on the floor, as he strode away, expressed a protest he dared not otherwise voice to his religious superior.

⁂

Eleanor closed the door, sighed with exasperation, and left her public chambers for the more private room just beyond. The effort to keep the sharp arguments productive between the two monks had wearied her. Before she proceeded to the next item on her mental list of tasks for the day, she knew she needed a moment to refresh her spirit.

Her private quarters were simple. She would have them no other way. The only ornament was an old tapestry of fine embroidery that depicted Mary Magdalene at the feet of Jesus. This she had inherited from her most immediate predecessor, and it hung on the stone wall at the foot of her narrow convent cot. Near that bed was a plainly carved prie-dieu, the wood polished to a warm glow from the touch of each woman who had lived in this room from the time of Tyndal's first prioress. It was there Eleanor went, knelt, and bent her head.

"May it please God," she murmured, "that a wise man be chosen as our next prior, and," she sighed, "that the election be confirmed without delay."

She had tried not to sway this election in any direction, but it was becoming more difficult for her to remain objective. When the news that Prior Theobald was dying became common knowledge, many of the monks had aspired to replace him.

Although Eleanor might have spent most of her twenty-one years in the cloister, she was neither naïve nor unskilled in politics. Perhaps the fires of worldly ambition should die when mortals take the cowl or veil, she thought, but the embers of those flames invariably flared when the chance for advancement in the Church added dry wood to burn. Church leaders might publicly turn their backs on these episodes of human frailty, but their silence did not mean lack of interest. Someone would be watching to see who won the contest and perhaps how skillfully she herself determined the outcome.

It was that final result that troubled her. Most often, when priors were finally elected, the gap between factions required little effort to bridge. At Tyndal, as the weaker candidates had joined the ranks of the two strongest, the debate had grown more strident and very divisive. A religious life required cooperation and selflessness to function efficiently. Political competition promoted neither.

Fortunately, one of the two major candidates was Brother Andrew, a man whom Eleanor respected and whose views were complementary to her own. Unfortunately, he was also the quieter contender. A modest man of thoughtful ways, he could not match the eloquence of his primary rival, Brother Matthew. Matthew was not only persuasive in his attempts to gather support, he already commanded a most fervent following. As her lack of patience with today's discussion had shown, Brother Matthew's approach to priory administration did not accord with hers.

In contention was the direction Tyndal should take as a house dedicated to God's service. Should they keep the hospital that offered cures to the sick and comfort to the dying? Or should they turn away from mortal cures and acquire a relic, thus making the priory a center for healing based solely in faith and the grace of a saint? These were passionate positions and, sadly, mutually exclusive.

Eleanor might argue that faith alone did cure many at Tyndal. The prayers of Sister Christina, the infirmarian, had proven that. For others, the priory also had Sister Anne, the sub-infirmarian, who honored God by using the talent with herbs and potions He had given her. Until Brother Matthew arrived, this reasoning had been accepted with more success than not, even amongst those who thought sickness was God's punishment on the evil-doer or that cures should be left solely to God's grace. With the monk's arrival, the latter had found their voice.

Apart from debate on what form faith should take in healing, the choice of hospital over relic had worldly consequences. The priory could not afford both. Although the hospital was often profitable, thanks to the fine skills and growing reputation of Sister Anne and her well-taught monastics, it was still a charitable institution and earned only what the grateful and more affluent chose to donate. Thus Tyndal's wealth, and resultant influence in the affairs of the Order, depended much on the skillful use of other land resources.

Housing a relic, on the other hand, was more reliably profitable. Floods of pilgrims came to shrines, leaving the silt of coin behind them out of gratitude or hope. In this, Brother Matthew was quite right. However, Tyndal encompassed a finite number of monastics, as well as lay people. Thus the priory could not care for the sick at a hospital while also sheltering pilgrims, guarding any relic from theft, and examining the validity of all cures. A choice must be made. Brother Andrew spoke for those who wished to keep the hospital. Brother Matthew wanted to rid Tyndal of worldly cures and buy a relic.

Although Eleanor knew no one could ever bribe God, she sometimes found herself reminding Him that He had allowed Abraham to bargain over saving Sodom and Gomorrah. Might He not allow Brother Andrew to win the election, thus keeping the hospital for the godly work it did? Surely the priory could find some other project to do solely for His glory, she argued prayerfully.

No matter which monk won the election, she would remain the head of Tyndal in this daughter house of the Order of Fontevraud, but her role as leader of both men and women was unique in a world that saw Eve as the lesser vessel. If Brother Matthew were elected prior, an eloquent man of strong opinions in direct opposition to hers, she would be hard-pressed to maintain her actual authority. She had little doubt she would succeed but resented the energy and thought the struggle would require when both could be put to better use in more profitable activities.

She sighed. Whatever the final result, the election must take place soon. The prior had a significant role in the daily running of the priory, especially amongst the monks and lay brothers. The anxiety of not knowing who would direct them and how their lives would be affected had fractured their usual peace.

She also needed the position to be filled by someone of competence. Problems cried out for immediate attention and she could not do everything. She had appointed a series of acting priors, who did provide some direction while avoiding any hint of partiality on her part, but temporary appointments did nothing for continuing efficiency.

Once the election was over, she would quickly decide how to handle whatever choice God gave her, but the current uncertainty was not beneficial to her priory. She might well prefer Brother Andrew, a man generally respected by all, but Brother Matthew had also demonstrated his ability to lead others. She might dislike the man, but she had to concede he was capable.

As she made the sign of the cross, Eleanor rose from her prie-dieu and listened to the rain's rhythmic tapping against her wooden shutters. Tyndal's lack of ease about its future direction was much the same as England's, she realized. The rumors that King Henry III was gravely ill were growing apace, and his eldest son, Prince Edward, had yet to return from the Holy Land where he had gone on crusade.

In his last missive from Wales, her father had reported that the current mood at court was calm, but, he said with his characteristic sarcasm, only old fools like himself tried to predict the future. The heir had not yet safely returned to England, and, were he to do so before his father's death, there were questions about Edward's final position on the demands for baronial reforms when he became the anointed king. The prince had shifted between both sides of that issue with dizzying frequency. Nonetheless, Baron Adam wrote, Edward was a clever man and, although much like his dying father, unlikely to make the same mistakes. So the powerful were poised to leap whichever way would keep them in control; the powerless would remain frozen like prey in the fox's path; and those on England's borders would watch for the new twists emerging in the diplomatic games of thrust and parry. "As you must have learned as well as I, my beloved daughter," the baron wrote in conclusion, "someone will shed blood when men joust for power."

Thus Eleanor did wonder what the future would bring, not just to her small priory but to England itself.

Chapter Three

Ralf the Crowner knelt on the sodden ground and cautiously put a hand against the neck of the fallen man. The skin was still warm to the touch, but there was no pulse.

"Quite dead, Cuthbert, but not long so," he said in low tones to his sergeant, then fell silent as they both listened for any noise from the surrounding forest. All they could hear was the birds' dissonant rejoicing in the brief break from the interminable rain.

"Could a murderer still be close?" Cuthbert whispered.

Ralf nodded.

The sergeant stood, unsheathing his sword as he studied the brush bordering the road where the corpse lay. All din from the woodlands ceased. Cautiously, Cuthbert walked to the edge of the clearing, then slipped sideways into the dripping, vine-choked undergrowth, and disappeared.

Ralf listened for a moment longer, then turned his attention back to the corpse. The man was lying on his stomach. Could he have fallen from a horse, or had robbers attacked him?

The crowner felt the bones of the dead man's neck. Not broken nor was there any horse nearby. The mount could have been stolen. He bent down to check the wear on the man's boots. No horse for this one, he decided. Judging by the badly mended holes, this corpse had walked much while he still breathed, unless he had lucked upon a passing wagon.

The crowner grabbed the man by the shoulders and rolled him over. As he did, glistening intestines tumbled away from the body. Feces and blood seeped out as well, their stench as strong as that of a badly gutted deer. This was no accident. Unless the man had killed himself, this was murder.

"Ugly way to go," Ralf said companionably to the dead man as he studied the jagged gashes in his belly. A few diligent insects had braved the damp and gone to work already in the raw wound. "And not the usual style of robbers," the crowner continued, glancing up at the forest edge.

He could hear Cuthbert crashing through the branches and thick brush. When he and his sergeant had come across this man lying at the side of the road, the birds had been chirping with good enough cheer. Now they were silent.

Ralf rocked back off his knees into a squat. The victim could not have been killed long before they had discovered him, and these woods were far too thick for a man to escape quickly. Unless the murderer had been mounted, the crowner concluded, he could still be close by, although his sergeant's failure to find a suspect by now argued otherwise.

Ralf glanced down the road. There was a small pile of greenish dung, but fresh horse droppings on a road leading to the priory hospital meant little. Murderer or no, a rider might well seek shelter at Tyndal for the night. Dark came quickly this time of year, and the everlasting rains made byways especially dangerous. Puddles hid deep holes, and one slip in the mud could break a horse's leg. Since Tyndal was the last stop for dry shelter and a hot meal for many hours, a wise man would take advantage of monastic hospitality and avoid injury to his steed. Even a fool would have stopped for a bracing drink of ale, and Brother Andrew, the porter, might remember which strangers had just come by.

He looked back at the corpse. This was definitely not a local man. Since he had grown up here, Ralf took pride in being able to call each villager, monk, nun, and lay brother or sister by name. "Unlike my brother, the sheriff, who rarely visits his shire," he muttered. "He that frets only about wine stains on his fine robes and the latest turn of the political worm at the king's court." To offset his eldest brother's overweening ambition, Ralf had always worked hard to bring local justice to those he called friends.

"And not long ago I would have heard straight away about strangers like you," he complained to the corpse. "But that was before so many began coming to Tyndal's hospital and soldiers started returning from Outremer. Now men arrive and go before I even see their faces." This man was one who had escaped Ralf's notice. Although that had become frequent now, he was still not resigned to it. He shifted to look more closely at the man.

"With that broken nose and thinning hair, I doubt many would call you a handsome fellow, but perhaps some woman did and you have now left a host of orphans to mourn you." The crowner lifted the man's upper lip with the tip of one finger. Several teeth were missing. A couple jagged off at different angles. "Bit hard to chew your meat with those," Ralf said, then sighed. "Nay, corpse, I know you not."

Sticking just above the neck of the man's cloak was the high collar of a quilted but stained and torn buckram, suggesting the man was a foot soldier. His kettle helmet had rolled off to one side and lay like a tilted kitchen bowl in the grass. Above the hacked belly, a dagger protruded from the man's bloody chest. The evidence argued much against any conclusion of a grisly self-murder.

"Odd," Ralf commented aloud. "Stab a man, then disembowel him? Or disembowel him, then stab him in the chest for good measure? Why?"

He felt around the man's waist. Any purse the man might have attached to his braies was gone. Someone had taken it either because robbery was the point of the attack or because the murderer had wanted whoever found the victim to think just that. Given this corpse was a stranger, the easy conclusion was that the murder was a chance act by unknown thieves, preferably ones just passing through Tyndal. In the past, his brother had always liked effortless answers. As a consequence, or at least in part, Ralf never did.

Cuthbert emerged from the sodden brush. Great patches of damp dotted his shoulders and chest. As he walked toward the crowner, his broad feet squashing the wet and rotting forest floor, he wiped bits of vine and leaf from his sword. "Nothing. Absolutely nothing," he grumbled. "Not a footprint, although one would be hard to find with all that standing water, nor any torn clothing caught on a bramble or branch. Nothing dropped." The man turned pale and glanced over his shoulder. "You don't think one of Satan's followers did this, do you?"

"How many bodies have we ever found killed by demons?" Ralf grunted as he stood up and shook the stiffness from his legs. Although he might still be a man of reasonable youth, few on this damp coast escaped the stiffening of the joints for long. Perhaps Sister Anne at the priory would have a remedy? He quashed that thought before painful longing clutched his heart with its familiar, stubborn grip.

"This could be the first…"

"Hold your tongue!" Ralf barked, then gave his sergeant a sheepish look. He had not meant to take his vexation out on the man. "If Satan's imp was after this one," he continued in a more civil tone, "he used a mortal man to do the deed."

The expression on Cuthbert's face suggested he might still think otherwise.

"Smell anything strange?"

The sergeant gave him a weak grin. "Other than our corpse here, just your sweet self."

Ralf gave him a friendly shove. "No smoke? No stench of Hell? No other signs of the Evil One?"

"Still…"

"Besides," Ralf said, pointing down the road, "with our holy brothers and sisters at the priory just there, would the Devil or any of his court dare come so near?"

"Aye, well, you might have the right of that." Cuthbert exhaled with some relief. "Do you think this is our relic seller?"

Ralf shrugged and gestured at the intestines spilled on the ground. "That was an act of great anger. If this were our relic seller, I'd say he asked too much for a fake splinter from the True Cross, then got even more than he expected for it." He knelt back down and fingered the knife. "Nay, the man we are looking for was not described as a soldier like this poor fellow." He bent closer to study the knife. "But do take a look at this, Cuthbert. It is passing strange."

Cuthbert knelt near enough to the crowner but at some distance from the pungent corpse. "What is?"

Ralf ran his fingers over the handle. It was wooden and bore a strange, cursive design on one side. Taking hold of the hilt with a firm grasp, he wrenched the weapon out of the body.

A cold sweat broke out on his forehead as he looked at the blade. This was not like any knife he had ever seen. It was short, wide, made of bronze, and had the same cursive design running down the bloody surface. This was no English weapon.

He reached over and touched a fold of the man's cloak. Odd, too, that a common soldier would wear something made of such good cloth. Perhaps he had stolen it, or… He flipped the fold over. Hidden there was a carefully sewn red cross.

"The man's not just a soldier, he's been on crusade, Cuthbert," Ralf said, then showed him the pattern on the blade. "I do not like what this suggests at all."

Chapter Four

"You are deep in thought, my lady?"

Prioress Eleanor was lightly tracing the semi-circle of ox-blood red in the very first letter of the intricately illustrated text. The manuscript on the table in front of her was a copy of the Epistles of Saint Paul on loan from her aunt at Amesbury.

"These details are so carefully done," she said to Gytha, the Saxon girl who had served her for over a year now. "Look at the tiny lines on the face of this elderly man and the clarity of leaf green in his clothing." It was a pity she knew no one with the talent to do this kind of work at Tyndal. Beautifully decorated manuscripts were unquestionably honorable work for any monastery and could even be quite profitable...

Gytha stooped to look carefully at the figure in the manuscript. "Pretty enough, my lady. God must surely be pleased with such work done to His glory." Gytha tossed her blond braid over one shoulder. "Although few men except bishops can read Latin."

Eleanor held back a laugh. She had grown so fond of this young woman who spoke with blunt honesty but had a kind heart. "You could have learned it but decided to become skilled with numbers and writing instead. Quite skilled, if I am to believe Sister..."

"I'd rather learn skills that will help my brother in his business. Latin would do little good there."

Skills that would also assist a merchant husband, Eleanor thought. Gytha was now of marriageable age and several men had already approached her brother, or so Tostig had told the prioress when he came to discuss their ale partnership. Although two had been landowners of sufficient rank, Tostig had rejected them. Eleanor suspected neither had been to Gytha's taste, and her brother would never agree to a marriage she did not want. When a suitor did come who met with Gytha's approval, Eleanor knew she would lose her maid. She might well find another competent woman to serve her, but she could not so easily fill the empty place Gytha's departure would leave in her heart.

"Did I offend, my lady?"

Eleanor shook her head and patted her maid's shoulder with affection. "I was just thinking that Brother Matthew has argued one point well. Tyndal should not be just a manor house with profitable sheep and a religious vocation. We should gain esteem from things with a holier purpose."

Glancing back down at the cursive letter, the prioress knew that Gytha's comment about the limited audience for this work had merit. As glorious as the manuscript might be, these things were for the few, and she did believe that Tyndal had a duty to all mortals. Perhaps performing instructive liturgical plays would be better?

"You won't bring some relic here, will you, my lady?"

Eleanor raised a questioning eyebrow. Did her maid have some useable objection to the relic? Although their Order did not approve of turning their religious houses into pilgrimage sites, she could not use this as an argument against those who preferred the relic. Most Fontevrauldine houses did not have hospitals either. Tyndal had been an exception. When it was still a Benedictine monastery, it had had a long tradition of serving the sick and dying. Later, after the Order of Fontevraud resurrected the priory, the abbess had agreed to allow the hospital to remain because this had been the desire of the benefactor's wife, who became the first prioress. If one argument had been successful on behalf of the hospital, surely another could be made for a relic.

"You seem opposed to the idea, Gytha. Why?"

Gytha reached for the broom she had set aside, then rested it over one shoulder. "My brother believes they lure criminals and told me about the self-styled pilgrims who swoon over the sainted bones only to bite or pinch off bits of the relic, hide them in their mouths with cunning skill, and then sell the stolen parts elsewhere at extraordinary profit. He has heard many such stories from our crowner and passing travelers from Norwich."

"Your brother is well-informed." The prioress fell silent as she put the manuscript away with great care. "Has Brother Matthew's desire to purchase a relic become common knowledge in the village?"

"The good brother and his opinions have become familiar to all on market days. There are many who wish he showed some modest hesitancy about expressing his views."

Particularly on the new inn, Eleanor thought, something he most especially hated. She pictured Brother Matthew just outside the door to the place, preaching on the fires of Hell to those who had just enjoyed warmth of a more worldly nature. According to Tostig, who sold priory ale to the inn, a handsome young woman named Signy not only served pots of the brew to inn guests but was also rumored to offer other comforts. Eleanor chuckled. How this must enrage Brother Matthew!

Gytha giggled as if she had read the prioress' mind.

Eleanor felt her face turn warm. Was she so tolerant of men's lust because she was equally guilty of carnal longings? And might others recognize the cause of her blindness to this sin? If Brother Matthew did, he would surely use it without scruple to win support for his cause and eventual control of the priory. "You have ceased to be a child, Gytha," she said with a smile to hide her thoughts. "As to the purchase of a relic, what do the villagers think?"

"Most agree that the hospital should stay. There are few that have not benefited from the prayers and potions. If you chose housing a relic over keeping the hospital, many might say that Tyndal would need more cats than even your fine red fellow can sire to catch the two-footed rats we would attract."

"Honest words, Gytha, for which I thank you. Do tell your brother that I will consider what you have said with due care."

Gytha picked up her broom and bowed with courtesy, then skipped through the door into the public chamber. Eleanor was pleased to note that the child had not completely deserted the nascent woman.

⚬⚬⚬⚬ ⚬⚬⚬⚬ ⚬⚬⚬⚬

Eleanor walked over to her window and breathed in the brisk autumn air. Gytha's comment about Arthur, her cat, fathering enough kittens for rat catching might have amused her, but another problem now deeply troubled her.

The problem was Brother Thomas and her unrelenting lust for the man.

Although she might be a respected leader at her priory, Eleanor was fully aware that she was also a woman, subject to strong passions. She knew her vocation to be a true one, but Thomas was also a most attractive man.

"And he will be returning soon," she whispered aloud, her emotions quite mixed at the thought. "His absence over the last few months has given me much peace."

From the day the auburn-haired priest had first arrived, she had been in love with him, a feeling she would never allow herself to express outside the confessional. Daily she had battled against her lust, but despite lying face down on the cold stone of the priory chapel for an hour each evening, her longing for him had brought vivid dreams on many nights of the sweet pleasures she had once so willingly vowed to cast aside. After months of this torture, her body was exhausted.

"Perhaps I should ask our abbess in Anjou to transfer Brother Thomas to another priory?" She directed this question to the darkening sky outside her window. As she stood there quite alone, this seemed to be the best choice. She knew that whatever calm she now felt would flee the moment she saw Thomas. How long could she continue to win the battle against carnal joy? In addition, she now realized, she must also worry about Brother Matthew discovering her sin and making use of it against her.

"My resolve can withstand only so much assault! Even stone crumbles when battered by the sea," she lamented, pressing her eyes shut with her fingers. Then she turned from the window and looked back at the cross hanging on her wall over the prie-dieu. "If my woman's weakness were the only consideration, I would not hesitate to send him away." She pressed her hand to her heart. "Sadly, that is not the case." It was times like these that she hated her fondness for the balanced view.

There were excellent reasons not to send the troublesome brother away. The strongest argument involved Sister Anne, Eleanor's confidante and dearest friend. Anne relied on Thomas' competent and sensitive help with her patients. Equally well, Eleanor knew how much the nuns counted on his common sense as their confessor. Sending him hence just because she longed to bed him would be a most selfish choice.

"I should count myself blessed to have a man like this amongst my monks," she growled, then added with bitterness, "and equally cursed."

As she thought more on the consequences of the monk's return, frustration and fear began to flood through Eleanor, then hot anger at her own frailty. Pounding her fist on the prie-dieu, she rushed from her chambers. The door banged with so much force behind her that the wood trembled.

Gytha stared at the door and frowned with concern.

Chapter Five

Brother Andrew rested one hand gently on the calf of the ripening corpse. The horse that bore that unwelcome load nickered hopefully as Andrew watched Cuthbert take his own mount off for stabling. When no one moved to take this foul burden away, the beast snorted with equine disgust.

"A crusader who survives the Saracens only to die at the hands of one of his own countrymen? A sad commentary on our dark days, Crowner." The porter shook his bald head in sympathy.

"The murderer may not be a subject of good King Henry, Brother Porter. The dagger in his chest was not one I have ever seen made by an Englishman." Ralf stroked the skittish horse with a calming touch, expressing sympathy that the creature was forced to carry such a dead weight.

"For cert?"

"You were a soldier once yourself, were you not?"

"Had I not been, I would not have this limp."

"You might know the make."

"My war was on English soil, Crowner. Nevertheless, show me the knife."

Ralf passed the weapon to him, hilt first. "I fought far from England's shore as a mercenary but never saw this kind of thing in the hands of any Christian man."

Andrew squinted, then held the darkly stained knife at arm's length from his eyes, turned it over, and silently considered the design. "Only once have I seen markings like this. They are not something one forgets easily. A man in my village had an object with similar engraving and told me it was a war trophy from his grandfather who had served under King Richard in Outremer. The script was Arabic, he told me." He handed it back to Ralf. "This may be a Saracen weapon."

Ralf frowned as he looked down at the knife. "I feared as much." Then he glanced around to see if there was anyone within hearing. "I have heard tales of men called *Assassins*," he said with soft voice. "The tellers say that no wall is thick enough nor castle strong enough to keep a man safe once these murderers are set upon a killing. Nor do they care if they lose their own lives in the act. I mention this to you, Brother, because you are a man who is not inclined to believe fables men tell to frighten others and thus are unlikely to be alarmed without need. But to you I confess that this dagger troubles me in light of these stories, and I do wonder if…" He stopped and put the weapon back into the pouch on the horse. "Has any stranger passed your gate today or stopped at the priory…?"

"Not with a hue darker than that of an Englishman who has spent too long in the desert sun, my friend." Andrew shrugged. "Nor would it be likely that a man like that would seek hospitality in a place dedicated to the service of a Christian God. Nay, no Saracen will be found, still on his knees in the front of our altar, praying for forgiveness."

Ralf flushed. His smile lacked humor.

Andrew clapped his hand on the crowner's shoulder. "But you might have the right of it, Crowner. If a man were as clever as those stories would have it, he might well bow down to our God and thus hide within the shadow of the unexpected to avoid detection. That aside, we have had none of foreign visage come to our gate and your question was, after all, about strangers in general."

"I agree that the latter is the more likely suspect, despite the evidence of the knife. Strangers, then, of any ilk, especially those coming from the west?"

"Strangers." Andrew looked toward the hospital with sadness. "When do we not have a stream of unknown men nowadays?

There have been an ever-increasing number of returning soldiers and a grim and silent lot they are. I do wonder how the war goes in the Holy Land."

"Their arrival here does not surprise me if they are sick or wounded. Many may well thank God that your prioress had the wisdom to recognize Sister Anne's healing talents and allow her to teach others her skills."

"Aye, some do come, having heard of her reputation for cures. Others stop only to rest on their way to Norwich. There they hope the bones of the sainted William will bring sight back to their empty eyes and restore arms or legs left behind in Outremer."

Ralf snorted. "And those who are too weak or poor to make the journey to the English shrines are waylaid by sellers of relics. Forgive me if I sound impious, Brother, but my men have found enough splinters of the True Cross being sold on the nearby roads to build our king a holy fleet. In fact, we were hunting one such fraud today when we came upon this corpse." He gave the thigh of the dead man a brisk slap.

"Selling false relics is a sin, Crowner, and I applaud your efforts to protect the innocent. I grieve over this abuse of the faithful." He raised his eyes with a quick glance heavenward. "And I pray we continue to hold fast to the Fontevrauldine tradition of rejecting the housing of any relics in our priory. If Brother Matthew has his way and does bring a relic here, that would certainly add to your problems by drawing the sellers of fraudulent items as well as forcing us to examine carefully each alleged miracle for validity." He took a deep breath. "But I should not trouble you with priory squabbles, and I fear I have, once again, gotten away from your question about strangers at our gates today." Andrew closed his eyes in thought. "Most who have come are known to us. A few not."

"Can you list them?"

"A few mothers brought their children with running noses and sore throats. It is the season for that according to Sister Anne. An old woman brought her husband. His lungs were full from the damp. He came to die, I do believe." Andrew was counting on his fingers. "Some courtiers from Westminster, but we were given advance notice to expect them with their attendant. One suffers from the gout and another from swollen veins." He chuckled. "Sister Anne will put those two right enough while our stables give their horses much needed rest from the weight of their masters! Oh, and one villager came with tertian fever. Only one. A minor miracle, that."

"Perhaps we can ignore those you have named. Methinks they are more concerned with their suffering children, bilious humors, and God's judgement than committing murder with an infidel's knife. But no one else has come?"

"Some soldiers came early this morning. One may have leprosy and has been separated from his fellows. Another is so ill I am surprised he survived the trip. Others suffered less dire ailments and were not ill enough to warrant immediate attention. These men are, of course, unknown to us, but if you follow me to the hospital courtyard, I could point them out to you. Perhaps amongst them are travelers who have come along the road from the inn." He nodded at the dead man. "And bring your corpse for Sister Anne. Even her fine skills could not bring life back to this ravaged body, but she might have some observations about how he and his soul were parted."

As the two men turned toward the hospital, Andrew suddenly brightened. "I almost forgot to give you some good tidings! Word is that Brother Thomas will soon be home. One of the villagers told me yesterday that someone had seen our brother on the road from Cambridge."

"That does cheer my heart! I have missed his wit." The crowner grinned. "He has an agile mind and a soldier's courage, as I remember well from that sad affair last year."

Andrew nodded concurrence.

"Your mention of the inn reminds me that Brother Matthew spends more time at its door than is meet for a man who forswore the world."

"He may bear little love for our hospital, but he hates the new inn more. I am told he stands on a small rise near the entrance and berates those who go inside for bone-warming ale." Andrew's laugh was less than monkish.

"Perhaps he hopes that someone, for a prayer, will give him a free drink," Ralf replied with scorn. "I, for one, am grateful for the place. The innkeeper gives good value for the coin he takes. I see no sin in good ale and a decent stew—or, for that matter, in enjoying the sight of Signy. Her beauty is a credit to God's skill in creation."

Andrew smiled but chose not to comment further on God's craft. "With the roads to Tyndal crowded with so many coming here to seek our cures or travelling to Norwich to visit the relic, our good brother fears an increase in drunkenness and lechery because of the inn. Thus he takes on the burden of seeking both sinners and the holy alike for long talks on their spiritual needs on fair-weather market days."

"Our Brother Crow has cawed in my ear as well when I have gone to take some ease at the inn," Ralf grunted. "How can anyone avoid him?"

Andrew clapped the crowner's shoulder with good humor, then gestured toward the hospital. "Come to the one place he rarely visits, my friend."

Chapter Six

The man from Acre looked around the crowded hospital court-yard, his mouth twisting with contempt. What mewling and weeping! Did these fools truly think their living bodies had ever been anything but decaying flesh? He could understand those awed into silence by imminent death, but he felt only disdain for the ones who squalled about it like spoiled children. Why did they imagine that God paid any more heed to mortal whining than He did to the sound of wind over an empty sea?

A sharp pain stabbed through one eye. Once. Twice. He held his breath to keep from groaning. For him, the act of living had become too hard, and he longed for the hour when only flies and worms made his rotting carcass quiver. The knife-like jabs stopped. He breathed in deeply, but the cold air now burned his lungs like ice on skin.

Yet there had been a time when he'd believed as they did. He fought the onrush of recollection, but the pungent scent of green English earth was too strong an ally to his bitter memory of hope. A drop of blood crested on his lip, broke, and wove slowly down his chin.

That day the silver-tongued priest had come to preach the crusade had been a fair one, sweet as only an English spring could be, damp and soft with the scent of expectant life. Although the man of God had spoken to many, his words had challenged *his* manhood, filled *him* with lust to fight for His glory in Outremer.

Thus he had knelt before the priest, pledging his sword for the Cross, and taken the pilgrim's staff with joyful conviction. Long before the king's own son had done so, he had set off for Acre.

With high passion, he had battled against the infidels, sending scores to Hell with his sword while the red cross of the true faith burned over his heart. After this combat, his body might have ached, but he felt only profound satisfaction. Nor was he alone in that. Knowing they had survived another day's slaughter brought greater pleasure than any woman's body ever could. Those evenings, he and the other warriors still living had drunk deeply, singing with joy.

Then God had abandoned him. His lips twitched as his mouth filled with a sour taste. His company of soldiers had been ambushed, and he was gravely wounded. Was it an imp of Satan who brought the Saracen woman to him? At the time he thought she was the instrument of God. She had saved him, dragging him from the bloody earth into her hut and caring for him with kindness and skill. Her faith demanded mercy, she told him once. When the fever left him and his manhood returned, he had taken her with gentleness into his bed, and they had loved each other most tenderly.

Later, when his Christian brethren retook the land, he had saved her honor and life, claiming her as his property and swearing that she had begged for baptism. He did so love her, as she had him, and, in the sweet darkness of their nights together, he had begged her to convert so they could marry. She would be safe, he promised, as a Christian and his wife. In the bright sunlight of the day after she had done so, he did indeed marry her—in secret.

He ran his hands down his face, the tips of his bent fingers snagging in the deep furrows of his forehead. How could he have done otherwise? If he had openly taken her to his bed as his lawful wife, his fellow soldiers might well have killed them both as they lay in each other's arms. Or so he had believed.

Bed the Saracen if you must, they'd have shouted at him. Breed bantlings on her. But *marriage* to an enemy woman, one whose kin has killed ours? That is treason!

Never again would they have trusted him in battle, a man who had taken an infidel to his heart. Thus he had left her with the other Saracen women captured by the Christians. It would be safer, he told her, and she would be happier with others who spoke her language. Soon they could reveal their secret union. Soon.

What a madman he had been, dreaming that he could some-day bring her home to England and that any son of theirs would inherit the manor lands despite his eastern hue. If he could not admit the marriage to his soldiers, why had he imagined his family would have greeted her with any joy? *Fool* echoed through his head like the chant from a choir of demons.

He shuddered. An ominous chill had wrenched him back to the present, and he turned to stare at the courtyard entrance. In the shadows, he could see the figure of a monk, behind him a man with a horse. He recognized neither of the men, but the horse bore a burden he did know well and hated even more.

Hate? Did he still? He remembered how he had quivered with a small joy as he pressed the knife into the soldier's soft lower belly, then ripped it upward. And had he not felt a twinge of pleasure when he saw the soldier's eyes widen and his hands flutter to catch his own steaming guts as they tumbled out just before Death snatched his soul?

With a vague sadness, he remembered a time when he had not hated that soldier. They had both come to Outremer from the same village, and, although different in rank, were kin as all men are in battle. So would this man have purposely chosen his wife to rape and butcher, or were the acts some random whim of the Devil? Would he ever know? Did he even care?

Unable to turn his eyes from the corpse in the shadows, he closed them, but now his dead wife stared back at him against the backdrop of his lids, her mouth stretched wide with the howl of the burning damned. God had not blessed her for denying the faith of her fathers, he heard her scream. Hadn't he promised that baptism would protect her from harm? Why had he lied?

"I did not lie," he whispered. "I believed what I promised was true."

He put his fingers against his lids and forced them open. Now his wife's ghost faded and her voice was silenced, but he could still smell the smoke she had brought with her from the infernal world.

He looked back at the corpse on the horse. Nay, he no longer hated the man he had killed. He felt envy. The soldier was dead while he still remained in the cold sun, a twitching piece of clay longing for the warmth of Hell.

Chapter Seven

Eleanor hastened across the cloister garth, through the gate kept locked to protect her nuns from intrusion, and into the public grounds. She often hurried, for that was her nature, but the passion of anger now drove her.

"When will it please God to free me from this sinful affliction?" she muttered. Her confessor had urged patience on her, warning that lust was often a stubborn thing. Being of an admittedly determined nature herself, she understood the nature of obstinacy, but the comprehension gave her little comfort.

The rain had stopped, but the air remained cold and heavy with dampness. She slowed her pace and glanced around her, clasping the hood of her robe more tightly around her neck. The lush flowers that gave her joy in summer were gone, leaving only thorns and twisted branches that had turned black with this never-ending seacoast rain. Even the snows of winter had a soft beauty, almost like the entrance into Heaven, but this season reminded her of the act of dying, not its rewards. She hated autumn.

"I am a poor one to lead this community of faithful," she said, her feet crunching loudly as she continued on her way along the gravel path. "Honored though I was by King Henry's choice, I fear my appointment was not a wise one. Tyndal might well have been better served by Sister Ruth, a woman with little carnal inclination if I am any judge."

The prioress of Tyndal marched on through the thick mist toward the hospital. Once a day, she went there as a service to the suffering. Her prayers were not really needed. Sister Christina's, with her gentle faith, offered more kindness. Indeed, few could equal the infirmarian's ability to paint so sweet a picture of Heaven that those who were healing sometimes envied the dying. Nonetheless, Eleanor could perform one critical service. She knew how to write, and that skill was of increasing value.

Many knights who now came to Tyndal were from distant parts of the realm and were either too ill to travel farther or dying. For the former, she could sometimes send families hopeful news. On behalf of the latter, she would send their last words, their prayers to children and parents, wives or betrothed. That message might well be the only thing left of their loved one that they could clasp to their hearts. If nothing else, knowing that a loved one had died in God's grace was better than knowing nothing at all.

Eleanor wished these acts were pure and selfless gifts, but she was rarely blind to her own mortal frailties. The solace she provided gave her comfort and hope as well. For more months than she cared to count, no one in her family had heard from her eldest brother, Hugh. Each day she hoped some soldier might have news. She tried not to think about these things, but she feared he had died of some fever or festering wound in Outremer. Although she prayed for his safety, God had remained as silent as her brother.

When she entered the hospital courtyard, she reckoned how many were waiting for care. The growing numbers concerned her. As she gazed on those who twisted and moaned, endured in silent pain, or lay dying but longed for reassuring words from one of the religious, she clenched her fist with renewed determination. There were relics enough for the faithful in East Anglia, but only Tyndal had Sister Anne's skills with herbs and the caring prayers of Sister Christina.

"My longing to love-joust with a handsome monk shall not distract me from the coming fight," she muttered, "and, when Brother Thomas returns, Brother Matthew must not see any wavering of my gaze nor telltale blushes that might betray me.

My authority at Tyndal shall remain as strong as the walls of Wynethorpe Castle," she continued. "I may be a woman, but I am also my father's daughter."

⊙⊙⊙ ⊙⊙⊙ ⊙⊙⊙

"Sister?"

The voice jolted Eleanor back to the moment, and she looked for the speaker.

Two men sat on their haunches but a short distance from her. It was the older man who had spoken. "I beg pardon, Sister, but…" His head was bowed.

"How may I serve you, good sir?" Eleanor glanced around to see if anyone was coming to help them, then turned again just as the older man adjusted the hood over his younger companion's face so the rain did not fall into his eyes. The tenderness touched her. "Has anyone attended you?"

The older man now faced her, and she saw that he was missing one eye. The hollow was inflamed as if angry at the loss. His other eye was so deep in its socket that she could not tell if the color was brown or black.

"Nay, good sister, they have not."

Eleanor glanced quickly at the younger man, and her heart beat with fear. He was of her brother's age with almost the same coloring. Across his face, from forehead to chin, ran a deep and horrible scar. Of course it was not Hugh, she realized, but tears nonetheless burned at the corners of her eyes.

The young man ignored her and stared up at the gray, shifting heavens. When he did look at her, the anguish in his eyes was palpable, and his sigh was a sound so tortured that Eleanor wondered if he had other, more mortal, wounds.

"Are you in pain?" She moved nearer.

The elder man jumped up, barring the way. "Come no closer, Sister!"

Eleanor stopped.

He shook his head. "I mean no discourtesy, but he grows quite agitated with those he does not know."

The young man's eyes had widened with that look of a deer facing an archer. As Eleanor backed away, his expression grew more peaceful and his breathing quieted.

"On his face you see an old wound," the older said, noting the direction of her gaze. "That one may be healed, but his soul is crushed. Therein lies his mortal pain." He gestured for her to move back still more. "I mean no insult, Sister, but please stand farther away still."

Eleanor inclined her head in silent question as she watched the young man's eyes flit back and forth at the milling crowd, then close as if he longed to shut the world away.

"You frighten him," was the only answer given.

She retreated several steps. "I have no wish to do that, nor am I offended. We are here to heal what we can of body and soul, with God's grace. If a woman disturbs him, a lay brother can…"

"I must demand the assistance of a lay brother, Sister, a gentle man who will take my direction. As long as that is done and I remain by his side," he said, gesturing to his companion, "he will have some peace. I regret the trouble this causes."

"Good sir, we serve a merciful God here at Tyndal and no mortal soul in need causes any problem for us. Since strangers agitate his spirit, I will direct my sub-infirmarian, Sister Anne, to speak to you alone. Although our lay brothers are most competent, I have learned to trust her skill above any in this priory. She can best direct others in whatever treatment might be of benefit."

The older man blinked, then bowed. "My lady, I fear that I mistook you for…"

"My soul rejoices that you thought my rank one more worthy of entering the Kingdom of Heaven. Sadly, it is not. I am Prioress Eleanor of Tyndal."

"This, my lady, is Sir Maurice, my master and a knight from the far north. I am called Walter, if a name is required."

That tale did not quite ring like true coin, Eleanor thought as she held the man's boldly fixed gaze. Few servants, no matter how concerned with the health of a master, would behave in so arrogant a manner to a nun whose profession, and most likely birth, demanded more courtesy. His master's name should be sufficient to gain whatever assistance was needed. Nor had he spoken with the tone or the accent of one born to serve. She considered the quality of his dress. Although he did not wear a cloak against the rain, the cloth of Walter's robe seemed no less fine than that of the man he called *master*.

What was their relationship, she wondered, if not servant and master? From the tenderness Walter had shown Maurice, they might be father and son, although the age difference between them did not seem quite great enough. Perhaps they were cousins, Walter springing from a younger branch of the family? She did not see any great resemblance in features between the men, although the loss of an eye in one and that terrible scar on the other might make a similarity hard to see. Surely Walter would have said if he and the young man were related.

Nor did either bear the crusader cross. How odd, she thought. Not all warriors did, but the omission was rare, and the visible wounds on both were unusual for men of obvious rank not coming from battle. Why not wear their badge of honor if they were coming from Outremer? And why lie about their relationship? What a very odd pair, she concluded, then looked toward the hospital. A lay brother was approaching.

"This is the man I shall assign to you," she said as Brother Beorn reached her side. "In the meantime, I will seek out Sister Anne. You may explain what is needed to her, and she will arrange for proper care." She turned to the lay brother and continued. "Gentleness is required, and you should take direction from this man in all matters pertaining to the care of his master. If there is any other immediate need…"

"Nothing, my lady. You are most kind."

"God is kind. We are but His instruments," Eleanor replied, then turned away, still perplexed. However courteous you make your words, she thought, your tone is still that of a man more accustomed to command.

Chapter Eight

From the shadows of the courtyard entrance, Ralf cupped his hands over his mouth as if he would shout at the prioress disappearing into the darkness of the hospital interior.

Brother Andrew grasped his wrist. "I fear she will neither hear nor see us." He opened his mouth, perhaps to rebuke the crowner for his intended rudeness, then shut it as if deciding he should forgive the crowner his lack of manners. After all, what man cheerfully brought a corpse-bearing horse to any woman, including a prioress?

"Satan's tits," the crowner muttered with irritation and shook off the monk's hand.

The porter shrugged. "Come now, Crowner! Our lady was on the other side of the courtyard. Even your roaring could not reach her ears in this noisy crowd."

Ralf turned his head away to hide his embarrassment. He had played the fool once already in front of Andrew when he voiced his ill-considered suspicion that an Assassin might be hiding at Tyndal. Now he had behaved like some rough boor.

He had meant no discourtesy by yelling at the prioress, but he also had no wish to lead this horse, with its bloody burden, through a courtyard filled with sick people. He shook his head. Nay, that was not the reason for his behavior. He was never at ease when he came to Tyndal where he might see Sister Anne and was even less happy when he had to seek the sub-infirmarian's advice about a corpse.

Wise though the consultation might be, he preferred to avoid the good nun entirely. It was the only way he could handle his painful longing for her. Now that he was here and must see her, he had grown impatient to get the unpleasant task over with, a situation that tended to chase away what little regard he had ever had for fine manners. "Get thee behind me, you daft devil," the crowner muttered, hoping that Satan might decide Ralf's bad temper was not to be taken lightly even by the Prince of Darkness.

"Are you troubled by something, Crowner?"

Not willing to give Andrew yet a third reason to think him a fool, this time for talking aloud to himself, Ralf quickly searched the courtyard for a distraction. "Aye, I am. That man." He pointed. "The one over there. Has he just arrived today?"

Andrew frowned as he followed the direction of the crowner's gesture. The man thus indicated did stand out. Skeletally thin, his robe hung on him like an adult garment on a little boy. His face was the mottled purplish-red of one who might have enjoyed much wine during his indefinable life span, and his rough, undyed robe was so stained it resembled a sad copy of Joseph's coat of many colors. Tufts of pale hair spiked at uneven angles around what was either an oddly shaped bald spot or a tonsure of unusual pattern.

"I do not remember him passing the gate either today or yesterday." Andrew hesitated. "Although I have been called to meet with our prioress several times and might have missed seeing him. Still, he is a man I should recall and do not. I will ask others who might have seen him pass."

"He's just the sort who is either a total innocent or a wily criminal," Ralf said. He might have picked the man out to shift the monk's attention away from his outburst, but now that he thought on it, the man did have a dishonest look about him.

Before Brother Andrew could reply, the man, who heretofore had been standing quietly with arms crossed, began to scream. Those surrounding him were startled, their eyes widening with fear. People drew back as the man began to jerk in a strange dance. Raising his hands heavenward, he waved them as if greeting a friend who stood at some distance.

"Get thee hence!" he sang, repeating the words like a chant at the top of his lungs.

An old woman, with her back to Ralf, crossed herself several times. "He's possessed," she hissed, loose skin wobbling under her chin as she looked to her left, then right. "And wouldn't you know it? Not a priest in sight. I swear by all that's holy, you can never find a man of God when you most need one!"

"He's seen the Devil! He's fighting with him!" a young man leaning on a crutch began to shout. "I see it all too. It is…" But words failed him and he gestured in circular motions as he struggled futilely to come up with details of what he was sure he had seen.

The attention of the crowd shifted away from him.

Ralf looked around quickly for a lay brother or monk, but Brother Andrew had anticipated him and was hurrying toward the jerking, chanting man. As soon as the porter laid a gentle hand on him, the dancer stopped twitching, dropped his head into his hands, and appeared to be praying. Andrew whispered something in the man's ear. Without protest, the man let the monk lift him to his feet, then pull him toward the hospital.

The excitement over, the crowd gave a collective sigh and began to drift about as they had before. The young man sagged back on his crutch, his features once more pinched with the pain of his affliction. The woman with many chins had grasped the arm of her nearest neighbor and was continuing to complain about how badly priests protected good Christians when the Evil One and his imps attacked.

Ralf watched the hospital door, waiting for Brother Andrew to return. On his trips to Norwich, he had seen too many who earned a fine living by faking similar afflictions at the shrine of the sainted William; thus the crowner was not convinced the rough-robed man was either possessed or insane. At least this one did a rather entertaining dance for his supper, Ralf thought. Most just foamed at the mouth and rolled around.

"You missed a fine spectacle," Ralf said to his sergeant as the man returned from stabling his horse. Then, deciding that Brother Andrew might not come back any time soon to take him to the sub-infirmarian, the crowner passed the reins of the corpse-bearing horse to Cuthbert. "Wait for me here," he said. Perhaps he had best find Sister Anne himself and get this over with. He began to grind his teeth.

Chapter Nine

Thomas doubted he would ever be dry or warm again. His fellow monks had cheerfully greeted his return, made room for him near the fire in the warming room, then teased him about the amount of steam rising from his wet robe. After he had changed into dry garments, their jesting lapsed into a stream of questions about any news he'd brought from the outside world. Men might give up the secular life but not their curiosity about it. Thus Thomas satisfied his fellow monastics with a few good stories while he chased away the chill and, if truth be told, an uneasy sense that something was not quite right.

When he first came to Tyndal, he would have understood the feeling. He had hated this priory for its remote North Sea location, the pervasive smell of rot, and the deadening silence when wet fog rolled over the land. Since then, he had become fond of the place and now considered it home. Today he had been so eager to return that he had taken a shortcut through the dripping wood to the mill gate, a route that left him soaking wet, short of breath, but happy to be back within the priory walls. So why did he feel so uncomfortable?

"You have not told us how your sick brother fares." A milky-eyed monk, his voice gentle with concern, rested a shaking hand on Thomas' shoulder.

Thomas bent his head. "He did recover. For your prayers, I am most grateful."

The other monks murmured joy at the good news.

Thomas swallowed hard. He hated lying to these gentle men, but he had no choice. When his raven-clad spymaster had ordered him to York last spring to discover the instigator of a series of attacks against cathedral clerks, Thomas invented a sick brother who required his prayers and attendance. The work took several months, but no one doubted that a serious illness would keep him away so long. Perhaps, he thought wryly, it was reasonable to claim that some figurative brother had been cured. After all, he had successfully found the man who had infected the peace of his religious brothers with a most feverish plot.

Thomas rose and, with proper grace, left the warm company of his fellow monks. As he entered the cloister, a gust of wet wind hit his face. He rubbed his eyes with the sleeve of his habit, then blinked. It had not taken long for the damp air to mist his dry robe.

He had just started down the path to the hospital when he stopped and looked back toward the mill. Few should be out in this weather, he thought, squinting into the drizzle. There was perhaps one lay brother near the stables? Nonetheless, the unease he felt earlier returned. Had he been followed?

Why would he have been, Thomas wondered? On the way to York, he had grown his beard, let his tonsure fill in, and then traded his cowl for the modest dress of a servant. Once the crime was solved, he had shed this disguise, and although his auburn hair was distinctive, he had covered his head when he left the city so early that next morning. No one should have recognized the bumbling servant in the clean-shaven Fontevrauldine priest.

Nay, this could have nothing to do with the work at York, he decided, for he had not even felt this discomfort until he left Tyndal village for the priory. Perhaps Satan had decided to taunt him for the lies he must tell on his return? That wind along the main road before he turned into the wood had certainly been unnaturally strong. Maybe it was the Devil who had been following him!

Thomas shivered, then continued on his way to the hospital. He wanted to see Sister Anne.

When he reached the courtyard, he stared in amazement at the long lines of sick waiting to be seen. He began to wend his way through the crowd, greeting several villagers he knew. There were women seeking advice on soothing babes whose first teeth were coming or curing children of rashes and scabs. One had brought her carpenter husband who must have gashed his hand. With sadness he noted a man and a woman with the pallor of death already on their faces, here to beg entrance for the peace of their souls.

In the past, all had been quickly seen. Today, despite the miserable weather, the line wound around the courtyard. Some of this increase must be due to the dampness that brought with it aching fevers and congested chests, he realized, but not all this crowd had come for ease of seasonal ills.

Sitting above the general throng, there were many on horseback. At the front of the line, Thomas could see three finely dressed men of King Henry's court astride beasts with equivalent adornments and just as impressive bloodlines. The sight of the occasional courtier had not been unusual when Thomas first came to Tyndal, but perhaps it had now become rather more common? Equal all Christians might be in the eyes of God, but, in the world of men, these warranted the attention of the infirmarian herself.

To give her fair due, Sister Christina did not make these worldly distinctions and served all that needed her prayers. Thomas had concluded early on that, if anyone at Tyndal were headed for sainthood, it would be that round and ardent sister. Nonetheless, Sister Christina was most biddable, and the sub-prioress, Sister Ruth, had assigned one lay person to turn the nun's attention, gently but promptly, to those arrivals of high secular rank.

Thomas turned his attention away from the courtiers and looked around for Sister Anne. She was not at the hut where the sick were first assessed. While her superior concentrated on praying for the greater wisdom of God, the tall sub-infirmarian did the more worldly work of supervising hospital care. Not that Thomas ever doubted the power of Sister Christina's influence with the Almighty, but Sister Anne's God-given talent with mortal medicine never ceased to amaze him and had done much to raise Tyndal's reputation for healing. Perhaps she was tending someone inside the hospital, he concluded.

As he moved toward the hospital building itself, he saw men with faded and torn crusader crosses on their garments, some on foot, a few on horseback. In this late autumn of 1271, these soldiers were most likely returning from Outremer with far greater ills than they could ever have imagined when they first left England.

On his way back from York, Thomas had overheard some say, in hushed tones, that the crusade had been a failure. Others more loudly claimed victories. All concurred, however, that Jerusalem remained in infidel hands. Any conclusion on the success of Lord Edward should be left to those more knowledgeable than he, Thomas decided. In any case, he saw no joy shining from the eyes of the men returning from Outremer.

Those soldiers who had sought him out for words of religious comfort had most certainly lost their early zeal. The tales of the heat and how they had cooked in their chain mail under the desert sun were bad enough. The stories of how they had watched friends, fathers, brothers die of unknown plagues, their corpses melting quickly into a stinking mess within hours of death, both shocked and sickened his soul.

Perhaps it was his imagination, but Thomas also wondered if there were more lepers on the byways, their clappers shattering the calm of well-escorted travelers who had little reason to fear robbers but now trembled at the sight of these poor creatures. Once he had rounded a bend in the road to see some merchants taking whips to the suffering as if chasing them from sight would banish them from existence. He had shouted at the men to have mercy, but their fear deafened them. After the riders had passed on, the lepers swarmed back across the road, searching the earth for a coin or a bit of bread dropped from a kinder hand. That night, wracked with dreams and sleepless horrors, he had wept.

In the line today, he saw two men with possible signs of the disease, and Thomas wondered if there were truly so many sinners, cursed by God, or if the lepers were meant to warn England itself of her sins. Looking into the frightened eyes of these two, Thomas found himself hoping that such suffering was not the result of any man's sin. Perhaps the clerics who claimed the disease was a blessing, one that brought the victim closer to Heaven, were correct. Somehow that seemed the kinder conclusion.

Some battle-mutilated common soldiers were waiting to be seen: one missing his nose, another with features melted by fire, a third without eyes and one hand missing. Would these die of starvation in the coming winter, their families too poor to feed them, Thomas asked himself? By all rights he should offer faith's solace and kneel with them, repeating the required litany, but Thomas wondered if he would ever have words enough to comfort them. He did know he would never have sufficient tears to soothe their wounds.

Thomas shook these thoughts from his head and looked again without success for Sister Anne in the throng. Close by Sister Christina and the courtiers, he saw a familiar lay brother standing with two men dressed in secular garb. Brother Beorn was talking to the elder of the two, but the younger captured Thomas' particular notice.

This man stood with arms folded, head bowed. He was dressed in a dark cloak, his hood tossed back despite the weather, and his hair blanched almost white. From others he had seen, Thomas recognized that as a familiar mark of Outremer's blinding sun, yet the man did not bear the mark of a crusader.

Suddenly the man looked directly at Thomas, his eyes slowly taking him in from shoe to cowl. The monk felt his face turn hot, as if a woman had come upon him while he was naked. Then the man turned aside and stared toward the hospital entrance.

Thomas relaxed and studied the man's face. He would have been most handsome once, but the wide purple scar that ran diagonally across his nose from forehead to jaw made a mockery of the beauty God had given him. How could the man have survived a blow that had almost cut his head in two, Thomas wondered?

The monk looked back at the older companion. Although he was still talking with Brother Beorn, the man glanced around the courtyard as if he were seeking an enemy hidden in the crowd. Once his look rested on Sister Christina where it lingered for a few seconds before restlessly moving on. The elder's face was several shades darker than that of his companion, with lines cut deeply into his forehead and around his mouth. He was also shorter, and a scattering of gray in his black hair suggested he was older than his lean, muscular body would suggest. As he turned toward Thomas, the monk noticed that one eye socket was black and quite empty.

Unusual wounds for men who were neither dressed as soldiers nor carried the sign of crusaders, he thought. Surely they had been in Outremer. Rare was the Englishman with such a tan or a youth with such white hair unless both had been exposed to that barbaric sun. It was strange that they did not wear the cross. Even those returning with much reason for grief displayed their red badge with pride.

As he waited for Brother Beorn to finish with the men, Thomas continued to study the pair. The one bore a vague similarity to the other, he decided. They might differ in hair color and build, but there was a certain likeness of feature. Perhaps they were brothers born to different mothers? After all, Thomas, especially with his distinctive hair, little resembled his siblings. Not only had Thomas' own father had more than one wife, he had casually coupled with a servant woman, the one who gave birth to Thomas. One of these two might have a similar parentage.

Whatever the truth there, their bearing proclaimed them men of some status, Thomas concluded. As one raised somewhere between the world of servants and that of the nobility, he recognized the stance. Men of rank inevitably stood firmly on the earth as if it were made of stone. Those of lesser birth shifted cautiously, their ground made of a more unstable substance perhaps.

The older man now turned away from Brother Beorn and touched the young man's arm with a poignant tenderness. When the latter turned unblinking eyes to him, the elder put an arm around his shoulders and directed him, much as a father would his small son, toward the hospital entrance.

How sad, Thomas thought. Was the world truly so disordered that older men must care for younger ones when youth should be tending to their elders?

Then he shrugged the thought away. Since Brother Beorn was too occupied to give directions, he would continue to hunt for Sister Anne on his own.

Chapter Ten

"Brother Thomas!" Sister Anne cried out with obvious joy, dropping her basket of herbs and extending her arms as if to gather the monk into a loving embrace. Suddenly mindful of her vocation, she lowered them, but the affection in her eyes remained. "Welcome home. We have missed you so." The fondness of her tone defied any monastic rule.

Thomas bent down, quickly tossed the herbs back into the basket, then handed it to the nun. "I have longed to return to Tyndal as well," he replied with a smile that matched her warmth. Had this humble and gentle woman not accepted him as the hospital priest, a morose man with an unknown past, he might well have continued to consider Tyndal no better than a prison. As a consequence of her unquestioning kindness, he had not only found a home but also learned to love and respect Anne as if she were a sister of the blood, not just of the faith.

As if of one mind, the two walked toward the hospital dormitory.

"We have had no word of you since you left. Has your brother recovered or…" A dark shadow drifted across the nun's eyes.

Thomas turned his face away so she would not see his discomfort. Of all people, he most especially hated to lie to Anne, but his work as a church spy was something no one at Tyndal could know. Not Anne. Not even Prioress Eleanor.

"You are kind to ask," he said quickly, fearing that she would mistake his hesitation for grief. "Time and God's grace were needed to cure the ill, but all is now well." If he must lie, he thought, he could at least phrase it with some ring of truth.

"God be praised! I prayed it would be so." Her tone was soft, but her eyes narrowed ever so slightly.

Thomas wondered if she suspected he had lied to her. "I do thank you."

She hastily bowed her head with proper reverence, but he had already caught her expression of doubt. He grew more certain that she was not convinced that his tale of the supposed family illness was true, but, as had been the case from the beginning of their work together, she remained silent about suspicions.

"Tell me what has happened at Tyndal since I left while you show me the patients I should attend," he asked, as they started down the two rows of beds in the dormitory part of the hospital.

At the bed of one fretfully sleeping old man, Anne stopped and laid the back of her hand softly against his sunken cheek, then shook her head. "Despite all our prayers for the recovery of Prior Theobald, they were not enough," she said in a low voice.

"May God be merciful to his soul," Thomas replied and was surprised that he felt sincere regret at the tidings. "He had taken to his bed before I left, but I did not know that death would be certain. Did he suffer long?"

Anne stopped and spoke briefly to a lay brother about the elderly man whose fever still raged, then continued: "He suffered like a saint. At the end, he had little flesh upon him except where his stomach had swollen almost to the bursting point. I do believe it was a malign tumor that killed him. I tried everything but, in the end, gave him only what would relieve the pain until God saw fit to release his soul."

"He may have been a weak man but not, I think, an evil one. Nor, I fear, did he ever recover from Brother Simeon's death."

"And he is buried next to him, as he begged just before he died. He said his sins were too great for his bones to rest with his predecessors as Prior. The prioress honored his wish and he rests at the edge of the cemetery next to Brother Simeon and at some distance from Brother Rupert."

"I understand."

"We all did, Brother."

Thomas felt the sharp twinge of sadness in his heart, then felt something softer brush his leg. He looked down and met the round yellow eyes of the large tabby cat that kept the hospital free of vermin.

"Now we must choose another prior," Anne said.

He bent to scratch the purring bundle of fur between its pointed ears. "And who are the strongest contenders amongst the monks?"

"Would you refuse consideration?" she asked, raising one eyebrow.

"Aye, without hesitation, but the community would not consider one who has come so recently to the religious life. Were the circumstances different, I would still refuse. I am not suited to administration." In fact, he had no ambition to rise beyond his current status, which was wise as well as true. Thomas knew his dour spymaster would find some way to make sure he never became prior at Tyndal even if he were selected.

Anne smiled. "Blessed are the meek for they shall inherit the earth."

"God knows full well that I am not humble, but do tell me which amongst our brothers are sufficiently meek that one might inherit the position of Tyndal's prior?"

"Many, in the beginning, but Brother Andrew and Brother Matthew are the only remaining candidates."

"That Brother Andrew is striving for the position surprises me. I never thought he was an ambitious man."

"Nor is he, but others are on his behalf. When he realized that many here wished him to be our next prior, he said that the final decision was up to God and he would honor His choice."

"Then may God grace us with Brother Andrew. Were He to choose Brother Matthew, I might wonder what sins we had committed to be so cursed. How could anyone even consider a self-righteous and shallow man like Brother Matthew for the position of prior? Have we not learned…"

"Hush! He is sincere in his beliefs and has far more ability than our last prior. Nor is he without thoughtful followers. There are many that would prefer Tyndal become a pilgrimage site, thus diminishing or even stopping our charitable work with the hospital. He has become the leader of that group."

Thomas looked around. "Cease this work? Diminish it? Do we not serve God when we ease mortal pain and help the dying into Man's inevitable fate? What quarrel could he or anyone have with that?"

"A relic cures men by faith and the good will of the saint alone. When we treat the suffering with remedies made by frail mortals, some do believe that we are going against the will of God."

"God would either stop us from finding the remedies or would at least wreak vengeance upon us for doing so if He found these things sinful." Thomas raised one eyebrow. "I confess that I suspect Brother Matthew had more reason than a theological disagreement when he joined this contest."

"I do agree, Brother, and suspect the underlying issue with him is authority. Two sisters lead the hospital. A shrine would require the oversight of the prior and an increase in the number of lay brothers who would be needed to guard the relics. His power in our woman-ruled priory would be enhanced."

"Surely those who agree with him are few."

Anne did not reply but instead gestured for him to come to one patient's bedside. The child's eyes glowed when he saw the monk, and Thomas greeted the boy with joy. After a horrible fall, he had suffered an amputation in the days before Thomas had left for York. All had feared for his life. Now he saw the lad healing and almost ready to return to the family, who had spent days holding his hand, their eyes dark with fear that they would lose their beloved child.

"A happy sight, that," he said as they continued through the maze of patients. "How could anyone doubt that God blesses our work here if they saw the smile on that child's face and the joy of the family who thought they would lose him so young?"

"Few would close the hospital, Brother, but many would love to have a holy relic."

"Who could not see that a shrine would take away people needed to care for the sick?"

"Sister Ruth is one. She agrees that we should keep the hospital but does not look unkindly on our good brother's other ideas."

"Our sub-prioress is often sotted by monks who speak eloquently but have little else to recommend them."

"Have you never been deluded by a fine speech yourself?" Sister Anne cocked her head to one side.

"Aye, you have the truth of that." Thomas shook his head. "I was as blind as Sister Ruth in that matter of Brother Rupert, but she and I have parted company on Brother Matthew."

"And our brother has just strengthened his position significantly."

"Is there no hope for us? I almost fear to ask what he has done!"

"He has found a relic for sale and has been trying to convince our prioress to buy it."

"Will she stand firm?"

"Have you ever known our prioress to do otherwise?"

Thomas nodded. "Have you no good tidings for me?"

Anne gestured at the yellow-eyed tabby that had been following them. "Our hospital cat was safely delivered of three healthy kittens."

"Now that is news indeed!" Thomas looked down at the great tabby. In their staring contest, however, he blinked first. "Did we not think the cat was male with so much fur and great size? Surely a birthing male is a miracle, or perhaps a sign that the end of the world is nigh?"

"Would that the end of war might be nigh! I do ask God sometimes whether men might think twice about ending life if they birthed it, then held it to a breast to feed."

"But surely wars against infidels are holy ones?"

Anne turned away.

Thomas sensed he should not delve into the meaning of that silent answer. "Are there not more soldiers at Tyndal's doors?" he asked instead.

"You are right." She gestured toward the courtyard. "You saw the number just today."

"Perhaps Prioress Eleanor's eldest brother will be coming home as well."

"She has had no word from him for some time, Brother. She says naught, but I know she is worried. When she comes here to comfort those men from Outremer, their grievous wounds to both body and soul break her heart, and I know she thinks the Lord Hugh may suffer similar ills. No one has any recent news of him, however."

"I grieve for her worry. Is she otherwise in good health?"

"Yes, but she also hoped for some word from you. She cared about any grief you might have faced..." Anne hesitated, then added, "On your family visit."

Thomas looked down at his feet. His shoes were still muddy from his journey. "There was no one coming here who could bring a message."

"I understand, Brother."

That she well might, Thomas thought, and, if she did suspect that he had lied, he hoped she was the only one at Tyndal who did.

Chapter Eleven

Thomas saw Eleanor first. Crowner Ralf was at her side. The crowner's presence never signified pleasant tidings nor did the prioress' stern look belie that conclusion.

"I fear something has happened," Thomas said to Anne, inclining his head toward the approaching pair.

Ralf bowed stiffly to the sub-infirmarian. "I regret disturbing you, " he said, his gaze targeted somewhere between Anne and Thomas.

"You are always welcome here, Ralf," Anne replied, her voice soft. "Although I fear you have not come merely to visit."

"You are most generous." Ralf was now studying his feet.

Anne gave her prioress a quick, questioning look, then continued. "I did wonder if your long absence from Tyndal meant you had followed your elder brother to court. Your manners, I note, are more polished than has been the case in times past."

"I am not one for the court." Ralf grunted, then spat. "I have brought you a corpse."

"For cert I did not think you came to grace us with poetry." Sister Anne's eyes shone briefly with mirth.

"To gift us with a corpse is more like the crowner we know," Thomas grinned.

Eleanor's gray eyes darkened. "I fear your jest is out of place, Brother. A corpse is not something to treat with levity." Her words cut like the edge of a sharply honed knife.

Thomas blinked. Hadn't Sister Anne said much the same as he? Why did the prioress single him out for chastisement? He had meant no ill with his remark nor had he taken the crowner's tidings lightly. Surely she knew that. "I beg pardon, my lady." He bowed his head to hide his confusion. "I grieve that any should die before reaching our hospital."

"And that he did, Brother," the prioress said, "but the cause of his death was not any of man's many mortal ills, unless you consider murder such a thing."

Anne turned pale.

Ralf bent toward them and lowered his voice. "Since the man died violently, a death that took place in the woods nearby, I had to bring the tidings to Prioress Eleanor immediately before rumor spread."

"Surely we have suffered enough bloodshed at Tyndal! Why should murder come to our gates again?" Anne raised her hands in a gesture of frustration, then crossed herself. "Forgive me. It was selfish to think only of our peace, not of the poor soul who has been robbed of life and without a priest to ease his soul."

"You have reason enough to be upset after the events of last year." Ralf reached out his hand as if to give Anne a comforting touch, then quickly dropped it.

"You did not say if he was a local man," Eleanor said.

"I do not recognize him." Ralf looked briefly at Anne. "Someone else might. His dress is that of a soldier, and, if the red cross on his cloak is a true sign, I would conclude that he must be a crusader just home from Outremer. My sergeant and I found him lying alone, not a half-mile from here in the clearing by the road that passes through the village. When we first saw him, we feared he had suffered injury from a fall or an attack. Instead, we found him freshly slain."

"Clearing by the road?" Thomas asked, his expression a troubled one. He, too, had just traveled that road but had left it before he reached the clearing to take the shortcut through the woods. Had he seen or heard anything untoward? Only the scream of the high wind that he had taken for Satan's laughter. Could that sound have been human, not demonic?

"I have failed to welcome you home, Brother," Eleanor said, breaking into his thoughts.

Thomas looked at her with puzzlement. Her voice fell like a drop of chill water on his ears. Why so cold to me, Thomas wondered? Not only had she rebuked him unreasonably, she had certainly failed to welcome him, a most unusual breach of courtesy from his usually gracious prioress.

"The nuns have prayed for the speedy return of their confessor, and I am sure Sister Anne is grateful as well that you are back." Eleanor hesitated, thoughtfully studying the monk. "All Tyndal has missed you. Sorely."

Thomas bowed in silence. Although her words now expressed kind concern, her tone suggested but a token interest. Had he somehow fallen into disfavor in his absence?

Sister Anne looked confused as well. "His brother was ill…" she began.

"Forgive me, Brother Thomas," Eleanor said, flushing despite the autumn chill. "I fear these tidings of murder have so taken me by surprise that I have been discourteous. How fares your brother? We have all prayed for his improved health."

"I thank you for that, my lady," Thomas muttered, then willed himself through his litany of lies. "Your prayers have been heard, and my brother is fully recovered."

Did she suspect or had she even learned that his story was false? When the man in black had sent Thomas off on this latest mission, the monk had warned his spymaster that this pretense could not continue forever. Prioress Eleanor must be told how else he served the Church. If she found out that he was a spy, placed in her midst without her knowledge or consent, the prioress' anger over the deception could have unpleasant consequences.

On the other hand, he had said, she could prove a valuable ally if she knew what the Church required of him, but his black-clad master had only waved a dismissive hand when Thomas mentioned all this. The monk hoped the man fully understood what a dangerous enemy Prioress Eleanor could be if crossed. Not only had he seen how wily she herself could be, he also knew that her father was a powerful man in King Henry's court and her brother a close friend of the Lord Edward. The Wynethorpes were not a family one could offend with impunity.

"The monk has a brother?"

"And what do you mean by that, Ralf?" Anne frowned.

Ralf cocked one eyebrow with an exaggerated gesture. "Only that I am now assured he was born of woman and must share some vices with other mortal men. I had some doubt."

"That I was born or that I have vices, Crowner?" Thomas was grateful for the gentle jesting. "There is no doubt that I was born of woman. That I have sinned as much as you, Ralf? Of that there may be reasonable question, for you are a most worldly man."

Ralf threw his head back and roared. "How I have missed you, monk! Even Brother Andrew has not your quick wit."

"But you speak of murder?" Thomas countered, still feeling the sting of his prioress' recent reproach.

The crowner swiped his sleeve across his nose. "Aye, the man was gutted and abandoned in the woods like an illegally slaughtered deer."

A most vivid image, Thomas thought, and swallowed hard.

"Brother Andrew said that you were seen on the road from the west. When did you return, Brother, and by which route did you come to Tyndal?" Suddenly, the crowner's tone lost all warmth.

A shiver of apprehension went through Thomas. "Why do you ask?"

"I seek information. You may have seen something."

"After I left the village near the inn, I followed the road to the turn, then took the shortest way through the forest by the stream. I entered the priory at the mill gate and so never came to the clearing of which you speak."

"You neither heard nor saw anyone on the road?"

Thomas shook his head.

"Odd, that. You must have come near enough to the corpse." Ralf studied the monk in silence. "You noted nothing at all?"

The crowner might be his friend, but his questions were sharply asked. Thomas felt a cold sweat breaking out on his forehead. Once before he had been questioned in like fashion, then thrown into a prison where he had nearly died. This questioning brought his hideous memories back with so much force that his head now spun. "For cert, Ralf. As I said, I left the road just before…" Now his voice was rising in panic. He must calm himself!

"You returned when?"

Thomas could smell his rank fear. He closed his eyes, reminding himself that this was Tyndal, not London. "I stopped at the warming room, then I came to the hospital…"

"To hear a confession?" Ralf asked, sarcasm quite palpable in his voice.

Thomas looked nervously from crowner to prioress. What did all this mean? How had he offended his prioress? Why was his friend treating him like a suspect in a crime? He swayed backward as if he had come to the edge of Hell, then seen the twisting bodies of the burning damned. Someone put a steadying hand on him. "I wanted to find Sister Anne and return to my work," he whispered.

"That is enough, Ralf," Anne said, dropping her hand from Thomas' back.

"Forgive me, Brother." Ralf's voice softened. "As Sister Anne often reminds me, I fail in civility, but I am desperate for information."

Eleanor nodded. "This was a grisly crime. Anything you remember might be of help."

Thomas shook his head. The terror receded slowly. He nervously rubbed his eyes with his hand. "There were other travelers on the road earlier in the day, but I believe I was alone after I left the village. Those with whom I had journeyed thus far stopped for refreshment and lodgings at the inn. The weather had turned most foul." He took a deep breath. Should he tell Ralf about his strange feeling that he had been followed? Nay, he decided, for he had no wish to speak of York or his imaginings about the Prince of Darkness.

Ralf stared up at the bracing of the ceiling like a builder studying his work, then glanced down at Eleanor. "Cuthbert has the corpse tied to his horse, my lady. I was hoping Sister Anne might examine…"

Eleanor looked first to the sub-infirmarian, then turned to the crowner. "Of course, Ralf, but there are some without who have most pressing need of her attention…"

"As soon as I have tended to them, my lady, I will be happy to be of whatever small assistance I may be in this case."

"Then have your sergeant take the sad burden to the outside entrance of the men's chapel, Crowner. We will have a trestle table set up so Cuthbert can put the corpse there and cover it for decency's sake."

"I am grateful, my lady," Ralf replied.

The prioress smiled, then gestured to Anne, and the two women left.

Although the crowner bowed his head, Thomas noticed that Ralf's eyes followed the nuns until they had disappeared from sight around a pillar. When the man still did not move, Thomas coughed.

Ralf turned red and looked at the monk as if he had forgotten he was there. "Will you come to the hospital chapel, Brother?" he quickly asked. "After Cuthbert lays the corpse on the trestle, I would be grateful if you looked upon the body. Perhaps the man was among those with whom you traveled earlier."

"I shall, Crowner," the monk replied, briefly closing his eyes with weary relief. Would he never be able to forget his time in prison, his body abused and bitten by rats while he lay in his own filth? For the moment at least he had recovered from the horror of old memories, and perhaps he could be of help in this current matter. He shook all thoughts of his past from his mind and accompanied Ralf to the chapel.

Chapter Twelve

Eleanor spun around. She saw nothing untoward in the murky shadows beyond the hospital entrance. Why then this prickling at the back of her neck, she asked herself? Was she so filled with dark sin that she thought some mocking imp might be prancing behind her?

She shivered, then continued rushing along the path to her chambers. Sin, indeed! Her body ached, not with the autumn chill but with a longing she had little will to fight. The unexpected sight of Thomas at the hospital had sent shocks through her, reigniting the fires of her passion, causing her knees to weaken, and banishing any hold she might have on rational thought. Angry and humiliated, she was disgusted by her frailty.

"Get thee behind me," she growled at whatever frolicking imp might be near. She could not afford this teary lovesickness. Not only must she emerge victorious in her struggle with Brother Matthew, but she now had a murder committed all too near her priory, news that must be handled with both delicacy and firm reason. She could not continue to suffer these hellish agonies whenever she was in Thomas' presence. Earlier she might have thought she had a choice in this matter of the comely monk. Now she was convinced he must be sent away.

As she marched along, oblivious to the water she splashed through on the way, she swore that she would remain in command of her reason. If the murderer or murderers did seek shelter here, as Ralf had suggested when he first told her of the crime, she could not indulge in womanly weakness. She was Tyndal's leader; thus she must have a man's stomach.

She felt cold, then glanced at her shoes. They were soaked.

She walked on. Could these killers have gained a haven at Tyndal's hospital? If so, she must help the crowner ferret them out. Although she had much confidence in his ability to find the perpetrators, she could not, as leader of this priory, remain passive in this matter. She represented the authority of the Church on these grounds. Thus she could not ignore any evil in her midst, even a criminal who fell under secular law.

Suddenly she realized the direction her thoughts were going and stopped her headlong rush through the cloister garth. She found a dry spot on a stone bench just under the covered walkway and sat.

"Must it take murder to chase lust from my loins?" she asked aloud with grim humor. Raising her eyes to the slate-dark heavens, she continued. "May You send me a kinder remedy, for my soul's cure should not bring more bloodshed to an already violent world!" In truth, the news of this murder had seemed to burn away her woman's softness, at least for the time being. She did not think any of them in the hospital had suspected her longing to take Thomas into her arms, nor noticed how she had studied his face for any sign of grief at a brother's death. Once she had felt her face flush, but she believed she had hidden her feelings with a brusque tone and even discourtesy. Better she be condemned for insensitivity, even cruel indifference, than lust.

With this foul murder to solve, she might be able to delay any decision on Thomas' future at the priory. She did believe in a God of consummate compassion, and surely in good time He would give her guidance, some insight on what she must do with a priest who served Tyndal well but wracked her soul with longings she had once so willingly forsworn. Perhaps the answer would come when she spent her hour of penance on the chapel floor. "Thy will be done in this matter," she said, head bowed as she rose from the cold bench.

In the meantime, she would spend some hours with her account rolls, leaving time for Ralf to study the corpse with Sister Anne. Then she would return to the chapel herself and see what stories the victim might have to tell the prioress of Tyndal.

Chapter Thirteen

The man from Acre slipped into the shadows and leaned his forehead against the rough wall. With a muttered curse, he slammed his fist against the stones.

How dare they bring that hell-bound corpse into a chapel and lay it before the cross? It was blasphemy! They should have burnt the rotting thing in the forest at midnight, then left the ashes for Satan's imps to dance in.

He hit his head once against the masonry, then turned his gaze upward. Dust motes were falling slowly in the feeble beam of light from the window just above him. They reminded him of sand, of Acre, then of blood.

"The man did take the cross," he snarled, sliding into a crouch. "He is probably in Heaven now, laughing and enjoying God's favor, while my wife jerks and twists with the flames of Hell."

His eyes burned with pain, and he longed to close them. His body cried out for rest. The empty place where his soul had once been ached like a festering wound. He wanted to die, but he could not.

He had given his word not to commit self-murder when they took him off the ship in Sicily and said he must make peace with God. When they finally let him finish his voyage to England, there had been days that he regretted his promise, especially when he stared back across the ship's wake toward the land where his wife had died. Nonetheless, he had sworn an oath.

He leaned against the cold, rough-chiseled stone of the hospital wall. Turning his face away from the chapel, he watched the movement in the light from the window, his vision blurring as he stared. The specks of dust were now dancing with so much innocence and grace that he smiled in spite of the throbbing between his eyes. Nay, they were not bloodstained bits of sand, he thought. Might they not be tiny saints?

Had it not been for the man who had been kind to him in the days when he rolled in the dust of Outremer, screaming for miracles, he would not have come here at all. It was that man who promised him God was good, that He would heal him of his pain and guilt. Nonetheless, he still wondered if he might not have found a greater peace, sitting at the grave of his wife until the sun baked his body into a brittle shell and released his soul to join hers.

A tall nun walked by. She looked over at him with a questioning glance, but he shook his head and she went on into the chapel. Might she be the one who was supposed to heal him? Or was it the round one, the one with closed eyes who twisted her fat, white hands as she spoke to those soft-robed cokenays on horseback? It could not be the short one, the one who claimed she was prioress of this place.

He shuddered.

That woman's eyes were the color of hot ashes. When she had looked at him, her eyes had reflected hellfire, burning through him with searing pain. She was no healer. He doubted that she was even prioress here. Nay, she was one of Lucifer's minions hidden in this cloistered place to fish for weak souls. The heat of that gaze would cause any monk's chaste vows to shrivel and his forsaken manhood to swell!

He bit his thumb and felt a chill sweat break out on his forehead. Had they lied to him? If God would let Satan send such a creature to seduce him, then He was no kinder here than He had been in Outremer. The memory of the hot-eyed woman pounded in his head like the banging of a condemned man's fists against his prison door.

Ah, but had he not struggled well in their silent wrestling match in the courtyard? God may have given him up to be the Devil's plaything, but he had won the fight, despite his weariness, even when she had summoned the naked apparition of his wife.

"A woman's body is but a supper for worms," he had roared at the hellish phantom of his wife. "Even yours," he had howled as tears of longing fell from his burning eyes. It was then that the fiendish creature had stepped back, and his wife's spirit had vanished.

Memory of that conflict now melted into a haze of pain. He yearned to weep, but he had no more tears to shed. Although he had triumphed over Satan's forces, his exaltation was short-lived, and a profound sadness darkened his heart.

He knew that the vision of his wife, with her yearning look and out-stretched arms, was only the Devil's painted fantasy. Yet he had hungered to hold her body against his, to join with her in loving passion just one more time. That had been denied him. Despite her ghostly touch, his body had remained cold, his manhood as dead as the woman he had loved.

Twisting with impotent longing, he cursed. For stealing that little comfort from him, he would never forgive that demon, the one who dared call herself the prioress of Tyndal.

Chapter Fourteen

Thomas and Ralf walked along the row of small, screened rooms just behind the dormitory beds in the hospital. The only sound, besides the moans of the suffering and the whispering of the lay brothers, was the soft crunching of their leather shoes on dried and scattered herbs.

"I owe you an apology," Ralf said at last. "I meant nothing by my harsh-spoken questions. Surely you know that."

That I did not, Thomas thought, then replied with greater composure than he felt. "I did not think you were accusing me of murder, Ralf, or of lying for that matter." He had imagined just that, of course, but the crowner need not know why this thought had leapt to mind.

The two men continued on without speaking until a scream from a man nearby startled them. The force of another's most mortal agony chased Thomas' own fears aside, and he realized there was something else that had troubled him about the crowner's remarks, something perhaps more important than his prison memories. He laid a hand on his friend's sleeve.

"May I be frank with you, Ralf?"

"We are both honest men, monk. There is no need for evasion."

"When you asked if I was returning to the hospital to hear a confession, whose did you think I came to hear, and what did you think it would be? Was it a woman's? A particular woman?

I knew from your tone that you did not mean any confession I might hear as a priest."

Ralf turned his head away as if he had been struck.

"Anyone who has said that the relationship between Sister Anne and me is less than chaste is a fool," Thomas said. "If there is sin in respect and friendship, we are guilty of it, but only of that." Looking around, he dropped his voice. "As we both well know, the only man Sister Anne has ever loved was the one she called *husband*. That has not changed, my friend."

Ralf's weather-roughened face turned an uneven red. "Truly, I have never thought otherwise," he replied, his hoarseness betraying swallowed tears. "When you told me you had come to the hospital to see her, the arrow of jealousy did strike my heart. I quickly plucked it out and know full well that there is nothing untoward between you." He cleared his throat. "As you might guess from what I have just told you, I have loved this woman since before her marriage. Only you and she know this, monk, for I have long hidden my feelings."

Thomas struck his friend's shoulder with affection. "Your secret is safe, Ralf." He did not believe, however, that the crowner's love for the sub-infirmarian was as unknown as Ralf thought it was.

"Nor do I doubt that you honor your vows, Thomas, although I confess I have never understood what called you to the religious life. You do seem a most unusual monk."

"Do you think Brother Andrew's calling strange as well?"

"He was a soldier. I understand his vocation." He studied the monk. "Have you ever been in battle, Thomas?"

"Nay."

"But you have bedded women."

Thomas nodded.

"Then you will understand when I tell you that war is like a skillful whore. Some return to her again and again until they die in her arms, exhausted with sated longing. Others may ride her with joy for a few hours, only to flee her embraces to save their souls. No man, however, ever rises from her bed without some mark to show he has lain with her. I see the mark on your porter. I'm sure he sees the same on me."

A fine speech from a man better known for a rough manner and even rougher language, Thomas thought, with surprised admiration.

As if he had just read the monk's mind, Ralf grinned. "That was childish babble. What I mean is that I understand why a former soldier is here, and I respect Brother Andrew for his choice. What I do not comprehend is why a lusty young man like you should have taken to the monkish life."

Thomas fell silent, choosing his words with care. "Perhaps, Crowner, a worldly life and war are both wily whores, seducing men with pretty promises of adventure and excitement. Each does mark any man that lies with her." Thomas hesitated, looking steadily into the crowner's eyes. "Some the whore kills. Some escape. Many she drives to the edge of madness, robbing them of all happiness with her cruelty. Among these are men who seek the monastery. Others may fall over that cliff, their souls breaking on the rocks where they remain, convulsing until they die."

Ralf said nothing, then nodded.

For a moment, the two men looked at each other, agreeing without words to ask nothing further: the one having no desire to speak more about his feelings for a now-encloistered woman; the other not wishing to explain his love for another man.

Of course the crowner was right to be suspicious of his calling, Thomas thought with some bitterness. Had he not been caught in the act of sodomy and thrown into prison, his body tortured, his spirit broken by suggestions that an influential man of God wanted to burn him at the stake, he would not be here. That no man had yet been burned in England as a sodomite was irrelevant. Supporters of the punishment were growing in influence and favor. One day, Thomas believed, someone would burn; he had had no reason to think it would not be him.

Thinking back on the horror of his prison time, he wondered if he had finally retreated from madness or if he was still at the brink. When he first arrived at Tyndal, he knew that he wavered on the edge. With night's darkness came the demons. Some bore the guise of his jailer who had raped him. Some were but voices, the worst being that of Giles, mocking his love. Now he did sleep most nights, but all life had fled his loins. Mad or not, he might as well be a monk. Aye, the edge of the cliff was still visible, but he did think he had stepped back.

"You are deep in thought?" Ralf's voice broke through the musing.

Grateful to be dragged from his bleak memories, Thomas grinned. "A rare enough thing, you'd say. Still, I fear that others may suspect that there is something unchaste in my friendship with Sister Anne. I would not be the cause of any shame for she is a most honorable lady."

"Nay, Thomas. Her honor is safe. Not once have I heard ill rumors about either of you. Were they even started, Prioress Eleanor would put a firm stop to them for she trusts and respects you both. As do we all."

After her cold reception, Thomas was no longer sure that his prioress either trusted or respected him. He shook his head.

"You do not believe me?" Ralf put his hand on the monk's shoulder and looked at him for a long time.

"I do, Crowner…"

"I have good sources from inside Tyndal, Thomas. To prove that, I will tell you that I know about your cleverness in the matter at Wynethorpe Castle last winter."

"Then you have an unreliable resource, Ralf. My part was modest. A man must find something to do, stuck on the Welsh border in the middle of a snowstorm. Having a murder to solve might have kept my blood from freezing, but it was our prioress who led us to the truth, not I."

"Careful what you say about my source, monk! Tostig is not one to cross, and his source is his sister. He believed everything Gytha told him. So do I, for she is a most honest woman."

Thomas laughed. "If Tostig and his sister told you those tales, I would not say otherwise, although I might suggest that they were too generous…"

"A spy could not have better informants."

Thomas winced at the reference. "Let us go to the chapel and view your rotting corpse."

Ralf stopped near the entrance to the chapel and winked at his friend. "After the effort of caring for your brother, this murder may prove as much a potion for you as the one in Wales."

"Then let us go in, Ralf," Thomas said with a laugh, then looked around his friend into the chapel. "Sister Anne awaits."

When she heard the two men enter, the sub-infirmarian covered the dead man, then turned around and smiled at the crowner. "How thoughtful to bring a corpse, just fresh from his killing, to greet our brother on his return," she said.

Ralf stepped back as if she had slapped him. "Annie, this was not of my planning!"

"Nor did I think so. Peace, Ralf, I was but jesting."

The crowner was quite stricken into silence.

"Yet a corpse there is," Thomas said to Anne, "and Ralf may have brought me to see it, but it is your opinion he hopes to get. I fear I might not remember the man even if we did pass on the road."

As he watched her looking at the crowner in silence, Thomas saw a strange look race across her eyes and wondered if he had been wrong in what he had said to Ralf. He was certain that Anne had loved her former husband, as she did the welfare of her soul, and had seen proof enough that she still did. Nonetheless, there was something between Anne and Ralf, something more than what lay between a woman, who was kind, and a lover she had rejected. Perhaps she had loved him once? Not that it would make any difference. Thomas had no doubt that Sister Anne was now quite firmly wedded to the religious life.

"He should hear from both of us, Brother," she said, her voice soft with whatever memories had just come to her. "As we learned last winter at Wynethorpe, your observations are most thorough."

With that, Anne beckoned them to come closer and view the corpse.

⚭ ⚭ ⚭

On a trestle table lay the body, hidden by a rough cloth. Despite the chill, an over-sweet stench thickened the air.

As the men came forward, Anne carefully folded back the cloth that had been placed over the face of the murdered man. She could not have been gentler if the man had been sleeping.

When Thomas looked down at the gray face of the corpse, mortal time slowed like the heartbeat of the dying. The man might be dead, he thought, but he would have sworn that the widened eyes of the corpse were turning, turning to stare at him.

He blinked.

The man's mouth twisted into a snaggle-toothed grin, and the tip of his tongue seemed to flick in and out with lewd suggestiveness.

Thomas gasped and staggered back.

"By all that is holy," Ralf cried out, reaching for his friend. "What is wrong?"

Ralf's words sounded as hollow as speech heard from the depths of a pond. Thomas' head began to spin, his legs lost all feeling, and he knew he was slowly sinking into an ever-growing hole. "God help me!" he whispered as velvet darkness slipped over him and he lost consciousness.

Chapter Fifteen

Thomas awoke to find himself lying on the ground while Sister Anne held a foul-smelling concoction under his nose. He sneezed.

"He's alive!" Ralf exclaimed, dropping the monk's head with a thud.

Had Thomas felt better, he might have laughed.

"Sit up slowly." Anne nodded at the crowner for help.

May this be the last day so full of lies, Thomas thought, as Ralf lifted him back on his feet. "I fear my faintness must have come from hunger, nothing more," he explained with some truthfulness. "Since the sun rose, I have traveled far but had nothing to eat except a bite of bread given to me by a pilgrim on the way to Norwich." He gently shook off the crowner's arm. "As I promised, I will look upon that corpse."

"Can that not wait…" Anne began, but seeing the expression on the crowner's face, she fell silent.

Thomas walked with the careful step of a weakened man back to where the corpse lay. He most certainly did not want to see that face again yet knew he must force himself to the task. Surely he had only imagined what had gripped his heart with chill horror and caused him to faint from the sight?

With his back to Anne and Ralf, Thomas closed his eyes tightly. His heart pounded loudly in his ears, but as he pried his eyes open and stared down on the corpse, a sigh of relief escaped his lips.

The man was not his former jailer. Fighting his old terror, he studied the man with care. Although the head shape and mouth were much the same, the body was too short. He picked up one of the hands and examined the fingers. These stubby things were nothing like the long claws that had squeezed and scratched at his genitals. Even knowing that this man was not his rapist, the similarity was not vague enough. The gorge rose in Thomas' throat, and he quickly looked away.

"Do you recognize the man?" The crowner was watching him most carefully.

Anne slapped Ralf's arm. "Enough! Our brother has just regained his senses and is still weak. Let him take his time. Perhaps he is not as ready or eager as you are to deal with rotting bodies, no matter how important you think they are."

"I am grateful for your kindness, but I am recovered enough." Thomas turned away from the body but caught hold of the table for balance. Hoping Ralf had believed his story of weakness, he now looked steadily at the crowner, willing himself to say what he must with the firmness of truth. "I do not believe I saw this man on the road."

He failed. He had faltered in mid-sentence, his voice rising as the force of his old memories grabbed him by the throat. Had he heard this from another man, he would have suspected him of lying, or at least saying less than he knew. Ralf was no fool. He would hear it too. Thomas grimaced.

⚭ ⚭ ⚭

Ralf was deeply troubled. Before Sister Anne would discuss the dead man with him, she had insisted that he take Thomas safely back to the monks' quarters. This he had been glad enough to do, but, as the two men walked out of the chapel, he glanced over at his friend. Thomas had fallen deep into one of his black silences.

Early in their acquaintance, Ralf had noticed that Thomas often suffered from fits of melancholia. These, according to Sister Anne, were caused by an imbalance of the humors. Still, humors became unbalanced for good reason. Even he knew that. What had caused this shift now?

He thought back on the day. Thomas had been cheerful enough when he had first seen him, jesting as was his wont whenever the two men were together. Of course, he had been upset with the news of the murder. So had Prioress Eleanor. Yet he had recovered from that and his spirits had risen until…until he had seen the corpse. Then he had fainted. Was there something about the dead man that had caused the monk's humors to go out of balance?

The crowner continued to study the tall, broad-shouldered man walking quietly beside him. Not that he suspected Thomas of anything untoward, but Ralf was too experienced with the solving of crime not to question when something did not quite fit. Thomas' vocation, to his mind, had never fit the man. Most men would have claimed, readily enough, that they had had a vision or a calling or had lost something of so much value on earth that they had retreated from the world. Thomas had never done any of these things, although his suggestion that both war and the secular life were alike might suggest the latter. In the past, there had been no reason to discover why Thomas had chosen a contemplative profession. Was there now?

The monk's manner and speech were courtly enough to suggest high birth, although the crowner suspected his friend was a by-blow. Perhaps his father's rank was too low to provide a clever son with more than this simple priesthood in the Order of Fontevraud? Ralf doubted that. There was a confidence about Thomas that made the crowner guess that the man was not just the son of a scullery maid, fathered by some minor knight. The sheriff, Satan take his soul, might know more of this Thomas of London. Were Ralf inclined to speak to said cursed brother, he could have asked him. He was not, however, so inclined.

Whatever Thomas' past, the crowner reminded himself, the monk had a soldier's proven courage. This was no delicate fellow who would faint from the stink of a drawn corpse. What was there about this particular one that had sent his friend's humors into rebellion and caused him to call out in agony for God to save him as he fell into blackness? Ralf shook his head. Had his friend suffered some secret wound that only his confessor had seen, and, if so, had it been caused by this soldier of God? And why had he so carefully examined the dead man's hands? Had he seen him on the road, his face would have been all he would have noted.

Ralf clenched his fist. Anger flooded his heart. A soldier had been butchered, a man who had gone to serve God in Outremer. He would find the foul killer of this brave man. On his oath, he would! And if Thomas knew…

A shout put an end to the crowner's thoughts.

With no warning, a figure leapt out of the shadows.

Ralf reached for his sword.

Thomas grabbed the crowner's hand, thus keeping him from drawing his weapon. "He means no harm," he said, as the figure bowed and danced in front of them.

"We are well met, good fellows, are we not?" The swaying man hid his face behind his hands, then began to sing in a high-pitched voice. "A man whose fruit has been plucked." The dancer cupped his genitals. "A servant of the law who cannot find justice." His voice dropped as he danced in a circle in front of Ralf. "And a jester with no king to hear his jokes." The dancer pulled one side of his mouth into a distorted grin as he shifted from foot to foot. "Alas, such lack!"

"Satan's tits," Ralf exploded. "It's the wild man I saw when I came here with the corpse."

"Mad, methinks."

"Or possessed?"

"He does not blaspheme as do those possessed," Thomas said as the man turned his back and danced away from them. "And he dances rather than foaming at the mouth and rolling on the ground. I wonder if he is afflicted with the dancing mania?" He frowned. "Yet I see no others so touched. Sister Anne once told me that these most often come for care in numbers, not alone. She might find this one most interesting."

"If he can be caught." Ralf pointed to two lay brothers running down the hospital aisle.

The object of their frantic chase danced in ever decreasing circles and laughed with crazed merriment. "Monks here. Monks there," he sang.

"Do you get many mad ones here, Brother?" Ralf asked, scratching his head.

"'Tis rare. In London we had more..."

Ralf snorted. "London *is* a house for the mad, my friend."

"The inhabitants often come from the country, Crowner. Like this one..."

"They've caught him." Ralf nodded as he watched the lay brothers leading the man away, his head now bent, his body limp and docile. "I never understood the pleasure men find in visiting the mad," the crowner said. "It is cause for grief, not laughter, when men lose their ability to reason."

"Perhaps they jest out of gratitude that God has not chosen to curse them with similar suffering?"

"Then they are mad to do so. The difference between a man possessed of his wits and one whom God has cursed with the loss of them is this thin." Ralf held two fingers but a fine line apart.

"In my absence, you have become philosophically inclined, Ralf."

"Never, monk. This beastly rain must be blamed for washing too much reason from my head."

Thomas nodded, then turned back to watch the madman. Suddenly, the man looked around. His eyes widened as if in terror as he stared at the monk. Thomas shuddered. "Why look at me so?" he whispered.

Ralf, too, had noticed the madman's look.

Chapter Sixteen

Ralf looked up at the darkened sky. Not only was the rain relentless, the sea wind gave it a cutting edge. Shivering, he scurried into a sheltered spot in the hospital courtyard. He had a job to do, and cold work it was for cert.

Surely, the murderer must be here. Only a fool would have continued on in this weather. Scrutinizing the few people that still moved about in the dimming light, Ralf decided that the clever man would have feigned some illness, when he saw the crowds at the hospital gates. Thus he would have found a safe haven, hiding amongst the many sick, while getting a hot meal and a dry bed in the bargain. He might even have persuaded Sister Christina to pray for his bloodstained soul. With that thought, Ralf's mood turned even grimmer.

Aye, he was convinced this is where the murderer must have come and that no sensible killer would have drawn undue attention by asking for a traveler's shelter here when the inn offered not only clean accommodations but food and drink more congenial to the secular taste. Even pilgrims, many of them families escaping the smithy or the shop to refresh their spirits at some holy spot, preferred a meaty stew and good wine or ale to the lean monastic diet offered by Tyndal Priory. In fact the prioress had confirmed, with an expression suggesting no regret, that the new inn had certainly taken that custom away. Few healthy people, except an occasional monk, had requested shelter for months. If truth be told, she had added after some thought, not many monks had either over the last several weeks.

Thus he had sent Cuthbert off to the innkeeper to ask about travelers arriving this day or if any others had returned to the inn after leaving it earlier. There were none of either, the innkeeper had confirmed. The foul coastal weather had not only kept his own custom from leaving, but it had prevented others from arriving. Those staying on had more than made up for any new travelers, the innkeeper had added, patting his stomach in satisfaction, for they chose to sit downstairs, where he kept a fire roaring, and cry out for drink to warm their damp bones where the fire could not.

Ralf shook his head. He'd rather question healthy strangers in a comfortable inn, where he might enjoy a hot stew with good ale himself, than examine the sick for any well enough to slice into a man as if he were cleaning game. Since he had been the one to conclude that the killer was here, he would take the responsibility for searching Tyndal. Of course, he could be wrong and have lost the killer entirely by looking no farther than the priory. Might he or the murderer be the more foolish?

Ralf growled to himself. He was not a happy man. When he had left Thomas at the entry to the monks' quarters, he soon fell into a particularly foul mood. After seeing what violence mortals did to each other during his years as a soldier and then as crowner, Ralf doubted that fork-tailed imps ever leapt out of smoky holes to do evil unto men. Nonetheless, he did suspect that invisible ones were sent by the Prince of Darkness to invade even honest men's souls, troubling their spirits so they could do naught but cruel and sinful acts until the imp was satisfied.

Ralf knew that he had most certainly done and thought things he should not, only to feel the shame of his sin when reason chased the fetid stench of evil from his soul. Even today, within a few hours, he had not only lusted after a nun but had felt base desire for Gytha, the sister of his childhood friend. When she had brought him a hearty meal of bread and cheese, teasing him as she was wont to do about the roars of his empty belly keeping godly souls awake, he had suddenly realized that she was no longer a child but a finely formed woman. As she walked away, he had enjoyed the sight of her rounded buttocks and slim waist, then recoiled in horror when his manhood had stiffened.

I may be more sinful than most men, Ralf thought with embarrassment, but surely the Devil's minions make as merry with monks as they do with crowners. Had a like creature dug into Thomas' soul like some demonic weevil, causing corruption there? Was the monk not hiding something? Why had he behaved as he did with the corpse? And what of the madman? Why had he looked on Thomas with so much terror? Was there a connection or were these incidents quite coincidental, meaningless?

"'S blood!" the crowner spat with anger.

A man nearby jumped as if he had just seen Satan himself.

Shoving aside lingering thoughts of soft breasts for the rougher lure of solving a murder, Ralf ignored the fellow and walked into the hospital. He was wasting time watching these pitiful few, so desperate that at this late hour they still stood soaked and chilled, waiting for someone to see to their pain and ills. The murderer would have long since found shelter inside.

⚬₪₪₪⚬ ⚬₪₪₪⚬ ⚬₪₪₪⚬

The crowner shouted to a lay brother.

"Aye, Crowner," Brother Beorn said as he gestured for a woman with six children to come closer. Even in this poor light, one could see that the children's faces were covered with little red spots.

"Your madman. What have you done with him?"

"He sleeps, praise be to God!"

"I would speak to him."

"Let him be. Sister Christina has calmed him with her prayers. He makes little sense and awake would once more cause havoc amongst us all. Have mercy on the dying and the sick, Crowner, if not on those who must tend him."

Brother Beorn knelt down in front of one child. Just as he did, the little girl vomited on his robe, then raised her face to the sky and wailed. The man took his sleeve, gently wiped her face clean, and shrugged as if it were nothing when the mother wrung her hands with frustration and embarrassment.

Ralf frowned. Was he mad to think that questioning someone so bereft of wit would be of any value? Then he shook his head as he thought about his last encounter with the man. Surely the fellow was not mad at all, despite his odd dancing. The words the man had spoken held more wit than the speech of many who claimed greater ones. Had Ralf been one to play at dice, he would have bet that the dancing was an act, and that act did not ring like any king's freshly minted coin. Besides, Brother Andrew had sent word that he could find no one who had seen the man enter the priory gate, and Ralf did find the encounter with Brother Thomas most curious.

That settled it. He would talk to the madman even if doing so meant the man would scuttle up the walls to the wooden beams above, dance on those rafters, and wake the dead in all the graveyards of Tyndal Priory.

Ralf lifted his fist and shook it at the lay brother. "See this? Should he show signs of straying, I will make him sleep once more."

Brother Beorn grimaced, then spoke to a lay sister about the children and, with weary resignation, gestured at Ralf to follow him.

⌘ ⌘ ⌘

Ralf shook his head when he saw that no one was on watch at the private hospital cell. "You left none to guard him despite his wildness?" he asked the lay brother.

"We have few enough to care for these." Beorn gestured at the rows of sick, moaning and praying for respite. One man sat up, gasping for air, and a lay brother rushed to his side. "We are healers, Crowner, not soldiers guarding prisoners."

"You have not even sent a priest to exorcise him?"

"Sister Christina will see him again soon. Her prayers heal as often as exorcism. After her last visit, he fell into a sleep more peaceful than either the mad or possessed are wont to do." He glared at Ralf. "We had considered that a blessing."

Ralf ignored the hint. "I will send word for you to come when I leave so he will not be left unattended."

Beorn's eyes narrowed and he hesitated as if he would say something further, then turned and marched away in silence.

⚭ ⚭ ⚭

The man was truly sleeping, if his loud snores were genuine. Asleep, he did not seem any different from other men, Ralf thought as he studied the man's face. Perhaps sleep, like death, healed the mortal ills of many men?

"Fa!" he muttered. "I am beginning to sound like one of my courtly brother's foppish poets." He spat, then took a few more moments to look the madman over carefully.

The fellow did not appear to be a wandering felon. Both ears were intact and his nostrils were not slit, although the nose had been broken just below the bridge at some time past. Had he been in a street brawl or had he been a soldier?

Ralf studied the one visible hand. All fingers were present, although crisscrossed with many white scars. This was a man who had worked with knives, perhaps, or other sharp things. Had he been a craftsman before he had, willingly or not, discarded his reason?

The man shifted from his side onto his back. There was no sign of a crusader cross, nor was there any other indication that he had been a man of arms. The cut of his robe was monkish in its simplicity with a bunched cowl around the neck and a rope tied around his waist. The cloth was unbleached, dirty and rough, but bore no mark that would distinguish him as belonging to any particular Order.

The faded reddish color of his face did suggest to Ralf that the man was either fond of drink or had spent time in a more southern climate. Perhaps the man was one of those wandering preachers like Peter the Hermit who had taken aged men, women, and even children off to Outremer to fight with just their staves, fists, and faith, then left his followers to die or be sold into slavery. Peter the Hermit, unlike his converts, had escaped.

Ralf shook his head. He had only contempt for those who drew the ignorant and innocent into mad plans that brought only sorrow to the followers. He hoped this man was not such a creature. If so, the crowner might be sorely tempted to give him a taste of what the man had left others to suffer.

Suddenly Ralf realized that the man was now quite awake and staring at him.

"You wish to speak with me?" The man's voice was hoarse, as if he were unaccustomed to using it or else had done so far too much. As he pushed himself upright, he pulled his cowl over his head, then quickly shoved it back with an inexplicable change of mind.

"You are not mad at all, are you?"

"What is madness, Crowner?"

"I did not come to play with words. What do you call yourself?"

The man spread his arms. "Adam? Jesus? Beelzebub? All suit."

Ralf grabbed the man by the collar of his robe and pulled him upright. "Do not play the fool with me. Your time for feinted babble is over. Oh, you may dance for me if you will, but, as you prance, think on this: those that dance for me usually do so at the end of a rope."

"Gibberish may be my tongue, but the gibbet will never be the ceiling over my head. What words would you have with me in the English tongue and under this holy roof?"

For all his cocky words, Ralf saw fear flicker in the man's eyes and he was pleased. He pushed him back on the bed. "Who are you?"

"No one of note. I am a free man, a pilgrim seeking a cure for an invisible wound."

Aren't we all? Ralf thought. "Surely not madness," he said with contempt. "Why play that game?"

"Is it madness to fear Satan's henchmen hiding in the forests along the road or cutpurses amongst bands of travelers? I have been left in peace while others have been attacked. Knowing that, which would you say was mad?"

Ralf visibly clenched one fist, relaxed it, then clenched it again. "What road did you take to Tyndal?"

"The one that runs by your village."

"No one saw you enter the priory gates."

"Am I to be condemned because mortal men are blind? I am here, am I not? I did not float over the walls like some hellish imp. Satan would not want this thin soul of an honest pilgrim when there are fatter souls to fry."

Ralf waited. The man said nothing further. "Whom did you see between the village and the priory gates?"

"None."

Ralf bent over the man, his nose almost touching the other's. "I smell the rank stench of a liar. A man has been murdered on that road, and, if you do not cooperate, I assure you that slowly pulled teeth will hurt less than my methods."

The man drew back, his color now quite white. "Do not press me so, good sir! Some madness I may feign, as you say, but only to save myself from harm. Yet not all you see is false. Did I not tell you that I suffered from an invisible wound?"

"The stench grows, knave!"

"Have mercy!" the man whined. "If the sainted William is to cure me, I must not offend either the saint or God. Surely I would do so by pointing an accusing finger at one who may serve Him."

"And what mean you by that babble?"

The man tried to turn away from Ralf, but the crowner grabbed him again by the neck of his robe. "Speak!"

"Do not hurt me! I will tell you," he whimpered. "A monk. I saw a monk on the road to Tyndal."

Despite the chill that ran through him, Ralf begin to sweat. He pushed the man back. "Describe him."

"You stood by him near the chapel. A tall, broad-shouldered man with hair the color of red gold. Early today, I saw him standing at the bend in the road, near the clearing."

"What more!"

"The wind was howling like the screams of the damned. The monk was so tall, his hair the color of flames. I feared he was no monk at all but the Prince of Darkness himself. Fear turned my feet toward the woods and I fled, coming by accident upon the mill gate entrance. That is why no one saw me at the main gate. I know nothing more, Crowner. I swear it!"

Ralf's shoulders sagged, but he said nothing further.

Slowly the man backed away, watching to see what the crowner would do. When Ralf did not move, the madman rose from his bed and once more began to dance. This time, his feet moved slowly as if his silent harpist played a most melancholy tune.

Chapter Seventeen

"I swear to you, Ralf, that I did not see him!"

Thomas and the crowner were standing outside the parish church where the monk had just emerged from the sacristy. Cuthbert stood at a discreet distance.

"He described you."

"I do not doubt it, but he also saw me when we were standing together near the hospital chapel. If the man is mad, as he appears to be, he could have taken the reality of one sighting and made a fantasy for a prior one. I did not notice him on that road."

"The man's madness comes and goes. He may be as mad as you or I."

"If he is neither mad nor possessed, then he may have other reasons for wanting to cast some suspicion upon me. Perhaps he is the murderer."

"I have made inquiries. Brother Matthew told Brother Beorn earlier that he had found the man in the village, unable to travel farther due to his affliction. According to the lay brother, your fellow monk believes the man to be a true penitent who, quite sadly, must travel to Norwich for a final cure at the shrine of Saint William. In the meantime, he sent him here, claiming that Sister Christina's prayers might give him a short respite so that he could continue on to Norwich."

"That does not mean he did not commit the crime."

"Look at him, monk," Ralf said impatiently. "He is as tall and slender as your Brother Matthew, not a man likely to win a struggle with a soldier. Besides, he was sweating like a horse when he told his tale about you and wailed like a child that he would be sent to Hell for pointing any finger at a priest. As I told him, monk, I am in no mood for word jousts. I have a murder to solve. What did you see on that road that you have failed to tell me?"

Thomas fell silent. "I am trying to remember if I passed him or..."

Ralf cut him off. "You are sure you did not pass by the clearing? You are sure you saw no one?"

"As I have said, I also took the shortcut through the woods to the mill gate. I did not go around the bend in the road nor see the clearing. Perhaps he was behind me and I noted him not, but he was wrong if he claims I went farther than I did." The monk's mouth twitched with the effort to retain self-control.

"Do you have witnesses?"

"Only God," the monk snapped.

Ralf said nothing in the face of his friend's anger. He stared at the ground and began grinding his heel into the earth with a circling motion. At last, he looked up, his expression both troubled and cold as stone. "Thomas, you were much disturbed when you saw the murdered man. You examined him at greater length than a man would who was trying to remember a face. You were seen near the body. I believe that you do know more than you are telling me."

"For the love of God, Crowner, I did not do this deed!"

"My heart may believe you, Thomas, but there is something you are refusing to tell me. Perhaps you did not kill the soldier, but I cannot ignore either what this man says or your unexplained behavior." He raised one hand in protest. "Nay, do not give me the story about your weakness from hunger. I have yet to know any monk who failed to find bread when he needed it." Then he hesitated, dropping his voice. "I must say something further. Will you hear it?"

Thomas nodded with angry reluctance.

"You know me to be a man of justice as well as your friend. If you are in any way involved with this murder and tell me so now, I promise you will not suffer cruelly for it. If you are protecting someone…" He waved his hand as the monk began to protest. "Very well, but if you have important knowledge and do not confess it, I promise I will render full justice on you myself. What friendship there was between us ceases."

Colors from the white of rage to the red of humiliation waved through Thomas' face. At last, he took a deep breath. "I tell you truly that I fear death and God's judgment like all mortal men. Had I killed the man that lies within, I would never have returned to Tyndal. No one expected me to arrive when I did, and no one would have been the wiser had I changed course and taken a boat to France. Nor would anyone on the ship question why a man with a tonsure was going to the Holy Land. No, Ralf, I did not kill the man no matter what evidence to the contrary there may be."

Ralf studied the hole in the ground he had dug with his heel. It was filling with rainwater. "But you know something of it."

Thomas shrugged with contempt, then turned away.

Ralf gestured at his sergeant to come forward, then reached out and seized the monk by the arm, twisting it ever so slightly behind him as he pulled him back. "On any hope I may have of Heaven, I wish to believe you, Thomas, but your actions belie your words. You know that dead man or something of him. Why else would you act as you did?"

"Of that, I shall not speak," Thomas snarled.

"Then you leave me no choice but to take you into custody."

With that, Cuthbert bound the stunned Thomas and led him away into the night.

Chapter Eighteen

"He is innocent." Eleanor struck her fist on the arm of the chair. "There is no question of it."

Ralf bowed his head. "My lady, no one could wish him innocent more than I. Nonetheless, I fear there is doubt about his involvement."

"Doubt? Are we speaking of Brother Thomas, a man we know well?" The prioress enunciated each word with angry precision.

Ralf spread his hands in frustration. "I must keep him in custody until he explains himself. He was seen too near the place where this murderous act took place not to have witnessed something, yet he swears he knows nothing and squirms like the most guilty of men as he does. Beloved though Brother Thomas may be by us..."

"Once again, Ralf, you are following a road no one else would even think of taking." Anne's voice shook. "How could you believe the word of a witless man or, if possessed of his wits, possibly the guilty one himself? Brother Thomas would have confessed the crime had he committed it, and that he has not."

"I did not say he had actually done it, only that he knows more than he will say. Do you not care as deeply as I that an innocent soldier was gutted just outside this priory?" His voice began to rise. "As for confessing to such a deed, Annie, not many men, however honest, would willingly admit to the brutish act."

Anne folded her arms. "Brother Thomas would. He is a monk."

Ralf stared at her as if she had just changed shape in front of him. "Have you forgotten what happened here last…? Nay, you surely cannot be so foolish, Annie! Monks are like any other men except for the tonsures they bear." Then the crowner slammed his hand down on the table. "Or have the cold vows you took frozen your reason as they have that of your fellows in the Church?" he shouted. "A tonsure has never stopped a man from committing crime, and it is time the Church realized the king's right to punish those who do."

The air's heavy chill was matched only by the silence that fell on all in the room.

It was Prioress Eleanor who spoke first. "I think we were speaking of Brother Thomas, Ralf."

The crowner flushed. "Please forgive these rude words from this sinful man. As you must know, I honor you both and have been humbled, not just by your devotion to God but by your equal dedication to mortal justice."

Anne turned her back to the crowner.

"Your words are forgotten," Eleanor said, knowing that few did ever forget these outbursts. Indeed, her own anger was hot, but the pain she saw in Ralf's eyes began to soften her heart with sadness. She had long suspected the love he bore her sub-infirmarian and knew well the troubled relationship the crowner had with his two elder brothers, especially the one in the Church. "If you do not believe that our good brother killed this man," she went on, "please explain why you put him under guard in a priory cell. Placed there, I might add, without my permission." She sat back and met the crowner's gaze with firmness. "Need I remind you that I am his superior here and the only one with the authority to say that this might be done?"

Ralf bowed with profound respect. "Thus I came to you immediately, my lady. If you will, set aside my own suspicions. Would you not agree, however, that it would be most foolish to ignore Brother Thomas' presence near the place where the killing took place?"

Eleanor said nothing.

"The monk turns pale." The crowner's tone was tense. "He faints when he sees the dead man. Then he not only looks at the face, sweating as he does, but he studies the man's hands as if he were looking for something specific. Is this what you would do if you had only seen the man in passing, a man who meant nothing to you?"

The prioress did not move.

"Later, when I asked him to explain his behavior, he refused. Why? I swear Brother Thomas knows who the victim is but, for some unexplained reason, will not say."

"So might any man sweat and pale if questioned as if he were already judged guilty of the crime." Sister Anne had turned around. Her eyes were rimmed with red.

Ralf swallowed but ignored the remark. "Would I be serving justice if I ignored my observations of the good brother's behavior as I do most fervently wish I could?" Pleading with Eleanor, he stretched out a hand. "After all the years I have spent hunting those who defy the king's laws, I do recognize the behavior of guilty men. Surely you will acknowledge that."

The prioress nodded. "I respect your skill, Ralf. Nevertheless, might you not wonder more about this witness of yours as Sister Anne has suggested? Why do you not suspect that he is your killer?"

"I did not dismiss this conclusion." Ralf shifted uncomfortably. "Brother Beorn told me that some had noticed the man and his strange behavior in the village several days before the murder took place. The innkeeper confirms that the soldier was only at the inn two nights, and no one has claimed that the two ever spoke. If this fellow was behaving like a madman before the soldier even came here, I cannot conclude that his antics were intended to hide himself from suspicion."

Eleanor nodded for him to continue.

"He claims to be a pilgrim on the way to Norwich where he hoped he might be cured of his affliction. In fact, he freely admitted to me that he is not always witless, my lady, but rather suffers episodes of madness. Based on what I have been told, there is no reason to suspect he is lying. Finally, he did not say our good brother was the murderer, only that he had seen him standing near where the soldier died." He hesitated, then added quietly, "My lady, I would suffer reproach for letting Brother Thomas remain free in view of his behavior and proximity to the crime."

"And thus you took this stranger's word over that of a respected servant of God, a man who has also demonstrated an honest courage as you yourself well know?" Anne's words dripped with contempt.

Ralf bent forward with fatigue and braced his hands against the table. "It takes strength to mutilate a man as someone did our soldier. The madman is slight…"

"Unlike Brother Thomas?" Anne snapped. "So you are now saying that he could have committed…"

"One moment, please, Sister!" Eleanor looked with puzzlement at the crowner. "Ralf, you just said you would be rebuked if you did not take my monk into your custody? By whom? Surely no one in either this priory or village?"

Ralf shook his head.

"I cannot believe that you are being swayed by something other than the pursuit of justice. You have never been one to care much for anything else."

Ralf exhaled slowly, rubbing his eyes as if they hurt. "The victim was a crusader. As my dear brother would say in his quaint way, this fact makes the murder something more than a simple country matter."

"Your brother's views have rarely troubled you before, my friend. Why this sudden change?" Eleanor asked.

"Until now, the sheriff has stayed at court to increase his prestige, while leaving me to maintain order in the shire as I see fit. Now that our good king's health fails, there has been a change. In the last few months, my brother has demanded both detailed reports on shire crime and speedy punishment of malefactors. I suspect he fears that Prince Edward might not like sheriffs who are perceived as weak on crime."

"How can any man know which way our prince may turn?" Eleanor replied.

"Aye, but all may assume one thing with certainty. The Lord Edward is a soldier and cares much for the men who joined him in the Holy Land. Thus, the murder of any returning crusader on English soil will have the attention of powerful men even beyond the shire. If I do not pursue this matter vigorously, my brother will be counted as weak. That he will not tolerate. In short, my lady, I will be directed in this matter."

"Like our Lord, King Henry has shown mercy to prisoners and forgiven many who have repented their sins," Anne began. "Once on so godly a path, why would we change?"

"And our king has been roundly condemned as womanly for just these actions. I doubt the Lord Edward will be so soft, and my brother has made it clear that he does not wish to lose all by seeming lenient on crime and felons. If I should fail him in any way he deems significant, he has already said that he will replace me with one of his more pliant fellows. This killing of a crusader is this kind…" Ralf looked from Prioress Eleanor to Sister Anne. "Despite my rude ways, do you not think that I am still a better crowner than such a replacement?"

"Your brother is not the only one who hopes to be wearing the latest style when the season changes. No one, however, would ever accuse you of caring about the cut of your clothes. Aye, we all much prefer the crowner we now have, a man who has always worn the unchanging attire of an honest man." Eleanor paused. "The arrest of an innocent person may be swift, but I would hardly call it just. How could it satisfy the sheriff?"

"I have not arrested Brother Thomas, my lady. I have put him into cautionary custody in a priory cell that remains under your control. From my brother's perspective, a man seen near a corpse around the time of the killing, who has failed to act in a forthright manner even to someone he calls *friend,* should not remain free."

"A *monk,* not just a man," Eleanor added.

"Monk or no, my brother would find it unjustifiable to let him remain free. By putting Brother Thomas into custody, a most comfortable confinement in fact, I will have shown firmness in this matter. As for arresting an innocent man for the crime, I would never do that. Do you not both know me better than to think I would?"

Eleanor remained silent for some time, then reached out and touched the crowner gently on the arm. "You have logic in what you have done," she said. "Nonetheless, do not forget that Brother Thomas is under my jurisdiction as representative of Church justice. He is not under the rule of your brother or even King Henry, and I retain the right to overturn this act. Nevertheless, I shall allow it for the time being. If the confinement is brief and the true murderer quickly found, I would prefer you continue in your brother's favor. Should I find good reason to reverse this action, however, I shall. In the meantime, you are..."

"...continuing the investigation, my lady. I believe there may be others who traveled along the same road as our good brother and the man who identified him. Although I do not want to aggravate whatever ill brought them to your care, I beg permission to bring those who can walk to the chapel to view the corpse's face. Let us hope that one of them will know more of the corpse."

"You have my permission, and a lay brother will be assigned to assist you." Eleanor continued, "Should you wish to question any of the women on the other side of the hospital..."

"Few women travel alone, and only a man would have had the strength to do this deed. Thus I do not think..."

"Yet one might have been a witness. If you do judge it advisable to question any woman, I will make arrangements for it."

"As always, you are kind, Prioress."

Not kind at all, the prioress thought, for you know well that you are in my debt, not only for my concession in this matter, but also for my silence over that business last year. "As for Brother Thomas," she said at last, "I wonder if Sister Anne can get the truth from him. They have developed a friendship from their work together in the hospital."

"If anyone could, Annie might." Ralf looked sheepishly at the nun.

"Perhaps he will be more forthcoming soon, my lady." Anne ignored him, but her eyes suddenly regained some mild hint of humor.

"Whatever do you mean?" the prioress asked.

"When Brother Matthew learned that our good priest had been detained, he rushed to him, swearing to wrestle any devil from Brother Thomas' soul. I do believe they have been together for at least an hour now."

"An hour?" Ralf asked.

Eleanor cringed.

Chapter Nineteen

Thomas' knees were growing numb. His spirit, however, ached with fear. Although it was cold in the cell, he was sweating, and the roar of his beating heart resounded in his ears like the screams of condemned souls. He would have sworn the stone walls were leaning forward ever so slowly to crush him. Trying not to cry out, he bit his lip, drawing blood. He was still amongst the living, he realized, and took a deep breath. The howling in his head faded. He had not yet gone completely mad.

Nor had he been condemned, he reminded himself, and the man who had sealed him up in this cell was his friend, a man known to be just. He inhaled deeply once more. This air might be redolent of rodent, but the scent was of dusty fur and dried feces. Almost soothing, he said to himself, attempting to lighten his mood. These were healthy rats and mice, not vermin glutted with human flesh that had shared the cell with him in London. This was not the London prison, he willed himself to remember, although the effort to do so was increasingly difficult.

Thomas began to shake again. Nay, he would not dwell on London: the sweetish stench of ripe carcasses, men and rats; the pain of the rough chains rubbing his bleeding flesh from his ankles and wrist. Despite his determination, memory shattered his resolve. Foul panic now flooded his heart like night soil washing through the middle of a city street.

He forced his eyes open and tried to concentrate on his current place of imprisonment. This is no cell, he repeated slowly. This is a storage room for priory supplies.

Although there were no windows to let in light, Ralf had left him a cresset lamp, the curved depressions in the stone filled with oil and the floating wicks alight. The flames did cast shadows on the rough walls, and Thomas tried not to think about those shades, seeing mocking spirits and twisting demons in them. Instead, he tried to concentrate on the kindness of Sister Anne, who must have brought the lamp from the dormitory, and the man he still hoped to call *friend*.

Thomas slumped back on his heels, weary with his efforts to fight both panic and madness. This room might be a storage room, but it had a troubling past of its own. The last person held here had also been accused of murder. With that thought, Thomas bent over and moaned aloud, too exhausted any longer to hide his agony.

"Are you praying, Brother?" a reedy voice asked.

"That I am, Brother Matthew. That I am." Indeed, Thomas thought, if ever I could pray, it would be now.

"Then stop wriggling. A man filthy with sin itches only for God's forgiveness and thinks not of his weak knees."

Before Thomas could respond, the door to the storage room swung open. Framed in the light of the doorway was the outline of a very tall woman.

"Brother Matthew," Sister Anne said. "Our prioress has asked that you attend Sister Ruth. Our sub-prioress has a point of theology she has struggled to understand, and she begs for your wise teaching."

Brother Matthew uncoiled himself from his knees, then picked tiny bits of something from his robe. "I will come immediately. A worthy woman, Sister Ruth, one who knows the limitations of her sex." He gazed upward. "Would that all women were as wise as she." Lowering his eyes, he glared at the sub-infirmarian.

Someone, Thomas was sure, had just stifled a snort.

"You know the way to our prioress' lodgings. I would accompany you but our lady has asked that I see to Brother Thomas' needs."

"Even monks can be tempted by woman's wiles. A nun should never be alone with a man."

"Nor shall I," Anne said and turned to reveal the man hidden in the shadows behind her. "Our crowner will be with me."

Matthew shook his head in disgust. "Not only is he a worldly man but a rude one at that," he protested in tones much akin to his preaching voice. "No respect for the Church, if you ask me. Why our prioress allows him to profane our sacred priory is beyond my comprehension, but women do have little logic and less understanding…"

Ralf stepped into the room. "Be off to enlighten Sister Ruth, monk. We would speak with Brother Thomas."

"How dare you…"

Anne stepped between the two men. "Please, Brother Matthew! Sister Ruth is deeply troubled and needs your guidance before the next Office."

Matthew growled something under his breath. As he walked through the door, he pulled back his habit so that it would not brush against either Ralf or Sister Anne.

⚭ ⚭ ⚭

"Have you come to your senses, monk?" Ralf asked.

Thomas had risen from his knees and was sitting on the narrow bed provided for him. His face was turned away from them both.

Anne knelt in front of the auburn-haired priest and raised her hands as if in prayer. "Please talk to us, Brother," she said. "We believe you to be innocent of this crime but must know what knowledge you have of the dead man. Tell us and not only free yourself from this cell but help us catch the murderer."

Thomas remained silent. He studied all four walls of his prison as if the form of each was unique, even wondrous. Then, as he bent his head, tears raced down his cheeks.

With a beseeching look, Anne gestured at Ralf to come forward.

The crowner reddened, shook his head, and stepped back.

The nun sat beside the weeping man. "Thomas," she started, then hesitated. Once more she looked over at the crowner, her eyes begging Ralf to lend words filled with warm friendship to her pleas.

Ralf did not move.

With a dismissive toss of her head, Anne turned back to Thomas. "Tell us your grief," she whispered, then put her arms around the monk and held him close like a mother might her young son. "Ralf and I could not love you more if you had been born kin to each of us. Do not weep so!"

Thomas put his head on her shoulder as if he were her child in fact and began to sob, his great racking gasps most painful to the heart.

As he watched Anne holding Thomas in her arms, Ralf clenched his fists, then hid them behind his back. Friendship, jealousy, and duty fought for primacy in him. The struggle was apparent in the dark red of his face, noticeable even in the flickering light of the cresset lamp.

"Speak, Thomas," he finally said in a low voice. "Annie has the right of it. You are more a brother to me than my own kin, and I would not have you in this foul space for naught." He swallowed. "Do not make the same mistake as the man who was imprisoned here before."

Suddenly Thomas leapt away from them both and ran to the wall of his cell. "Leave me!" he panted, his back flat against the stones. "Get out of here! You may brick me up and starve me to death, Ralf, but you will hear nothing from me about your corpse."

Chapter Twenty

Eleanor stepped away from the dead man and drew the sheet back over the ravaged body. Above her, the wind hit the chapel walls with so much force that she wondered if all nature was outraged by this murder of God's soldier.

She turned to Sister Anne. "What strength it must have taken to slice through that buckram!"

"His armor was well-worn and ragged," Anne replied. "You saw the holes where the cotton stuffing had fallen out, but a most demonic power was still needed to dig through it, then rip into the body with these devastating results." She shuddered. "Could this have been done by one of the Evil One's minions?"

"My aunt did teach me that the Prince of Darkness usually commits evil with the aid of mortals," the prioress replied. "I suspect we must look for a killer with a man's flesh and form."

"And the meaning of this?" Anne pointed to the dagger found in the man's chest.

What of the knife with Arabic script? Eleanor asked herself. Should King Henry be warned that an infidel with malign intent was on English soil? "What do you know about these Assassins?" she asked Anne.

"Little enough, but I have heard that they do not attack simple men like this corpse once was."

Eleanor nodded. "Then I might say that this murder was committed out of great passion, perhaps anger." She touched the dead man's chest with gentleness as if she wished to chase the wrath away. "What did you do to so enrage your killer," she asked the corpse, "and what did he want to convey by stabbing you in the chest with that particular knife?"

"The wound from this knife did not kill him. From the dull look of the blade, I would doubt that it was the murder weapon. The length must be sufficient to penetrate as well. This knife did not pierce the chest very far, and the buckram was thinner there."

"Ralf did not think that this was a robbery gone awry or the knife stuck in the chest to suggest a false motive." Although it was the crowner who had just put her monk in custody, she normally respected his conclusions.

As if she had read Eleanor's thoughts, Anne smiled. "Ralf is usually right about these things."

"The nature of this killing and the extra time it would have taken to stab a dead man would not seem the style of casual thieves. If not robbery, then perhaps it was anger over some current deed, revenge for some deep wrong, or even prevention of some threatened injury or humiliation."

"And the dagger left because it meant something to both the victim and his killer?"

"Well said! Or even a sign that something had been resolved by the killing. When de Montfort was killed in battle, parts of his body were chopped off and sent across the land, not just to humiliate him and prove he was dead, but to establish that the threat he posed to the king's rule was ended."

"But this man was a common soldier." Anne frowned.

"Ordinary men shatter the tranquility of other ordinary men just as men of higher birth destroy the peace of kings. Perhaps, when the killer stabbed him with this knife, he meant to indicate that the end had now come to such disruption."

"Do you think they knew each other?"

"I would say so, but when they met and the cause of this act remain unknown." Eleanor fell silent. The only sound was the screaming wind.

"It is almost time for the Morning Office. Shall we…?"

"I will join you but wish to pray alone for a moment."

"I shall stand without," Anne replied and left her friend alone with the dead man.

                                         ᏳᎢᏳ ᏳᎢᏳ ᏳᎢᏳ

Surrounded by the reek of another's mortal corruption, Eleanor knelt on the stone floor of the hospital chapel and prayed that she might conquer her own. The pain she felt in her breast was like an unquenchable fire. Although she knew that the killer of this man must be found, she feared what she might discover in the search.

Ralf was right, of course. His seizure of Brother Thomas was the kind of gesture that satisfied the mighty while resolving little. If it gave them all at Tyndal time to find the real murderer while keeping their crowner, a man she knew to be fair and honorable, then the gesture served a good purpose.

Being neither saint nor fool, she would do whatever was necessary for the benefit of Tyndal Priory and having Ralf as crowner was definitely beneficial. Of course she could free Brother Thomas at any time. Ralf would not have protested had she freed her monk immediately. That was her legal right, and they both knew the crowner was in her debt for not exercising it.

Prudent though the gesture might be for those reasons, she could not forget that Ralf had also confined Thomas because he believed her monk knew something he would not confess. This troubled her more than any jurisdictional argument over who had the right to seize one of her monastics.

She bent over and moaned as her forehead hit the uneven floor. Tears finally flowed down her cheeks, and she looked back at the butchered body whose soul must be crying out for justice. "Is Brother Thomas as innocent as my weak woman's heart believes, or is he somehow involved, even guilty of this horrible crime?"

Was her willing ignorance of this man's past keeping her from seeing his evil nature? She did not know what had called him to the priesthood. If bastard-born, as she suspected, the Church must have granted him dispensation to enter holy orders, and that was not often done unless the father was of high rank. Surely she would have been told his lineage if that was the case, yet the abbess at Anjou had said nothing.

Of course she had the right to know about her priest's past, but Eleanor did not believe in digging out a soul's secrets just to satisfy a passing curiosity. Only when she sensed some contagion therein, something that might infect her priory with evil, did she pry into things usually left to the confessor. Might not this be just the occasion to ask?

"Could he be Satan's liege man, and I so blinded with lust that I cannot see the malevolence I have allowed into Tyndal?" Or was he an innocent man, albeit one born with an archangel's beauty? In that, as she well knew, there was no sin.

"Yet ask questions I shall," she whispered to the corpse. "I owe you that, and I will face my monk with fortitude. If he is guilty of any ill, I will make sure he is duly punished." Then she quickly whispered one more prayer. "Should he be innocent, please teach me the direction I should take. Must I keep Brother Thomas or send him away?"

With that, Eleanor rose to join Sister Anne and the rest of her nuns for the Morning Office.

Chapter Twenty-one

He shook with silent but frenzied rage.

That Devil's strumpet had not seen him standing in the dark, obsessed as she was with her hellish corpse. He longed to slip behind the cursed whore, grasp her neck, and shake until her bones snapped. Had it not been for the tall nun standing at the chapel entrance, he would have, but he had no wish to hurt that one. She had never done him harm.

The groans of the dying and sick intruded on his musings. From the deep shadows of the gray morning, he watched the outlines of the lay brothers as they went from bed to bed, offering potions and prayers. If he prayed at all, it was to go to Hell where he might find his wife and make peace with her at last.

Could he do so? On the ship to England, he had believed he might, but that profane prioress had caused their rift to widen, bringing his wife back to war against him. Could his beloved do otherwise, now that she owed fealty to the Devil?

He still had hope, however. Earlier this morning he had seen the ghost of his wife, drifting deep in the gloom near his bed. For once she had not screamed reproaches at him but had remained silent as if ready to hear his tale. He had risen and walked toward her, hand held palm up in a gesture of supplication.

Then that handmaiden of Satan, the one who called herself the prioress of this place, had walked by, and his wife's shade flew at him, whirring around his head and howling once more with rage. He had swatted at his ears, but the screeching continued until he had been driven nearly wild with it.

His mood darkened. He looked back at the chapel and silently cursed that evil spirit who had so roused his wife's shade to renewed fury. Nay, that false prioress was not praying, in there with the corpse, to anyone but the Prince of Darkness. She knew his soul's desire and would prevent him from making peace with his wife. Even Satan might be kinder and at least let him share a place with his beloved in eternal Hell.

"Be damned!" He heard his shout echo in his head, followed by the mockery of laughter. Damned? Wasn't the prioress already one of the Devil's own? He rose. He must destroy that vile creature!

Then his eyes fell on the nun outside the chapel. How could he slip by her? She might cry out. What choice would he have but to strike her? Nay, he could not hurt an innocent.

He fell back to his knees and began to weep, closing his eyes as he did. Once more, the shade of his wife floated toward him.

"I swear on the everlasting flames that burn you: I believed you were safer with the other Saracen women! How could I have known that such a monstrous thing would happen?" he sobbed.

A hand came to rest on his shoulder.

Chapter Twenty-two

Had Thomas ignored the bare walls, the narrow space, the lack of windows, he might have imagined that he was not in a cell. An earthen pitcher of Tostig's good ale from the priory brewery sat on the rough boards of his small table alongside a bowl filled with thick cabbage soup, still steaming from Sister Matilda's kitchen and fragrant with spices. Next to the soup were a loaf of fresh bread and a slice of good yellow cheese. Prisoner he might be, but Prioress Eleanor was making sure he ate well at his midday dinner.

But imprisoned I am, he thought, noting that there was no knife at his place. Despite the abundance set before him, he had no appetite.

Cuthbert coughed. "I will cut your cheese if you wish it," he offered.

"Like a rat, I'll gnaw it," the monk replied with a weak smile, "but I do thank you for your kindness."

"It may be of little solace, Brother, but many in the village grieve that this has happened to you. Those you have comforted in the past long for your release."

"The word has traveled then?"

"If you will forgive me for saying so, monks and nuns do gossip."

Thomas shrugged. "We are all mortal."

Cuthbert carefully looked around and listened for a moment before continuing. "Some say our crowner has been bribed to do this so that someone of rank will escape justice."

"What think you?"

The sergeant spat. "Ralf would sooner cut off his own balls than take any man's bribe." He looked up, turning red. "I spoke before I thought, Brother. Forgive me my rude language."

For the first time, Thomas laughed. "Then I assume our crowner's manhood is intact."

Cuthbert nodded, turning yet a deeper shade of wine-red.

"Since gossip travels swiftly in the village, I wish you would spread the word that I am in good spirits and know that our crowner will soon capture the man who killed this soldier. Thus my residence in this cell is but temporary, and I will soon be released."

"The villagers believe he arrested...?"

The monk shrugged. "Since men are sometimes placed in safe custody to protect them from harm, I believe Ralf fears that I know something that could put me in danger. In fact, I was on that road where the man was found, although I left it before the glade. You may also pass the word along that I know Ralf to be an honorable man who would never set justice aside for his earthly gain."

"That I will, Brother. Your words may save our crowner from an accidental shower of night soil as he passes through the village of Tyndal." Cuthbert grinned, then bowed out of respect for Thomas' vocation and left.

Despite the sergeant's sympathy, Thomas noted that the man did carefully lock the door behind him.

⚬₪₪⚬ ⚬₪₪⚬ ⚬₪₪⚬

Thomas sat in silence and stared at the meal in front of him. He still had no appetite. Briefly he might have broken the surface of his black pool of melancholy, but his head had slipped beneath it again. Even Sister Matilda's finest efforts now failed to restore his humors.

Suddenly rage filled him, and he struck the table with so much force that great drops of soup flew in all directions. "I am cursed," he cried. "Cursed!"

A knock at the door and a muffled question reminded him that Cuthbert remained near to guard him. He shouted back that he had accidentally bitten his tongue and all was well.

How he wished that was true! He must find some way out of this prison. He could not remain in it, haunted as he was by his past. If he were to stay, he surely would go mad.

Thomas closed his eyes. When Ralf reminded him about the last prisoner who had been put here, he had grown angry with passion fueled by the humiliation of his tears. Anne and Ralf had meant him no ill. He knew that and had apologized to them for his outburst before they left. Nevertheless, he had refused to tell them what they wanted to hear. What could he say? How could he say anything?

Nor, despite his speech to Cuthbert, could he easily forgive Ralf. Although he knew the crowner had not put him in this cell as a cruel jape, Ralf had been his friend and he had placed him here. Did friendship count for nothing?

Thomas knew that his behavior had been questionable and that he had been on the same road where the murder had taken place. The madman had been right, if he had seen him as he claimed. He could quarrel with none of this. What had hurt him was that Ralf had not set aside appearances and let the bonds of friendship weigh more heavily in this matter.

"Were I a better man," he muttered, "I would respect him for that. A less honest man would have ignored a friend's apparent guilt." The monk's shoulders sagged. "But I am not that better man."

The crowner might have proven his integrity, but that was cold comfort when Thomas did not know how he could explain the basis for his guilty behavior. It had been true that he had been so eager to return home that he had forsworn sufficient food that day. This omission had not given him the fortitude to withstand the sharp questioning from both his prioress and Ralf about the circumstances and timing of his return. Then he had faced the corpse and, with his humors set off-balance, had seen his rapist in the features of the dead soldier.

Nor did it help matters that he was in a cell once again, one that not only brought back London memories but also those from last year when he had chanced his own life to save another's. This last part Ralf might understand, but that alone was insufficient to explain all.

Thomas shook his head. Ralf was right. He did have something to hide, and he knew he could not blame the crowner for putting him in this cell, whether to keep him safe or to wear him down so he would tell what he knew. The crowner had been sharp-witted enough to sense the oozing fear when Thomas' past sorrows met with current circumstances. Ralf might be a friend but he was also the representative of the king's justice. The difficulty Thomas faced was how to justify what had happened without revealing things about which he had no wish to speak.

He could not confess to Ralf that he had been held so long in prison, and, even if he were to do so, he certainly would never admit he had been put there for an act of sodomy. If he admitted to the former, Ralf would surely ask why. In a land where sentences for minor crimes were usually quickly executed, the crowner might well wonder if Thomas had committed some grave, even treasonous act.

Were he to divulge the prison time and the sodomy, he would not only lose a friend, but Ralf could still ask why Thomas had been released into the priesthood when conviction for sodomy should have prevented that. This realization posed a more complex problem for the monk.

Thomas might hate the very sight of his sinister master, but he owed him loyalty. Or rather he owed it to that man's lord, the one who had ultimately saved Thomas' life. Although that man had never been named, Thomas had good reason to suspect he was of high ecclesiastic rank. Reluctant monk though Thomas might be, he had given his oath to remain silent about his role as a Church spy, as well as any secrets he might learn. Breaking any oath might be unthinkable, but telling secrets was rank betrayal. If one were a spy, the latter was also most cruelly punished. Thomas would keep his word.

No matter how independent the crowner seemed, Ralf had his own allegiance, and his was to the king. Since the secular powers were often in conflict with religious ones, Thomas knew that his loyalties and those of his friend might be at odds someday. Therefore, he could never explain why he was a monk or anything about his prison past to the crowner, even as a friend. He must find another way to escape this misery.

He began to pace the boundaries of his cell. His predicament was impossible, and his throat was dry from all the tears he had shed. At last, Thomas returned to the table, poured from the pitcher, and drained the cup slowly. The ale had a bitterness to it, albeit a pleasant one. The taste fitted his mood, and he poured another cup.

All of a sudden, a possible solution fluttered at the edge of his thoughts. Thomas looked down at the trencher and smiled.

Although Cuthbert had not left a knife, he had given Thomas a spoon. The monk picked up the implement and played with it for a moment as the idea took form. He dipped the spoon into the soup and swallowed.

Had Sister Matilda added garlic?

With the other hand, he reached for the bread. Grainy but sweet, he concluded after savoring a bite.

Sister Matilda was most certainly a wonder in her kitchen.

By the time Thomas had reached for the cheese, he knew what he must do, say, and to whom in order to gain his freedom.

Chapter Twenty-three

Ralf raced along the path, Anne's rebuke from last night still roaring in his ears. How dare she claim he was careless of Thomas' plight when the monk lay weeping in her arms? Had not Thomas' tears proven his innocence, she had asked. Why else would a man shed tears in front of another?

Women! Did they believe that men never wept? He had seen battle-hardened soldiers sob without shame. How could one not weep when friends and brothers screamed for their mothers as flaming pitch burnt their flesh all too slowly into ash or they lay dying from wounds that had turned their bodies inside out. "If God made Eve from Adam's rib, He must have failed to include his heart if her daughters think men do not mourn." He spat into a puddle.

Panting with anger, Ralf stopped to catch his breath. The rain had ceased for the moment, but the air felt cool against his hot cheek. He continued on at a slower pace toward the hospital courtyard.

Tears might well signify pain, but he knew that they did not always prove innocence. Although he loved Thomas more than he did his own kin, Ralf was convinced that the monk was guilty of something. He could not ignore that no matter how much Anne berated him.

As he entered the courtyard, an old woman from the village waved at him. He raised a hand in greeting but added no smile.

His hand ached. When he looked down at it, he realized he had been clenching it for some time.

Uncaring, was he? Did he not care about the man who had been cruelly murdered, a brave soldier who had gone to fight in Outremer? Why should he show Thomas mercy when none had been given that man?

"The monk knows something," he muttered, "and had you not given him the soft comfort of your embrace, Annie, he might have spoken the truth." Yet he knew that he would confess all his secrets and sins were Anne but to take him into her arms.

The crowner kicked at a rock in his way. "Oh aye, and I was jealous, Annie, seeing you holding him in your arms, but I fought the demon back." He cursed. "Why must I always be reasonable? Will no one grant me just mercy in return?"

"Watch your step!" someone shouted.

Ralf looked up. A young couple stood just in front of him. The woman, big with child, gestured at her belly. Her companion put his hand where she had indicated, then grinned with so much joy that even his rough features softened.

Walking around the couple without a word, the crowner felt a growing chill. His bleak mood deepened. Any autumn might be cheerless, he thought, but this one seemed especially so.

Just then, a familiar figure came into sight.

"Brother Beorn!" the crowner shouted.

"You wish to see the same man again, Crowner?" Although the lay brother came forward readily enough, his expression suggested that he was less than overjoyed to see Ralf.

"Not him. Your prioress has given me permission to order any travelers who came from the village yesterday to the chapel where they may look on a corpse. Perhaps one will recognize him." Ralf caught himself before he called the death "murder" since he had not asked if the prioress had told the priory about this tragedy or what she might have said.

Beorn muttered an almost inaudible oath. "We had so many at our gates. Without asking them, how can we tell which came by what route? Some were but children…"

"The men first, or at least those with one good eye who can walk without much assistance. If they had women or children with them, we may not have to trouble those, at least not now."

The lay brother exhaled a grateful sigh.

"I shall need your help in this questioning, however, for I have just sent my sergeant off to see a nearby farmer about a lost sheep."

Beorn briefly bent his head in prayer, then hesitated as if eagerly awaiting a response. When he looked back at the crowner, his expression suggested disappointment. "Whatever our prioress wishes, I shall do," he said.

"We should begin with any that bear the crusader cross. How many of those?" Ralf's chuckle sounded almost gleefully wicked.

"One has died already. Another is blind and would help you little unless he heard something helpful. A third has leprosy and will be sent to a lazar house in Norwich, but we will keep him here should you wish to question him." Beorn smiled back at the crowner with impish delight.

Ralf shuddered, then gestured for the lay brother to continue with his list.

"Thus ends the list of strangers who bear the crusader cross."

"I think we can leave the two still living in peace." However willing Ralf might be to drop a coin for the good of his own soul into a leper's bowl, he had no desire to come close enough to catch the disease. If he had to question the two crusaders, he'd leave the leper to the end.

"We had many from the village or nearby. Most were known to us…"

"And those men I leave to you to question on the route they took, when they did so, and what they might have seen."

The lay brother nodded wearily.

"Other strangers?"

"Three from court, men of some weight in both rank and person." A brief smile twitched at Beorn's mouth. "They needed assistance to dismount."

Ralf grinned. Although he and the good lay brother had often clashed over the years, he did enjoy Beorn's sharp wit. "Their weapons?"

"Bejeweled, I do think. The glitter, even in this weak light, blinded us."

Such men were not likely to attack anything with passion, other than a roasted pheasant redressed with feathers for dinner, Ralf thought. If he learned nothing from anyone else, he might question them later. "No one else?"

The lay brother fell silent for a moment. "Two in particular," he continued. "One was a badly scarred young man of some rank, if I might judge from the quality of his dress. An older servant with only one eye accompanied him. Neither bore the red cross, yet I did wonder if they had once been soldiers to have gotten those wounds."

"Let us begin with them."

Chapter Twenty-four

"The purchase of Saint Skallagrim's kneecap and thigh bone is a rare opportunity for Tyndal, my lady. If we do not buy now, the seller might go to Norwich with it. I beg you, make an immediate decision on this pressing matter!" Brother Matthew swayed like a sapling in a high wind.

Sister Ruth stared at him with unblinking eyes. Although most would conclude that her look suggested attentiveness, a few might wonder if it could be adoring.

Prioress Eleanor was not quite so wooed. "I was clear. We shall delay until we have a new prior."

"A prior who must await confirmation from Anjou, as you yourself so wisely noted." The monk smirked.

He has won that argument, the prioress conceded in silence. She nodded.

"Dare we hesitate so long? Think what prestige and coin other sacred bones have brought to blessed sites: Saint William to Norwich, Saint Thomas Becket at Canterbury." His voice slipped into an awed whisper. "Saint Frideswide to Oxford! King Henry himself has gone there and given gifts. Perhaps the king might grace us with a visit if we had a wondrous relic of our own."

Briefly closing her eyes, Eleanor imagined with horror the amount of work and expense required to receive a king.

"I do see God's hand in this. How else can we explain this sudden discovery of Saint Skallagrim's bones? How dare we turn ungrateful backs on this gracious gift?"

Sister Ruth blinked. "A whole thigh bone and kneecap! Think, my lady, what this would mean for Tyndal's reputation. Our good brother is right in this matter." There was none of the usual rasping malice in Sister Ruth's voice. As she continued to gaze upon the leggy monk, her tone was soft, even sweet.

Eleanor clenched her teeth. And what would it mean if she were foolish enough to consent? The monk would spread the story of how his superior arguments had vanquished her weaker ones. With this show of strength, he would surely win more support, become prior, and even do so with some appearance that she blessed the decision. On the other hand, if she were to refuse to purchase it, others might switch their allegiance to Brother Matthew out of anger that she had cast aside such a purported treasure. A dull ache began over her left eye.

"Shall I have the relic seller come to you, my lady?" Brother Matthew ground one fist into the palm of his other hand.

Eleanor watched the gesture, knowing it was she who was being ground down. "Your diligence has been most impressive and duly noted. Nevertheless, I do not believe the time is auspicious for a quick decision."

"I fear he may sell…"

"Norwich has its saint. A full body, I believe. Need I remind you that Tyndal is far from any major town, and there are no other religious houses or churches nearby that could afford an expensive relic. If your source is that eager to sell in this lonely area, he should be willing to wait a little longer."

"Nevertheless…"

The two monastics were watching her like hawks might a field mouse. "Please excuse me, Brother. It is late and I have vowed to pray at this hour." The pain above her eye was growing worse.

"My lady?" A look crossed Sister Ruth's face that suggested she was weighing the merits of staying behind to plead further on behalf of the relic.

"Alone. You may both leave with my gratitude. Your concern for the reputation of Tyndal is laudable." May the priory soon elect a man of sense, Eleanor prayed, for if Tyndal chose Brother Matthew, she might be forced to purchase these bones.

The two religious glanced at each other, rose in unison, and did obeisance.

As Eleanor watched them walk away, she caught herself muttering, "Why do they remind me of an old married couple, each having learned to read the mind of the other?" She took in a deep breath before turning to the ewer of ale on her table. Slowly she poured a cup and sipped. Her eyes burned. Her head hurt. Her heart? Ah, that.

A movement on the ground caught her eye. A cat with deep orange fur jumped up on the table. "Come, Arthur," she said, picking up the rumbling creature. "Sit with me and bring the wise counsel of your noble namesake. I am much in need of it."

She carried him to a chair, then sat. He circled briefly on her lap, then settled into the warmth of her woolen habit with feline contentment. As she rested her hand in the soft fur, Eleanor closed her eyes. The ache in her head eased ever so slightly. How she regretted not taking Anne's advice to take feverfew in time to ease this growing affliction, but despite the throbbing, the cat's happy purrs did soothe enough of the tension so she could think.

Although she had managed to deflect Brother Matthew and the issue of the relic for now, that difficulty would not go away, nor would the problem of Brother Thomas and the question of who killed the soldier. "What think you of this, Arthur? Could Brother Thomas be involved in a murder or am I so blinded by his beauty that I cannot see his evil nature?"

Protesting the pause in her attentions, Arthur pushed his head against her hand. "I do believe he is innocent," she said, rubbing the proffered head. "Satan's fire may have set my body aflame with lust, but the Evil One has not managed to reduce all my wits to ashes."

The cat rolled over, one claw catching the fabric of her robe. She eased it out. "The good brother is a man of courage and loyalty. You remember the bravery he showed when he first came to Tyndal, and I know I told you how steadfast he was at Wynethorpe Castle last winter. Had he not been willing to do what was needed to unveil a killer, my brother would have been hanged. When a man has proven he loves justice, how can he be guilty of a crime as horrible as the death of this poor soldier?"

Arthur shifted, raising one front leg so his mistress could more thoroughly rub his chest.

She smiled. "And what better proof of his virtue than your acceptance! I have seen you running after him with your tail held high with joy. That you approve of him is most assuredly unassailable evidence that Brother Thomas is an honorable man!"

The cat opened one eye and purred louder.

"Whereas I do remember that you have scratched Brother Matthew on more than one occasion."

Eleanor eased back into her chair. If the monk was innocent, as she did believe, what was he hiding? Did he know who the dead soldier was, and, if so, why did he refuse to identify him? She bit her lip. What if the dead man knew secrets about the monk's past, secrets that involved women in whose arms he had known joy? By any standards, Thomas was handsome, and, although there had been no rumors that he had been unfaithful to his vow of chastity since his arrival at Tyndal, Eleanor suspected he must have been quite a different man in the world. Women there must have been, or at least one who might have won his heart.

"May God forgive me! I am thinking like a jealous wife," she growled. What difference would it make if he had slept with every wife and daughter in London before he took vows? Since God would have forgiven that long ago, she should not be thinking on it. She willed her thoughts to another possibility.

Thomas did have family. Perhaps the secret he wished to keep involved them? She remembered that black-clad man of the Church who had arrived on a fine gray horse last spring and begged permission to take her monk away so he might care for his sick brother. Of course she had given it, then watched with aching heart as Thomas rode off with the messenger. At the time, she had thought it strange that Thomas' expression suggested more anger than concern for his brother when she gave him the news and her blessing to leave. "What rift from his family caused him to react so, yet feel duty-bound to attend when called?"

The cat yawned.

"Have I bored you, sweet one?" She gently rubbed his neck. "Very well, then, I shall confront Brother Thomas with a mother's stern face when I question him on behalf of that dead soldier's soul. As his prioress, I have sworn to be a mother to my monks as Our Lady was to the beloved of Our Lord. He must tell me whatever is troubling him."

Arthur slid one paw over his eyes with a show of some feline annoyance.

"What else might I do to discover the murderer in our midst? Ralf will question those who came by the same road where the killing took place. That is something he and his men can do more efficiently than I, and he will tell me those results as soon as he is done."

Arthur raised his head, extended one paw, and rested it against her chin. Slipping one finger under that foot, she let him grip her playfully with his claws.

"What of the man who saw our good brother at the turn in the road? Ralf believes that man too frail to have done the murder himself. He also believes him to be mad—yet not mad." Eleanor tried to remember if she had seen this witness, then shook her head. "Perhaps I should speak to Brother Beorn or Sister Anne about him. Our crowner may be correct in his conclusion that the man is but a witness and incapable of murder, but I do wonder how someone can be described as both mad and not so. If Brother Thomas, a man of proven honor, can be put into protective custody for what he may know, I do think we might consider whether a madman, who may not be mad, might have something to tell as well."

Eleanor lifted the cat from her lap and set him on her bed in a warm, roughly woven nest of woolen cloth she had provided for him. Then she bent down and nuzzled his soft fur with her nose. "While I go off to the hospital, sweet sir," she whispered, "dream of fat mice and…"

"My lady!"

Gytha stood in the open door.

Eleanor turned pale at the urgent tone. "What is wrong?"

"Please, my lady, you must come quickly! It is about Brother Thomas."

Chapter Twenty-five

Brother Beorn glared at the crowner. "Sister Christina is praying with Sir Maurice, and his one-eyed servant refuses to leave him," he snapped. "Although I will bring others to see your corpse, I shall not interrupt our infirmarian. The young man's spirit is in pain, and if anyone can draw God's healing beneficence to a troubled soul, she can. Question them when she is done."

Ralf shrugged. Although he was suffering from a most contrary mood, he knew there was little merit in countermanding Beorn's suggestion. The half-blind man and the youth with the shattered face could wait a while longer.

"Very well. Bring me other strangers who might have seen and remembered something." The crowner hesitated. Had he seen just the briefest sparkle of malice in the lay brother's eyes? "Barring the leper," he quickly added. "Of course, I shall want to know which ones you have omitted and the reasons for doing so." Both can play at that game, Ralf thought, not even trying to hide the spite in his voice.

Brother Beorn strode off without reply.

"I should not vex him so," Ralf muttered. "He is a good man, and there are others more worthy of my bad temper." Nonetheless, there was no one else at hand, and after all the pain and embarrassment he had suffered since the discovery of the corpse, the crowner was not in a charitable mood.

In fact, Brother Beorn should not be overly burdened, he reminded himself. Most villagers would have avoided the main road entirely and arrived at the priory gates by locally known shortcuts instead. These, and any strangers coming from the opposite direction, would not have any knowledge of the killing. Perhaps the man of rank and his one-eyed servant had also come from some other route and need not be troubled beyond asking which road they had traveled.

From Brother Beorn he had learned that the stout men of the king's court had come from an unsuccessful journey to the Norwich shrine of Saint William and therefore would have seen nothing. Depending on his mood, he might question them anyway, more for his own amusement than information. Doing this would surely irk his brother, something the sheriff deserved for all the trouble his newly found concern was causing Ralf.

The crowner had also established that only local villagers, or else the dead, had left the hospital today. Those living he knew well enough: women with their children, a few elderly, none likely to commit murder. Nor would any have traveled that road. Ralf was confident that the killer had not yet left the priory. Although that might be good news, Ralf knew he had little time to waste. If the murderer had come here for shelter, he would not stay long.

He cursed. If Cuthbert had not been out hunting wandering sheep, he could have helped, thus allowing the innocent to return more quickly to their beds and thus suffer their mortal ills in peace. Then the crowner shook his head with frustration. Perhaps it would not matter that his sergeant was unavailable. Only so many could crowd around the corpse to stare. This viewing would take time, time that was becoming ever more precious.

⌘⌘⌘ ⌘⌘⌘ ⌘⌘⌘

As Ralf had expected, there was much shaking of heads from those travelers well enough to hobble into the chapel to see the dead man. Their failure to recognize the corpse seemed honest enough. Most did study the face with dutiful concentration, and the crowner had made sure the grisly wounds were well hidden to protect the sensitivities of the innocent. Many of these men would have gone with anticipatory pleasure to a hanging or a quartering, but few cared to see similar sights against their will.

Only once did Ralf feel hope that the victim might be recognized. An old man, barely able to walk, had spent some time looking at the face, then touched the lank hair with a trembling hand. When the crowner asked him, with as much gentleness as he could, whether he knew who lay on that cold trestle table, the man had merely shaken his head and said there was something about the man that reminded him of his long-dead brother.

"Very well," Ralf said to Brother Beorn, as the last man was taken back to his straw bed. "We have eliminated most. Let us have your man with his one-eyed servant. Surely your infirmarian's healing prayers are long over and the pair improved enough to come speedily."

Brother Beorn cast a glance at the crowner that would have fried a lesser man, then turned abruptly on his leather heel and left the chapel. As he watched him leave, Ralf once again swore to limit his irreverent comments out of courtesy. He also knew that he most probably would not. Since boyhood, he and Beorn had always pricked each other.

⚭ ⚭ ⚭

The two men, who returned with the lay brother, did so without assistance. As he studied them, Ralf found it hard to believe that the younger was even alive, let alone able to walk. The sword blow that left such a deep scar from forehead to jaw would have killed most. Perhaps Sister Christina's prayers had worked a miracle. He vowed to remember this should he survive the nun and she became a candidate for sainthood.

The crowner bowed, his gesture perfunctory. "My lord," he said to the younger man. "I am Ralf, crowner for this shire…"

"I know." The young man's voice was deep, his eyes restless as a falcon's, hungry for a killing.

"You are called…?"

The older, one-eyed man stepped forward. "Sir Maurice of Carel is my master. I am Walter."

"I addressed Sir Maurice." The man might lack an eye, Ralf thought, but there was enough insolence in his look for two.

"I speak for him."

Ralf looked back at the scarred face. The young man's gaze was now frozen as if his eyes had turned to ice.

"You will understand why I do," the servant continued.

Surely this man must have known his place better when his master had had his wits about him, Ralf thought. The not-so-quiet arrogance in the older man's manner vexed him, yet he knew the servant probably spoke the truth. No matter how strong the master's voice might sound, his eyes reflected a hollowed-out man.

"I wish you to look upon a corpse," the crowner said to Walter. "Perhaps you have seen him."

The man shrugged. "We have not seen any dead men."

"Alive perhaps?"

"What reason would we have to remember if we had?"

The crowner's patience was diminishing with celerity. "I could ask the innkeeper whether you rested the night there and which direction you took when you left…"

"There is no need," Walter replied. "We did stay at the inn and traveled to Tyndal by the main road."

Ralf decided there was a steadiness of truth in the man's voice. "The dead man was found on that road you traveled yesterday. You may have seen him and perhaps any companions he might have had. We seek his identity."

"And who killed him."

"I did not say he had been murdered."

"You did not have to, Crowner. Your interest in this does not suggest the man died from old age."

Ralf raised one eyebrow. "I investigate any unexplained death, not just murders."

"Unless he bears an untoward wound, crowner, I doubt you would order this pilgrimage of the sick to view him."

This Walter showed too much boldness for a man who had supposedly spent his life serving the whims of the mighty. Whatever his bond to the man he called *master*, Ralf doubted Walter was any servant. "You have the right of that," he said with a mollifying tone. If their true relationship became significant in his investigation, he would question them further. If not, he would let them keep their secrets in the shadow. "Come with me, then. I would have you see the corpse."

Walter hesitated. "I will do so gladly, Crowner, but I beg you excuse my master."

"Why?"

"He is unwell."

"Others have been sick or wounded, yet they have come." Ralf gestured for the pair to follow him.

"I cannot allow…"

"Allow? Then I order it. In the king's name."

Walter reddened. "Do you know who my master is?"

"A knight home from the crusades, if I might guess, although neither of you wears the crusader's badge," the crowner snapped. "From the brown color of your faces, I would say that you have both recently spent much time in sunnier lands than England." Ralf watched the man's look grow guarded and wondered what he feared.

Then Walter shrugged, his gesture suggesting that any man with a full complement of wits could see that Sir Maurice was not a crusader. "A man who is close to Prince Edward," he answered, as if Ralf had asked.

"Not from Outremer, then?"

"We have traveled to the continent for my master's health. As even you must know, there are shrines there."

"And are you suggesting that your master has friends currently at court, not just the Lord Edward who is far from England, friends that this rough-edged country crowner might not wish to offend?"

"You show some astuteness, Crowner."

"More than you would be advised to ignore, Walter of wherever-you-are-from. Lest you blunder further in this badly stitched guise of a servant, I would suggest that you bring your master now. A good servant would not hesitate to do so at the command of a man standing for our king. Thus, out of kindness, I teach you how to play this strange game and leave you to hope that I do not press for any explanations about why you have chosen these ill-fitting robes."

The older man blinked, then looked over at the man he claimed to serve. A look of pity softened his features and, for just a moment, Ralf thought he saw tears rise in his sighted eye.

"I beg pardon for my rude manner, Crowner. I wished only to protect my master from grief. As you must realize, he suffers profoundly."

"The visage of death is not strange to any of us." Ralf gestured toward the chapel. "It should not disturb him more than any other man."

"When we leave our mother's womb, we may all come dressed with the flesh of mortality, but Death's features shine with an especially fierce light for some," Walter replied, taking Sir Maurice's elbow and leading him forward. "For these, the light may be both unbearable and blinding."

"He has you to aid him." Ralf walked to the corpse and laid one hand on the sheet covering the head. "Do you wish to view the man first?"

Walter shook his head. "We traveled together, Sir Maurice and I. What one saw, the other did as well."

Ralf whipped the sheet off.

Sir Maurice screamed.

Chapter Twenty-six

"My lady, I am grateful you came so quickly." Even in the wavering dark shadows of the hall, the young guard's long face was pale.

"Is our brother ill?" Eleanor hid her hands in her sleeves so the man would not see them tremble.

"I do not think so, my lady, but he did ask with some urgency to speak with you." The guard's voice betrayed his nervousness. "Cuthbert left me with orders to watch Brother Thomas with kindness, but I did not know whether I should ask the crowner first…I did not know where to find him…if I have done wrong in calling you here…."

"You were right to call me first." Eleanor stared at the wooden door behind which Thomas lay. "How did our brother seem when he made this urgent request?"

"*Seem*, my lady?"

"Was he anxious? Angry?"

"Neither, I think. He did beg your attendance with both calm and courtesy."

"Yet you are troubled."

The young man's eyes widened with fear. "Although the good brother's demeanor was tranquil, I have seen that kind of peace only on the faces of dead men!"

⁂

The cell door had opened with a loud creak, and the light of evening flooded the darker night of the cell.

Thomas looked up.

"You asked to see me, Brother?" Eleanor's voice was gentle.

The shadows from the flickering cresset lamp played lovingly with her features, softening the iron will that Thomas often found there. In this light, her gray eyes may have been black in color but they had the softness of velvet. Earlier, when he had first returned to Tyndal, he sensed disfavor in her cold manner. Now he heard a sweetness in her tone. Once before he had chosen to trust her and he had been right. Once again, he decided to trust his instincts.

"I did, my lady, and I am grateful for your kindness in coming so quickly." His throat was dry, and he coughed. "The time for these weak tears is done," he continued with a stronger voice. "I would tell you the truth that caused our crowner to put me here."

"Perhaps a priest should be called to hear you?"

"It is to you I must speak. As my prioress, you alone have a right to know the truth of this matter."

"Nonetheless, if there is a need for confession..."

Thomas shook his head. "My lady, please be at ease. There is little to confess, although much to explain. For cert, I did not kill the man who lies in the chapel." He took in a deep breath and waited.

"Do you know who he is?"

He exhaled. "I do not know this man at all."

"Yet you behaved as if you did, or so I was told."

Her gentle voice so caressed his ears that Thomas wanted to crawl like a small boy into her arms. Confessing the horrors he had suffered in prison, as he had done to the man in black before he entered the Order, should have brought him peace, but that priest's perfunctory forgiveness had not returned any warmth to his heart. Instead, chill and pain remained there and often tore at him like carrion birds.

Thomas swallowed. Tempting though it might be, he would say no more than required. No matter how much his heart longed for human comfort, his mind must still rule. He might believe she should be told far more than she had been, but he had no right to make that decision on his own.

"He reminded me of a man I might kill," he said slowly, "even now, were I given that chance."

"Why?"

The quietly spoken question soothed him like a mother's song. He would not weaken, he swore again. He must not! "The man I knew was my jailer in London."

Eleanor said nothing.

"He was a man who loved cruelty, my lady. I was not the only one to suffer from his mercilessness." Was she not a just woman? He must remember that, and, above all, he must stop his body from trembling. "I know it is wrong that I am unable to forgive, but surely there are sins so black that even God will not cleanse them white. If that is heretical, my lady, I will do my penance."

"The man that lies in our chapel is not the man you hate?"

"He is not, but my hatred for the man I thought he was disrupted the balance of my humors when I saw his body." He hesitated. "I pray that I never again see the man I believed him to be, for I fear what I might do." Had he gone too far in what he said? Thomas bit the inside of his cheek and winced. His blood, like his memories, had a bitter taste.

"A hard admission from a man dedicated to God."

Thomas said nothing as he listened carefully to her words repeat in his head. Nay, there was no judgement there, only a statement and an observation. From the day he had first met her, he knew she was not one with whom he would ever want to match wits. He had seen men far cleverer than he severely bested. Despite his trust in her sense of justice, he still felt like a man caught up in night terrors, waiting for an unspeakable horror to enter the room from which he had no escape.

"Should I know what cruelties he committed? Indeed, as your prioress, I must. Many of us may fail to forgive another, as we are required to do by God, but few would so willingly violate the laws against murder, one of the most precious commandments given to Moses in that desert land."

Could this woman, convent-bred as she was, ever understand the depth of his hate? Could any woman, who had chosen to reject all human passions, ever comprehend their extremes? Surely his iron prioress had never felt the power of love so joined to lust that rejection tore the heart out and left a mortal longing for death. Surely no one had ever so humiliated her, as he had been for one frail act of loving, that she would want to kill the perpetrator.

He shuddered, then realized she was still waiting for him to speak. He must choose his words with care and hope they were enough to gain his freedom while hiding his soul's rawest wounds. "He let a man die of starvation, who could not bribe him," he said, "then taunted him by placing a piece of maggot-ridden bread just outside his reach."

"And how did you know this?"

"I shared the cell with the pitiful wretch and watched him die." In the dim light, he saw her start.

"You could do nothing? Forgive me, Brother, for I have no wish to be cruel but I am naïve in like matters…"

"Few know of these things, my lady, and fewer still care to ask. For your questions, I do bless you. No, I could do nothing. Although I had my daily crumbs, he forced them into my mouth so I could not share even if I had been willing." Stop there, Thomas shouted to himself. Stop there!

"Then you had food…"

"For a price." He had gone too far. He had lost the battle over his heart.

"Surely, if you had the money for food, you had influence…"

"Neither influence nor money, my lady."

"Then…"

Thomas shut his eyes as he felt himself begin to sweat. Could he find words with enough of the truth but not so much that she would ask for more? "That I was fed while the poor wretch watched was part of my torture as well as his. I can never forgive the jailer for starving the man, and I will never forgive him for making me a part of the foul deed."

The silence in the room grew so heavy that Thomas gasped for breath. The blood pounded like ocean waves in his ears. He must not faint. Not now. Thomas slid to his straw bed as if weighed down with the chains he had worn in that London prison.

"You could not tell our crowner this?"

Thomas wiped the stinging sweat out of his eyes. "The Church chose to forgive me my past sins for reasons best known to God. In truth, my lady, I did not believe I could share this unique mercy with any man whose allegiance is to a secular lord, even though I call this man *friend*." He forced himself to look at the woman standing before him.

She seemed to study him for a long time in the gray light before saying, "I understand."

Had he won? If not, he was too feeble to fight his own weaknesses any longer.

"Brother, I must ask you one question, to which I demand a truthful response."

"And thus shall I answer you."

"Did you commit any act of violence, treason, or cruelty that led to your imprisonment?"

He took a breath. There had been only tenderness in his passion. As for treason, he saw no treachery in the love of one loyal subject of the king for another. What cruelty had he committed when Giles came willingly into his arms? "God may strike me if I lie, my lady," he said firmly. "I committed none of those acts."

"Then I require one promise from you."

Thomas wanted to cry from the relief that now flooded through him. All he could do was nod.

"Should you ever meet this jailer, you will not touch one hair on his body but will inform me immediately. In exchange," her tone dropped deep with fury, "I swear that I shall make sure he suffers in kind for the sins he has committed."

Thomas fell to his knees, shaking with sobs. "My lady, I do promise it. Most willingly do I promise!"

Eleanor called for the guard. As he unlocked the door to step inside, she laid her hand on the rough wood and thrust it open.

"By my order, Brother Thomas shall now be freed," she said. "Should any agent of secular justice dispute this, send him to me for I will be pleased to remind him that the law of God, not the king, rules at Tyndal Priory."

Chapter Twenty-seven

Were there any justice on earth, Ralf decided, he would be at the inn, getting roaring drunk, with buxom Signy wiggling on his lap and warming his very cold manhood. Instead, he was still at Tyndal, and his manhood was not the only part of him that was both chilled and shriveled.

The incident with Sir Maurice had brought lay brothers racing to the chapel from all over the hospital. It had taken four to wrestle the man to the ground as he swung wildly at everyone with painful results. Although he had no weapon but his hands, he did wield them with the strength of ten demons until he finally collapsed, weeping like a baby. As the knight was led back to his bed, Brother Beorn's rebuke was harsh enough, but Walter's silent look was filled with mortal hatred.

Surely that corpse was cursed. From the moment of its discovery, Ralf concluded, he had suffered only grief. Brother Andrew had made him feel the fool when he voiced his suspicion that an Assassin could be loose in Tyndal. The porter's teasing was bad enough, but the crowner's ever-weeping love wound for Sister Anne had reopened as soon as he saw her. As if the Devil was mocking him, Ralf was then seized with lust for Tostig's young sister and had capped his betrayals by imprisoning a friend. Like the fool he might well be, he had ignored Walter's warning, just because the man annoyed him, and freed whatever demons had settled in Sir Maurice's soul. Worst of all, he had failed to find the killer. In sum, Ralf felt like an apple picked in autumn but not eaten until the Lenten season. He cursed, but even that did nothing to improve his mood.

It was dark, and he had yet to talk to Sister Anne about the corpse. Although he dreaded facing her after the upbraiding she had given him, he needed her observations on the body, a discussion interrupted earlier by Thomas' fainting fit. Afterward, he decided, he would go to the inn for some good ale. Even if he did not find a wench willing to bed with him, getting drunk was a fine idea.

As he strode through the hospital seeking the sub-infirmarian, he looked over at the screened cells ranged against the wall. A tall, cowled figure stood near the one assigned to the dancing madman.

Had Brother Thomas been released?

Ralf stopped, started toward the man, then hesitated. Nay, he said to himself, no one would have done so without his permission. Despite his protestations, Brother Beorn must have found someone to keep the fellow in bed.

He continued on his way and turned toward the chapel. "'S blood!" Ralf muttered. "Must I be reminded of Thomas?" He wanted to believe that the monk was innocent of any knowledge or involvement in the killing, but he could not ignore signs that suggested guilt of some kind.

Thomas was not so womanish that he would sweat profusely, then pass out when he saw a corpse. The man had seen too much death, violent and natural, since his arrival at Tyndal and had shown only fortitude and courage. Something about this death had troubled the monk, and that Ralf could not set aside. Nonetheless, he hoped whatever his friend was hiding would be some minor thing. This was one of the few times he regretted being a crowner, but he was King Henry's man and had an obligation to put justice over personal feelings.

Taking Thomas into custody presented another problem. Those in the Church would certainly object to a secular man doing so with one of their own. With any luck, however, Ralf hoped he'd have found the killer, freed the monk, and made the issue as dead as the corpse in the chapel by the time the men of high church rank found out.

On the other side of that argument, his brother might be satisfied that he had taken the action, leaving him alone to handle matters in the future without interference. Ralf snorted. How odd that he might have pleased his brother for once. In this one thing, however, they had always agreed. Monks and clerics should suffer secular justice when they committed worldly crimes. Their other brother, a man of rising religious rank, would vigorously disagree that the Church had always been far too lenient with its own. "For brothers, we are most certainly a contrary lot," he said aloud.

Yet he could not have put Thomas into custody without Prioress Eleanor's concurrence. If the sheriff did leave him in peace to pursue this murderer, Ralf had her to thank. Whatever his feelings about religious and secular jurisdiction, he would never offend this woman, whom he did respect, to satisfy his brother, whom he did not. That the prioress had seen his plight and taken his side put him into her debt a second time in as many years. With anyone else, he would have feared what form reparation might take. With Prioress Eleanor, he had confidence that any repayment would be fair.

Jurisdictional debates, favors owed, and a crowner's duty all faded in the glare of one specific worry: the future of his relationship with Thomas. Perhaps he had had no choice but to put him in custody, but he hated doing so. If Thomas was found innocent of any involvement when the killer was found, Ralf knew that nothing might heal the wound he had inflicted on the man's honor. In imprisoning the monk, he might well have lost a friendship he had grown to value. Ralf cursed, then kicked at something in his path.

The hospital cat hissed and ran.

"Satan's balls! Can I do nothing right?"

"Occasionally, Ralf. Occasionally."

Ralf spun around. Sister Anne stood just behind him. Her smile warmed him more than ale ever could. "I kicked the cat," he mumbled, gesturing at the fleeing feline.

"She must like you, else you'd be missing a chunk of your foot. Did you come to see your corpse?"

He bit his tongue before he blurted out that the corpse could rot for all he cared and that he had come to see her. "Aye, and to hear your thoughts on it," he said aloud.

"Come then."

The crowner followed her through the chapel's gated entrance. Why was it, Ralf wondered, that he could only talk with her over a dead body?

They stood close to each other as Anne drew the cover back over the swelling body. "Not a happy death," she said.

"You are sure that he was gutted first?"

"You saw that mark on the back of his head, Ralf. Either he was hit from behind or he may have fallen backward, striking his head as he did. The skin is broken but I could detect no break in the skull. To bruise so, he was most likely alive when his belly was slashed open but I cannot tell how conscious he was."

"He could have bumped his head when he fell. The ground by the side of the road was rocky enough, but he was face down when we found him." He pointed to the man's chest. "What of the knife? What make you of that? Was he stabbed there first?"

"After death, I think. There was little bleeding about the wound, and I do not think that knife you found was the same blade that spilled his guts."

"My suspicion as well, but tell me how you came by that conclusion."

"Look at the blade." She handed it to him, hilt first. "It is so dull I could not cut myself if I tried. Another knife had to have been used. This one is more of an ornament than a weapon."

"Then why…?"

"A message of some sort? I do not know." She gestured at the body. "And this crusader has no more to tell me about it."

"Brother Andrew thinks that the knife may have come from Outremer."

"The script is Arabic. I believe our porter is correct, Ralf."

He looked at her with amazement. No wonder he had never stopped loving the woman. After all these years, she could still surprise him. "You recognize the design on the blade?" he asked.

"We have had many crusaders come through Tyndal of late, most with things they have brought back to remind them of their days in Outremer. This is not the first time I have seen this script."

He fell silent, lost in adoring fascination as her brown eyes changed shade like shadows in the flickering candlelight. He coughed and looked down. "Aye?"

"We have also heard many tales from returning soldiers about a sect whose leader sends men to kill, men who have no regard for their own lives. Assassins, I believe they are called. Had your corpse been a crusader of rank, I might have suspected that such a person had slipped into England to wreak vengeance for some perceived wrong. This soldier is of low birth, as Cuthbert did tell me. Surely this Old Man of the Mountain, as I've been told their leader is named, would not bother with a poor man."

"Might he not do so to spread fear amongst us? Might not this murder be an attempt to weaken our resolve in the Holy Land?"

"Only a fool unleashes the storm winds of fear, Ralf. Since no man has the power to direct how they may blow, they could just as easily destroy those who hope most to benefit from them, although the innocent always suffer long before that happens. Nay, from the tales I have heard, the Old Man of the Mountain prefers to send his minions against the powerful only."

Although he might disagree with her about the effectiveness of fear, at least Anne had not dismissed his concern about the Assassins as casually as Brother Andrew. "Then I must still ask why this corpse was stabbed with an ornamental knife from the Holy Land after he was butchered like a wild boar for the table."

Anne put one hand on her hip. "Answer that, Ralf, and you have your killer for cert."

Chapter Twenty-eight

He listened with affection to the staggered, harsh breathing of the dying around him. How could the living hate and fear these so as if they were the enemy? The dead would understand his fondness for them. Few of the living ever would.

Was it a frightened man, then, who had screamed in the chapel where that gutted corpse lay? Nay, that was not the howl of fear, he replied in his soul's silent place. That was the roar of rage. If God and Satan could bless one so wicked with hallowed death, then surely one who believed his sins might exceed those of the dead one could believe he deserved equal grace. Aye, it was fury in that voice, not fear. He, a coward that had led his beloved wife to slaughter, knew this to be so.

He rubbed his forehead, then studied a watery streak of blood on his hand and grieved. A contemptible creature, he still twitched on the earth. Not all the living were so loathsome perhaps. In some he saw a bright ember of pain at the edge of their souls. For those he prayed it would burst into a tower of flames and send them to death without memory. The rest? A few he pitied, for they had been blinded by conjured joy. Others were Satan's spawn.

The praying nun was one. Unlike the tall one who had kindly found a quiet place for him to sit and listen to the sounds of dying men, this one babbled on and on, her voice grating like a rusty gate in his ears. How dare she jabber endlessly about the kindness of God? A God there might be, but He had neither ears nor eyes, yet she knelt with her hands raised and eyes closed, her body swaying as if she expected Him to notice.

Whore! Did she think to seduce Him with her soft body and piteous cries? "God was not seduced by my wife when she raised her hands, begging to be saved from rape and an inconceivable death," he muttered. "Why should He listen to you?"

He began to sweat in the cold air, then snickered. Of course the nun might not know any better. She always shut her eyes while she whined her prayers. Thus she would fail to see God turn His face away. If she was to learn the lesson forced upon his wife, she must pry those lids apart and see all. His wife's eyes were wide open when she died.

He blinked. Perhaps the nun was no woman at all. If she were a demon, she could not bear to look upon God. Perhaps Satan's whore, the one he should have slain in the chapel, had sent her to him. Or had God Himself ordered a spirit to distract him from his desire for Hell?

Nay, she must be a demon. In her dress and manner, she resembled most her evil mistress. Besides, God mocked with silence, not with buzzing babble. Chattering was the Devil's tool, but one he would no longer tolerate.

With eyes burning, he stared at the masonry in a wall. The cracks wiggled like worms as the pain in his head grew worse. Which should he send back to their dark master first, he asked himself, the false prioress or her feigned nun?

Chapter Twenty-nine

The day had dawned as dark as night. Eleanor rose before the call to Matins and knelt at her prie-dieu in reverential prayer. Despite the disloyalty of her body, her soul once again willingly pledged fealty to the God she had sworn to serve.

The air had been so chill with coming winter that she had very quickly splashed herself with water from the basin near her bed. Perhaps, she thought with grim humor, she should wash herself twice daily in the colder seasons if doing so numbed her body this well.

When the bells did ring for Matins, she joined the nuns for prayer, then led them to Chapter. Yesterday she had given them the tidings about the murder in the forest. Unlike their response to that killing the summer she had first arrived, her nuns did not greet this news with wide-eyed terror, and the monks had responded more with grief at worldly violence when the acting prior told the tale on the other side of the priory.

Today, her flock remained calm. No matter how grieved the religious might be over this latest tragic act, they had received the news with relief, feelings some might call selfish but which most mortals would share. In either case, they did have cause for gratitude. This time the murderer had not broached their gates. God had kept their walls strong against the violent storms of worldly sins. Armageddon was not yet coming. They were safe.

Or so Eleanor allowed them to believe. The possibility that the murderer might be hiding within their walls was not a suggestion she wanted to voice. Panic would help no one in this matter, but the success of her deliberate silence was dependent upon a quick resolution of the crime. With the crowner roaming the hospital and questioning all, Eleanor knew that her flock would surely realize, before another night had passed, that danger skulked in the shadows of their passageways.

Although she had full confidence in Ralf's abilities, the crowner was not leader here nor was he ultimately responsible for the safety of the religious at Tyndal. Yesterday she had been unable to send her own wits as hounds to the hunt. After freeing Thomas, she had been summoned to see the cracked masonry in the parish church that threatened to fall on the faithful. By the time she had arranged for repairs, night had put an end to any questioning of men, mad or not. Today she would broach no further delay. After telling Gytha that all problems, except the most dire, should be directed to Sister Ruth, Eleanor took the path to the hospital.

Although the day was dismal and many shared the mood, Eleanor felt at peace. Her patient prayers last night had been rewarded with a balm of tranquility that had eased her into a soothing sleep. Thus she had risen quite refreshed. With some small degree of calm, she turned her thoughts back to Thomas.

She had believed his tale. How could she not? It was hardly a story a man would make up when the details could be so easily confirmed. At least by establishing both his innocence and ignorance of the crime, she had eliminated one unprofitable path to finding the killer.

Eleanor bent forward as a strong gust hit her. The raindrops stung her eyes and face. Should she have demanded more details of the crime that had placed Thomas in that brutal place, she asked herself? He had sworn it was neither a violent nor a political act, and she knew the Church must have forgiven him whatever sins he had committed. Last night she had decided the knowledge of that absolution must suffice for her as well.

Today, she was not so sure. Had her curiosity been idle, Eleanor would have set it aside. It was not, however. Unlike

the other members of her priory, she had been given almost
no information about Thomas' background since his arrival at
the priory. Nor had he been exactly forthcoming himself. Even
Anne, with whom he worked most closely, knew little about
him. Perhaps, she thought, her questions had less to do with
Thomas' past and more to do with why the abbess in Anjou had
told her so little of this man.

She shook her head. This was not the time to worry over this.
Whatever crimes Thomas may have committed, the Church had
chosen to forgive him and accept his vows as a priest. Of equal
importance, he had proven his worth to her many times over,
but his melancholic moods and troubled sleep suggested that
there was much in her monk's past, details that were probably
irrelevant at the moment. Nonetheless, she remained troubled
that someone had decided she should be kept ignorant of it.

Eleanor slipped in the wet gravel, then caught herself. There
was another reason to set aside these matters. By releasing
Thomas, she had imperiled Ralf. Of course she could recount
the tale her monk had confessed, thus proving his innocence,
but she would not repeat what she had been told in confidence.
Indeed, she had promised Thomas that she would say nothing
of their conversation. On the other hand, she did not want the
sheriff to replace Ralf because the elder brother decided the
crowner was weak in dealing with suspicious behavior and had
even allowed a woman to overrule him. Eleanor had no doubt
that she had done the right thing in releasing her monk, but now
the capture of the murderer was even more imperative.

⚭⚭⚭

"He weeps, my lady. He stares and weeps." Sister Christina was
wringing her hands as she stood outside the small cell. "Prayer
had brought him some peace until Crowner Ralf treated him
so cruelly. To force a man with such a troubled spirit to look on
a dead man's face was a brutal act! Shouldn't that worldly man
be hunting a killer and not troubling sick souls?"

Eleanor was surprised at the passion in her infirmarian's voice.
Usually she was possessed of a more saintly calm. "Our crowner

should not be here much longer," she replied, "but I gave him permission to question all travelers who came that day. We could do no less in view of this horrible death. Someone might have seen something of importance."

Sister Christina bowed her head with appropriate meekness, but Eleanor suspected that the nun would never agree that Ralf had any reason to be in the priory at all. She decided to ignore what her infirmarian might be thinking and looked over the round nun's head.

A screen provided some privacy, but the prioress could still glimpse the two men. Walter sat on a low stool, arms folded, eyelids shut as if asleep. Sir Maurice was stiffly upright on a simple straw mattress, staring intensely at nothing. Tears dripped from his jaw.

"What has been done for this man?" Eleanor asked softly.

"Sister Anne chose this secluded spot to give him some peace from the cries of the others being cared for here. The lay brother she sent to examine the young knight confirmed that he suffers from no open wound or fever, although the brother was amazed that the man still lived considering his past injuries. Later, I spoke with the servant about the signs Sir Maurice exhibits and do believe that the ill causing his distress lies solely with the young man's soul. Prayer is the best cure."

Eleanor nodded. "His man told me that the presence of a woman distresses his master. Have you sent one of our priests...?"

The plump sister was now looking heavenward, eyes shut, and her smooth skin glowed as she fell into spontaneous prayer. When at last she reopened her eyes, Sister Christina blinked as if she were amazed to find herself back on earth.

Eleanor waited for any revelation the infirmarian might have received.

"I believe Our Lord has called on me to pray for him," the nun said in a firm voice. "Although godly men are right to fear the lusty daughters of Eve, there is a special strength in the prayers of women who have given up the flesh. If this young knight is troubled by imps in the guise of demon women, my prayers will have more power to send these creatures back to their evil master."

"Then follow God's guidance, Sister, but do approach Sir Maurice with caution. Were you to do otherwise, the imp might choose to defend her territory most zealously. I would not want either you or the knight injured from the assault."

"God will protect us from such a thing, my lady. Nonetheless, I do beg that you keep the crowner away from this poor soul to whom he has already done much harm."

Repressing a sigh, Eleanor reminded herself that this woman might well be on the path to sainthood, a path that she, herself, would never travel. "I will speak to him, but, in the meantime, do not forget that God once held the Evil One in high esteem and for good reason. Satan is clever. You would do well to arm yourself with God-inspired caution as well as prayer."

Since Sister Christina's eyes were once again closed, the prioress was unsure that her advice had been heard, let alone heeded. If Sir Maurice had been so upset by the sight of the corpse, however, perhaps she should ask why. The madman could wait a bit longer, Eleanor decided, and gently pushed the screen aside.

⚬⚬⚬⚬ ⚬⚬⚬⚬ ⚬⚬⚬⚬

Walter was not asleep. His eyelids shot open the moment he heard her soft step. As he rose and bowed in silence, Eleanor studied his face. The empty eye socket and gray streaking in his hair she had noted before, but now she wondered if he might be ill himself. Although he was deeply tanned, pallor lurked beneath the high color.

"We are grateful for your hospitality, my lady," he said. "Our journey has been a long one from shrine to shrine. I feared we would not have the strength to travel farther without some care for," he looked sadly at the man sitting on the bed, "my master." His voice was heavy with fatigue.

"Perhaps your master has family to whom I could forward word of his presence here? If so, they might send men to help…"

"None."

Was it anger or fear that she saw? "The lay brother, who examined your master, said he suffered no physical ill…"

"I have already told you that I wish repairs for my master's sick soul, not the clay that imprisons it."

Eleanor felt anger explode inside her. His demeanor might be modest enough, but his bold speech and the mockery twitching at his thin lips were both rude and arrogant.

"With God's help, then, we shall seek the same," was her icy reply.

Walter dropped his head, falling into a study of his hands. He turned them over to look at his palms, then turned them back as if to see how the hair grew. The odd silence continued.

"What do you believe is the source of your master's ill?" she asked at last.

"Being mortal, my lady."

"We are all that, yet not all mortal men seek out Tyndal."

The man's one dark eye turned cold. "You are both mortal and far from home, yet you have come to Tyndal as well."

"I fear I do not know you, sir. Have we met in the distant past?"

"Nay, my lady." His expression softened. "Forgive me for being so rough of speech. It has been long since I had occasion to speak with gentle ladies."

"You and your master have both suffered grievous wounds. Have you been in battle?"

"A hunting accident." Walter pointed to his eye. "My master…"

Eleanor looked over at Sir Maurice. The young man stared at her, then turned his back. He had been a handsome man, she thought. With that God-given beauty, the angry scar that divided his face was a double outrage.

"Caring for my lord has been arduous, and I have lost the skill of hiding it. I do beg your patience," he said with a grimace.

Was he in pain, she wondered, or had some unhappy thought just struck him? Eleanor waited for him to continue, but the man said nothing more, bowing his head so she could learn nothing from his look.

It was obvious that he wished to avoid any further answer to her question. Despite this and his rudeness, she did not sense any real malice in the man, only a genuine concern for the man he called *master*. Tending him was clearly an onerous task, yet he performed it with gentle devotion.

"You are easily forgiven, but do say how else we may help your master. Prayers we do offer and potions as well; but, if there is something else, speak, so we may address it."

The man lifted his head, his look much softened with an obvious sorrow. "On my master's behalf, my lady, I am most grateful for your kind attention and that of Sister Christina."

"I have been told that Crowner Ralf caused your master much grief."

Walter said nothing.

"Was there something about the sight of the corpse that especially disturbed his spirit?"

"Does the sight of a butchered man give pleasure to any mortal?"

It was Eleanor's turn to fall silent.

"Very well, my lady, I will grant you that a dead enemy might give joy to a man's soul. In this case, my master did scream, but no one would claim it was a joyous sound."

And thus you read my next question and answered it, Eleanor thought. This Walter was a clever man for cert. "I feared that the sound of the dying would trouble your master since the sight of a corpse caused this much pain."

The servant nodded. "I would beg of you a separate place to rest, my lady, for Sir Maurice is troubled by evil dreams. On some nights, his howls would waken all. On others, he paces."

Eleanor gestured around the small space. "I fear this small, screened cell is all we have. We do not yet have guesthouses for those, like your master, who require them. The monks' dormitory would not be an adequate alternative either. From what you have told me, his cries and nocturnal pacing would disrupt the monks' sleep."

"Might you assign a lay brother to watch over him while I sleep?" The man staggered, his deep weariness now so very obvious. "Meanwhile, Sister Christina's prayers seem to be the balm my master needs as long as the crowner leaves him in peace. I tried to warn the man what would happen but he would not hear me."

"I shall do my best to find someone," she replied, knowing full well that she had few men to spare. "Of course Sister Christina will come for prayer, and I shall talk to Crowner Ralf about that unfortunate incident." She studied Walter in silence for a moment, wanting to ask more questions but deciding she would get little from a man so tired he was almost asleep on his feet.

Perhaps Ralf had already questioned Walter by now. After Sir Maurice reacted so strongly to the dead man, he must have. Thus she might be wise to talk to the crowner and find out what he had learned. It was, after all, the madman he had dismissed, not these men.

Yet she could not help asking herself if either the knight or his servant could be a killer. A dead-weary servant with a master who was little more than a mute child? Unlikely, perhaps, but she sensed there was much Walter was hiding. Although she might hope that they were as innocent of the murder as Thomas had been, she would return if Ralf had not spoken to them. Not only did she seek a murderer, she was also losing patience with secrets.

Chapter Thirty

Anger and black humors alternately boiled inside Thomas. Despite the damp air, sweat dripped down his sides as he paced the cloister walk. He slowed, wiping his face with his sleeve. It would be unwise to catch a chill, then die with the Evil One in control of his soul.

Although his prioress had ordered him to spend this day praying for the peace she believed God would grant him, his spirit had rebelled and driven him from his knees. In the past he would have gone to clean the stables, tend the beasts therein, and bank the fires of his choler with physical labor. Unfortunately, the buildings had been expanded in his absence, and the work, deemed too much for one man now, assigned to others. That saddened him for he could no longer go there for solitude. In this foul mood he most certainly did not want company.

"What have I done?" he moaned. "Have I given Prioress Eleanor the key to secrets I have no right to reveal? And how can I make peace with Ralf without telling him some fantastic tale?" Thomas ground a wet clod of earth into muddy bits. Had he betrayed his master or had he managed to keep the fine balance between deception and truth? Everything had seemed much clearer in that cell, his decisions so right. Now that he was free, he was filled with doubt.

The thick clouds above Tyndal were the color of slate. His mood took on the same hue. Perhaps he should see if the novices were practicing. That often soothed him. "Nay," he said, looking up at the heavens, "it may be too late for song, and with this humor I'd hear only the sour notes." He shut his eyes. They hurt. His anger had dried all his tears to rough salt.

Melancholia swung to choler and back again. He might go as mad as the one who had given witness against him, Thomas thought. Perhaps he should search out the madman and keep him company, one lunatic in conversation with another.

He walked over to the edge of the covered walkway, watched the rain tumbling from the sky, then winced as a drop hit his eye. In his panic to escape that cell, he had almost forgotten the fellow, but now he began to wonder why the man had pointed an accusing finger at him. Had the madman not been on that same highway, he would not have seen Thomas. Perhaps this fellow was the real killer?

He had first seen the madman, not on that road, but rather just after he had fainted. When he and Ralf left the chapel, the man had danced around them, making lewd and obscure jests. Not possessed, Thomas had said to Ralf at the time, but now he wondered if the man was even a lunatic. His dancing was strange but, as he thought more on it, his speech had suggested a man of more wit, not less.

Thomas turned toward the door leading to the priory's public lands and pulled his hood over his head as he started down the path to the hospital. He would seek out the madman and question him. If the man was truly mad, he would leave him to the prayers of Sister Christina and God's grace. If he was feigning, however, Thomas would learn why he had cast suspicion on him. Then he smiled with somber humor. He need not bother wringing the man's neck if he was the killer. The hangman would do it for him.

⁂

As Thomas reached the entrance to the men's side of the hospital, he stopped to listen. When the light dimmed toward the hour of dusk, the sick grew quiet and the dying slipped closer to a more profound silence. In Thomas' experience, this and the hours of early morning threatened life the most for those whose souls

God might want. Indeed, all men past the heat of youth found the darkening hours ones of weariness, for it was then that the labors of the day were felt in the bones and in the soul.

He turned away from the straw beds of the open ward and walked toward the private cells. Surely that was where the madman had been placed. Was he right to seek the man out now? he wondered. The dark hours brought not only pale horsemen seeking souls but also demons casting tares of doubt into men's hearts. Perhaps he should not speak with the madman when his own humors were so unbalanced. Could he question him fairly? Demons were known to play with a man, when one humor took precedence, and destroy his reason. How often had these imps chased him into the monks' cloister garth to pace under the cold moon's flat brightness until he could banish them?

"I am pleased to see you back in the hospital, Brother."

Thomas spun around.

"Am I correct in assuming you are seeking one patient in particular?"

"My lady!" Thomas was grateful that Prioress Eleanor could not see the flush he felt rising to his cheeks in the dim light.

The prioress' smile was gentle. "I was on my way to see this man who has led many of us in circular dances of his own construction. Now that I have met you here, I wonder if you might be the wiser choice to question him than I."

"As always, my lady, I serve your will."

"And I seek your opinion, Brother. If this man is guilty of something and believes he has cleverly cast blame upon you, he might say something useful out of fear if he sees you free. If he is innocent, then it matters not whether you question him or I do. In either case, I am a better witness to anything he might say since you are the one he claimed knew more than you would say."

Thomas bowed. "As is most often the case, my lady, you have the right of it." Indeed, his compliment was spoken with sincerity.

"Then I will hide behind the screen where I can listen to you both but where he cannot see me. Let us go quietly."

Thomas moved the screen aside and stood in the entrance to the small cell. What an odd motion, Thomas thought as he watched the fellow sway in absolute silence. This was neither a courtly dance nor some common man's caper. As strange as it looked, there was a grace in the movement, albeit an alien one.

"Peace be with you," Thomas said softly.

"Ah, the red-haired monk!" the man replied, his body twisting easily from side to side. "Sinfully conceived while his mother suffered her monthly courses, methinks."

Thomas ignored the insult. "You have recognized me, it seems, but I know you not. Who are you, good sir?"

"Cain," he replied, running one finger across his broken nose. "Or Abel, perhaps, for Cain may be Abel and Abel can be Cain. Does it matter to you which I might be?"

"So much wit is rarely found in lunatics."

"Perhaps I am a fool then. Fools may be mad. Or not. In this sinful world, are madmen and fools so different? Might they not be born of the same mother?" He rubbed his nose again. "Perhaps God marked me so he could tell me apart from my brother. Is God all-wise, do you think?"

"More than either of us or we would not be having this discussion."

The man's eyes twinkled with laughter. "Was God wise when He sat under the apple tree and made both maid and man?" He threw his arms up. "Oh, a pun! God be praised! You are right, good brother, I have not lost all my wits!" Then he bent double with an exaggerated gesture of sadness. "But I fear they are of little use."

Thomas lost patience with the game. "Wit enough, methinks, but enough of this foolery. Why did you say you had seen me on the road to Tyndal?"

"The road to Damascus, I think, Brother. We were fellow travelers there, although you did not see me. I thought you might be the one God chose to throw from the ass and render sightless with His knowledge, but you left the road and went into the forest of night. It was I who was left to find the blinding light."

Surely there is sense in these words, Thomas thought, struggling to find what it might be. "You were travelling behind me?" he began.

"Aye, but you left before you were granted the salvation He gave me."

"You saw me leave the road and go into the forest."

"Aye." The man began to sway once again.

"What did you see on that road to Damascus?" Thomas asked, deciding to enter into the man's feigned, or unfeigned, imaginings. This talk of Damascus might be odd, but he suspected there was some logic to it. If the man was only pretending madness, perhaps he was afraid of something but was trying to give Thomas a riddle to untangle without endangering himself. If mad, well then, there would be no harm in spending a few minutes humoring the fellow.

"What could a man like me see? God blinded me with the brilliance only a poor man can see. Afterward, I found this place." He waved his hands in circles above his head and moved his feet to the music of a harp only he could hear. "And that was enough."

However strangely the man might be phrasing it, Thomas was now convinced he had not told any more than the truth. The man had seen him on the road, something he could not condemn the man for saying, but the madman was not claiming Thomas had anything to do with a murder.

Had the madman himself seen the murder? What was this light of which he spoke? A vision? A flashing sword? What did he mean? "What blinded you, my friend?" he asked in a kind tone.

"Nothing more than I could have wished, then a safe place to lay my head. I did follow your path through the woods. You should be comforted that you did His will in leading me here, monk. More than that, you need know nothing else."

Thomas studied the man dancing in front of him. The man had not been upset at the sight of him nor did he see in the man's eyes the kind of evil capable of brutal violence. Such a conclusion might be called illogical by many, but he did trust his instincts when logic had nothing on which to lay hold. What would the prioress make of this strange conversation, he wondered?

The man must have seen something, however. How could he not have seen the corpse, even the murderer? He must have gone farther than Thomas had. Was the blinding light, of which he spoke, madness brought on by the grisly sight of the corpse? Or could the man not remember what he had seen because his madness would not let him? Or was he clever enough to deny all knowledge because he knew he would be the easiest suspect, a man of no rank or wealth who happened to be at the wrong place at the wrong time?

"A dead man? Did you see a corpse?" Thomas asked with intentional directness, watching for the man's immediate reaction.

There was none. "La, la!" the man sang in a low voice, repeating himself like a child who has just discovered a delightful word.

Thomas asked again, then again, and finally threw up his hands. He wanted to shake the tale out of the man but restrained himself. Perhaps the prioress could see the truth hidden in the man's strange story. Whatever had happened on that road and whatever the man may have seen were locked away in the mind of a man who was either mad or clever enough to pretend he was.

Thomas watched the man for a moment longer, then left.

On the other side of the screen, Eleanor was waiting for him. After they had walked some distance in silence, Thomas asked, "What think you, my lady?"

"I would not have dismissed him as a suspect as quickly as our crowner did. Whether he is a murderer may remain a question, Brother, but I do believe he is guilty of something."

Outside in the damp-laden air, the church bell dully tolled for prayer.

Chapter Thirty-one

Shivering with misery and cold, Ralf hastened toward the stables. Just above the horizon, a band of brilliant light lay between the North Sea and the black clouds that promised a coming storm. That glow reminded him of intense, dazzling days before the autumn frosts, days that deceitfully suggested brighter times than could ever come to pass. Tonight Ralf had no patience with false hope. Tonight he was going to get drunk.

As the crowner walked to where his horse awaited him, the dark stream flowing nearby mocked him with its babbling. Silently, he cursed its tactless joy. Lights from rushes and flickering candles began to dot the darkness that now cloaked the priory. At least they made no pretence of conquering the gloom, Ralf thought, then turned his mind to murder.

That dagger still haunted him. Sister Anne had confirmed, as Brother Andrew had suggested, that the script was Arabic. The porter had scoffed at the idea of a murdering Assassin, suggesting that a man like that could not easily escape notice in East Anglia. Anne had more earnestly considered the possibility, then decided against it as well. Should he, a rational man, dismiss the presence of any Assassin except as a fantasy useful only in scaring children into eating their peas?

"My dear brother would love the idea of an Assassin loose on English soil! He would make much political coin with that, calling for increased tallage or heavier fines on the Jews, there being no Saracens in England to tax." Ralf snorted.

Sister Anne and Brother Andrew must be right. Fear of the alien, the strange, should not blind him from reason. No Assassin had done this, but the killer must have wanted to leave a message for any finder of the corpse. What was meant? he wondered. Had it been intended to wreak havoc by sending men, like his brother, down the road to false retribution? Or had it a narrower significance, a more individual one? Whatever the truth, the murderer was still free. Somewhere near, the man must be holding his sides, laughing at Ralf's failure to find him.

He picked up a rock and threw it with anger in the direction of that merry stream, then squeezed his eyes shut. Mixed with the rain on his cheeks was the burning salt of his tears. With no one around to hear him, Ralf yelled at the dark heavens, "Rational I might be, but I am not made of iron."

Fear he had dealt with for years, both as a mercenary and as crowner. As any other mortal, he had suffered failure, and he had also learned to live with emptiness in his heart. Since the discovery of the dead man, he had suffered all these things in equal proportions and more than he could endure. He was weary of fighting his battles alone. "Satan can take that cursed corpse," he swore. After all, why should he not have what other men had to soothe them when burdened with difficulties? Why could he not have the comfort of a woman's arms?

He loved Anne. He had always loved her. There was no reason to think he would stop doing so. Most times he could set his longing aside. Tonight, he could not. Tonight he ached with it. He must find himself a woman, any woman who would hold him against the warmth of her breasts and make him forget everything for a few hours.

"And I shall," he said, shaking his fist against chill melancholy.

But it was not any woman he wanted. He wanted Anne as his wife.

"May Satan's balls fry!" he shouted into the misty quiet around him. Aye, he would go to the inn and get drunk, swyve any wench whose name he could forget and pretend he was content. If he were lucky, he would awaken the next morning alone, his head and stomach protesting against the abuses forced on them, and he would rise, throw water on his face, and pour out his foul mood on someone who deserved it.

Perhaps he'd find the seller of fake relics and make him swallow the saint's toe, the Virgin's nipple, or whatever fraud he was trying to pass off on the innocent. Better yet, he might find the poor soldier's killer. If that happened, he would take joy in making him beg for the rope. After all, a rotten mood should never be wasted when there were men of evil acts around.

Despite the deepened darkness, Ralf found his horse, saddled it, and mounted. If nothing else, he could always make life miserable for that sheep thief his sergeant was hunting, he decided. His grim humor growing ever blacker, the crowner rode off in search of the bright inn.

As he did, he failed to see two shadows emerging from behind the stables.

Chapter Thirty-two

A bolt of pain struck him, lodging between his eyes. He grabbed his head, tearing at his face, but nothing he ever did could drive away this agony. Why had the affliction returned with so much strength? He had not suffered thus when his wife was with him. She had always known what to do.

His wife? Where was she? As he looked around, he suddenly grew faint and reached out to brace himself against the stone wall. "She is dead, is she not?" a voice echoed in his head. He wiped the sweat from his face. Of course, she was. He had killed her.

His hand slipped and he lost his balance, falling to the stone floor. As he lay there, his cheek pressed to the rough coolness, a surge of hot pain tore through his eyes. He howled. The sound blended with the moans of the dying.

"I could not have murdered her," he cried. "I loved her!" He pulled himself to his knees. The pain eased ever so slightly, leaving him nauseous. "I must find her," he whimpered. "She will cure me."

A black shadow glided toward him. He stared, trying to see what it was, but his sight wavered. Everything before him rose and fell like waves. Quickly, he motioned the creature away, but, as he did, his hand passed through it as if it were fog. For a moment, the thing shimmered in front of him, then turned and drifted toward the glittering candlelight of the chapel. Slowly the phantom began to take solid shape against the yellow light of the entrance.

He crawled after it. The guise might have been deceptive, but Satan had underestimated him. He watched the figure fall to her knees in front of the altar. Why, he wondered, had the Devil dressed his wife as a sexless nun? Satan's strumpet, that creature who called herself a prioress, must have decided on this cruel jest.

It no longer mattered. He had discovered the truth. He knew that his wife would never have left him to suffer like this. "Look at her, praying for my relief!" he whispered, then vomited air. Perhaps Satan let her pray only that his soul might come to Hell, but that would be a joy.

The pain in his head returned. It flashed in his eyes like lightning. He groaned. Surely she must love him still, he thought. Why else would she kneel so near the man who had butchered her? She could not be praying for that corpse's burning soul!

"Why not? It was not he that was guilty of the deed," a voice mocked. "You were. Had you told your fellow soldiers of the marriage and taken me to your dwelling as your wife, I would not have been butchered as an infidel whore!" It was her voice, he realized, and the sound of it stabbed like dagger blows inside his skull.

Trembling, he wanted to cry out to her but held his tongue. She had still not forgiven him for his cowardice. Perhaps she did not know that he had taken revenge against her killer? Might she not be satisfied with his gutting of the man who had done those unspeakable things to her?

He must speak to her, he decided. He must tell her. Then she might realize at last that he was not the weak thing she had called him. Perhaps then she would return to his arms, warm his heart with forgiveness, and chase this violent pain away.

He pulled himself to his feet and walked into the flickering chapel light.

Chapter Thirty-three

"My lady!"

Deep in unremarkable dreams, Eleanor scowled.

"My lady, please wake!"

Eleanor opened her eyes. Why the wavering torchlight? Surely they had just returned to bed from the Night Office. What strange vision was this that her maid should stand so over her bed?

"Brother Andrew is at the door."

Eleanor sat up. "What has happened?"

"He said only that you must be awakened."

Arthur mewed in protest as Eleanor eased the disgruntled cat off to one side, then slipped out of bed. From her basin, she splashed icy water over her head, rubbing her eyes and face to bring alertness back to her sleep-dulled mind. In the moment it took her to dress, she was wide awake.

"I am ready to receive him."

Before she followed Gytha into the public chamber, however, Eleanor hastily tucked a warm blanket around Arthur and ran her hand over his soft fur. Perhaps now, she thought, she might be ready to confront whatever tidings the porter had brought.

⁂

"Sister Christina was attacked, my lady."

"How seriously…?" Surely not dead, she prayed. Not that gentle soul.

"She will live. According to Sister Anne, our infirmarian was unconscious when found but has suffered only cuts and bruises." He hesitated. "Nothing more, I believe."

"Who found her and where?"

"You must ask Brother Thomas for more details, my lady. After Sister Anne came to tend her, he sent a lay brother to find me so that I could bring you the news. He wished to stay with our sisters in case the attacker was close by."

"Has Sister Christina regained her wits? Did she see who injured her?" Eleanor started toward the door.

"I know little of that but was told that she has spoken but is still dazed and remembers nothing."

"Let us go to her, Brother. Gytha, would you bring me a torch?"

◠◠◠ ◠◠◠ ◠◠◠

As the two monastics made their way through the cloister, they remained silent as if any mention of this deed would trouble the innocent dreams of the sleeping nuns in the dormitory nearby. When they left the protection of the inner priory walls, speech became impossible in the howling wind.

The rain was falling so forcefully that the torch sputtered and died. Clinging to the hoods of their robes, they fought to stay upright against the fierceness of the gale. As the rain pelted down on her, Eleanor shuddered but more from fear of the malevolence lurking in her priory than from the cold.

At last they arrived at the shelter of the hospital entrance. Sister Anne and Brother Thomas were waiting for them inside.

"We came straight away," Eleanor said, shaking what water she could from her robe. "Brother Andrew told me that you had further details." She looked at Anne, then turned to Brother Thomas.

Thomas averted his eyes as if caught between the need to greet her with courtesy and his inability to do so.

"I did report that our dear sister would recover, but that she was too confused when she awoke to give information about the attack." Brother Andrew gestured to his fellow monk. "Brother Thomas?"

Eleanor had been watching the monk while Andrew spoke and realized he was frightened. What had they not told her?

"I would hear what you have to report, Brother Thomas," she said. "I would hear any observations you might have as well, for I respect your abilities in these matters." And, she added to herself, I am most grateful that you called for our porter, not Brother Matthew.

"You are kind to say so, my lady, although I fear I am unworthy of your confidence." This time he met her eyes and, briefly, smiled.

"Tell me what you have discovered." Eleanor quickly glanced at Anne as well, fearing that her expression might not be quite a motherly one.

"The man, Walter, found me in the ward and begged that I bring Sister Anne forthwith. As soon as I did, he took us to the chapel."

"Then he held us back until he looked inside. For our safety, he said," Anne added.

"When we entered, we found Sister Christina unconscious and injured but alive. Nonetheless…" Thomas hesitated.

Eleanor looked over at Brother Andrew. The porter turned his head away. Then she looked back at Thomas. "You both hesitate. Why?"

Thomas spat as if bile had flooded his mouth. "When we found Sister Christina," he said, his voice hoarse, "she lay on her back, her legs spread. Her garments were torn. We feared she had been raped."

Chapter Thirty-four

The infirmarian lay warmly covered in bed, her body rigid as a corpse. Although her face was pale, both eyes were swollen and ringed with purplish bruises. Her lip was cut. She clutched a wooden crucifix to her breast and thickly whispered a prayer.

Eleanor knelt by her nun, placed one hand most gently over Sister Christina's, and joined in the saying of the Morning Office. Behind her, the prioress heard rustling as Anne and Thomas knelt in the dried lavender scattered about to deter fleas. The muffled voices of the two, repeating the words in unison, were soothing in their ordered repetition. Even more comforting was the presence of the guard the prioress had ordered to remain outside Sister Christina's room in the hospital until the infirmarian could be safely moved to the nuns' quarters.

She had sent Brother Andrew off to a warm fire and dry clothes. She most certainly did not want her favored candidate for prior sickening or even dying from the damp. The idea of being left with Brother Matthew as the only candidate was not a happy one. Perhaps she should not think these things during prayers, she thought, and quietly chastised herself.

Nonetheless, while the infirmarian pursued her orisons with grim determination despite her wounds, Eleanor's mind stubbornly persisted in wandering. She tried once more to concentrate on the Office—and failed.

Perhaps Sister Christina had recovered her memory of what had happened? If God was willing, she might even know who did this to her and he could be bound over to the crowner before he committed yet another or an even worse offence. On the other hand, she hoped the young nun did not remember anything about the attempted rape.

Even that was puzzling. Sister Anne had determined that the nun's virginity was intact while Sister Christina was still unconscious. Thus her chastity had not been violated; yet, from the position in which she was found and her torn robes, the attacker had clearly tried to do so. Had he been interrupted?

Why had she been beaten and why was only her face injured? Surely such a gentle woman would not have made so violent an enemy. Each action by itself might suggest anger, personal vengeance or a Satan-inspired lust, yet only her eyes and lips had been bruised, and…

"My lady, you are kind to come." The voice was plaintive, like that of a child who has just discovered there is evil in her world and does not understand why.

"I wished to observe the Morning Office with you." Not the complete truth but a small lie with enough gentleness in it that Eleanor hoped her confessor would give her a lighter penance. "I see that you have the cross from your room."

The bruised eyes blinked with joy. "Sister Anne brought it to me."

For that kindness, Eleanor decided, Anne should be given more than a fingerhold on the edge of Heaven. For what she herself must ask next, little grace could be granted.

"Sister Christina, I beg your forgiveness, but I must ask some questions about your injury."

The glow left the infirmarian's eyes as she slowly turned to Eleanor, then that look of an uncomprehending child began to fade. In its place, a most beatific smile appeared until the pain of her cuts made the nun wince. "My prayer for understanding has been answered at last, my lady! You see, I did not comprehend all that happened, although I believed I had been granted a vision. Now I know the meaning!"

"Explain to us how you were so blessed, Sister."

"I was praying in the chapel when I heard Our Lord calling to me."

"Did He bless you with His presence as well as His voice?"

"Both, my lady." The nun had lost her pallor. Now she was positively radiant. "First, He called out to me as I was kneeling in prayer. When I turned around to see where such a beautiful voice was coming from, I saw Him behind me. His arms opened wide and He said, 'Come to me, my beloved wife. I have long wished to hold you in my arms.'"

Wife? How odd, Eleanor thought. Which patient might have confused the infirmarian with his spouse and committed this very mortal act of violence? "How did Our Lord appear to you?"

"As a man, my lady." The infirmarian frowned, puzzled at the question.

"I meant to ask how you did recognize Him. You said you heard a beautiful voice…"

"Never have I heard these tones from any mortal! His voice was so deep, I felt each word shake my body like thunder."

Eleanor raised one eyebrow. A most visceral vision, she thought, then rebuked herself. "Did He show you the wounds in His hands or the gash in His side?"

Sister Christina hesitated, then shook her head. "Nay, but He would not. I see little with clarity beyond here." She brought one hand to within a few inches of her eyes. "Our Lord would know that."

Eleanor had not realized that her infirmarian was cursed with such poor vision. That would surely explain her awkwardness in walking and the distant look she often had. Devotion to prayer did not account for all her ways, it seemed. "Aye, but do tell me what happened next."

"He stood with his arms open, calling me His beloved. I was overcome with awe and could not rise. My eyes shut to His glory, I crawled toward Him on my knees, weeping for joy and calling Him my Bridegroom! Suddenly, He kicked me." She pointed to her right eye. "Then again." She pointed to her other eye. "I cried out with the pain, but He grabbed me, pulled me to my feet, and ordered me to open my eyes. Then He hit me with His fist. He cursed me!"

"Cursed? Why?" Eleanor tried to control her outrage. No loving God would ever punish this unworldly and gentle creature so brutally. How dare this man take advantage of her soul's innocence!

Sister Christina blinked, but her eyes were still wide with wonder over the vision she thought she had been granted. "In my woman's frailty, I, too, failed to understand at first. Now I know that He struck me because I have failed to understand the suffering I bring to Him. We are all so cursed with sin. Were we not filthy with it, God would never have had to sacrifice His Son, a Lamb to be slaughtered to save us all."

Eleanor bit her tongue. "I am grateful for your wisdom, Sister." She waited until her anger had cooled enough so she could choose her next words carefully. "Do tell us more. Was he bearded? What color was his hair?" What else could a woman so poor of sight be able to see? "Surely you can share some detail with those of us who long to know more of what you saw."

"I saw little, my lady. He was in shadow, and it was dark in the chapel. My vision, well, then I remember nothing more. Yet..."

Something! Please, just one detail to pursue! "And that was?"

"His face had a strange hue, my lady."

"Hue?" Eleanor quickly looked over her shoulder at Anne and Thomas, her raised eyebrows asking a silent question. Neither indicated this had been mentioned before. "In what way was it strange?"

The infirmarian clutched her cross even more tightly to her breast. "His skin did not have the color of any mortal man, my lady. It was suffused with a purplish tinge." Then she cried out with joy: "By this noble hue, I knew He must be the King of Heaven's Son. For cert, I have been blessed with a vision!"

Chapter Thirty-five

Walter stood at the opening to his master's small room, arms spread as if to bar any entrance. "He did not do this thing!"

"Sister Christina said the face of her attacker had a purple cast. For one with indifferent vision, your master's wound might well seem so." Eleanor stood but a foot from the servant, her gray eyes hot with anger.

Walter gestured toward Thomas standing just behind the prioress. "Confirm my story with your monk. It was I who sought him out to help your injured nun, then readily answered all his questions. Surely I would not have done so had I thought my master the guilty one." He snorted with contempt. "If my master had done this, we would have escaped long ago as any guilty party would. Why do you accuse us when we have behaved in all respects as innocent men?"

"Can you assure me that you were with your master at all times last night? Will you swear that he could not have left this space while you slept? Have you witnesses?"

"I sleep little, my lady, although I confess I did leave him once to attend a call of nature."

"And when you returned?"

"He was lying as you see him now." Walter stood aside and pointed to Sir Maurice lying on the straw bed. With his hands crossed over his chest and his eyes unblinking, the man resembled the corpse in the chapel, a mortal shell awaiting reunion with the dust whence it came.

"Sister Christina came to pray with your master last evening, did she not?"

"She came, knelt by his side, and offered prayers. I believe she prayed for him rather than with him. My master rarely speaks, even to me, and he has been especially silent after the crowner upset him so."

"By his side? Do you not remember warning me to keep my distance from him?" Eleanor asked.

"With all due respect, my lady, I did not allow her to come any closer than I did you. I was in attendance at all times when Sister Christina was here to offer her healing orisons." Walter looked away. In the dark it was difficult to tell, but a tear might have escaped his good eye and tumbled down his cheek. "My master did seem more alert and attentive after her visits. I had hoped that she was bringing him a slow but definite cure."

"You have told me that your master is troubled by the presence of women. That, along with the color of his grievous wound, will explain why I must question you about the attack on my infirmarian."

"He is innocent."

"When did she leave your master last night?"

Walter shook his head. Either fatigue or weary impatience colored his voice. "I have no idea. She came. She prayed. She left. Perhaps you had best ask her, for I did not rush to take note of any moon or stars. I had no reason."

"Was it shortly afterward that you left him?"

"I cannot say!" Walter's voice rose with evident frustration.

"Nonetheless, you did leave him alone last night, however briefly, although you were aware that he often wanders as you yourself have said. Was there truly need to go to the garderobe when a pot has been provided for your needs?"

"Am I thus condemned for choosing where to piss?" he replied sharply, then gestured as if thrusting aside his rude speech. "Nay, I did leave my master but not alone. A man in monkish garb stood nearby. As you must remember, my lady, I did ask you for an attendant and thus assumed you had sent a lay brother."

Eleanor looked back at Thomas.

"I know of no such lay brother, my lady," he replied. "Sister Anne might have assigned someone while I was…while I was not here."

"I shall ask." Eleanor turned back to Walter. "Could you describe the man?"

"Were I able, I would have done so already."

Eleanor gripped her arms hidden in the sleeves of her robe and prayed she would not show her anger at the man's rough tone. She asked Thomas, "Was this man mentioned to you when the crime was reported?"

"I will answer for the good brother. I did not do so. There was no reason."

"Was the man still here when you returned?"

Walter hesitated, then shook his head with a brief negative. "Not by the entrance, but I thought I saw him near the chapel. My master would not have been unattended long."

A man in a monk's robe near the chapel? Eleanor knew of no lay brother or monk with a face matching Sister Christina's description. "Very well," she continued. "You came back from the latrine, found your master lying on his bed, and the lay brother absent. What happened next?"

"I have told all to yon monk."

"You shall repeat everything to me."

Anger painted his face with high color. "Why? I owe nothing to your family, nor am I required, like your charges here, to follow the rule of Eve."

"All this is true, but you stand on ground consecrated to God, and I am prioress here. As you owe God fealty, so must you obey me while you accept His grace here." Eleanor felt her own face blaze with rage. Were she wise, she thought, she would turn questioning over to Brother Thomas, who might get better answers from this man than she, but her insulted pride had just burned that logic to a crisp ash.

"Nor shall you leave until the crowner arrives," she snapped, then softened her tone. "We do you a kindness. Has your master's care so consumed you that you have forgotten what methods secular justice may use to obtain truth? To freely answer our questions is the wiser choice."

Walter's gaze shifted away.

Eleanor let him take as long as he needed to think this over.

When he finally turned back to her, his expression was most humble. "I spoke without thinking and beg your forgiveness."

"Granted. Continue."

"Since I was gone but briefly, I thought all was well with my master, then I came closer and saw that he was weeping." Walter put his hands to his eyes, rubbing the missing one as if it pained him. "He sat up, whimpering, his eyes wide as if a ghost had visited. His fear and pain were so sharp I could not bear to let him suffer and hurried to find help, a lay brother with a potion, a draught, to give him ease."

Surely he could not feign this caring, Eleanor thought. Could he?

"I passed by the chapel and looked in, hoping that someone, perhaps the man I thought had been sent to watch over my master, was there. It was then that I saw your nun…"

"Your hesitation is understandable. Her state has been described to me."

"As your monk can attest, I came to seek help for her forthwith."

"And left your master alone."

Walter looked outraged, as if she had just slapped him. "The crime had been committed, and none other has occurred!" he roared, then dropped his voice. "Perhaps I was in error when I sought aid for your nun without thought of my own lord, but I cannot be condemned for leaving him alone when nothing else untoward happened."

"Nor are you." The raw outrage was palpable. Either his master was innocent of the attack against Sister Christina, Eleanor thought, or Walter was ignorant of Sir Maurice's guilt. The former was possible, the latter unlikely, she decided.

But Walter was not done. "As to what may have happened between the time I went for a piss and returned to find Sir Maurice lying here, I humbly suggest that you look for the one who stood without when I left."

"Or perhaps we should ask your master more of what happened this night." Eleanor looked back at Thomas and nodded. "Brother Thomas would ask the questions, not I."

Walter opened his mouth, but whether he intended to agree or protest was irrelevant.

A high-pitched wail shattered the air.

Sir Maurice stood, staring wildly into the blackness above. "Angel! Angel of Death!" he screamed, throwing wide his arms as if to embrace the creature. Then he fell to the ground, clawing at his chest as if something were trying to rip his heart out with its talons.

"Brother," Walter cried out, gesturing in supplication to Thomas. "Save him from the demons!"

Chapter Thirty-six

As Eleanor walked into her public room, she halted so abruptly that Gytha trod on her heel. After the attack on Sister Christina and Sir Maurice's demonic fit, the last thing the prioress needed to contend with was Brother Matthew.

That determined monk knelt beside Sister Ruth. Their eyes were tightly shut, and their lips moved with silent, indomitable intensity. Lying on the table in front of the praying pair was a rough-hewn box. The lid had been removed and set to one side. On a worn piece of discolored silk, placed at the very edge of the table for optimal viewing by the kneeling monastics, rested a chalky white thigh bone with kneecap attached.

Eleanor prayed for forgiveness to whomever the bones might belong. Whether saint or sinner, either would understand her frail impatience after such an eventful morning.

"I could not keep them out, my lady," Gytha whispered to the prioress, then put the orange cat she had been holding down on the ground.

Arthur strode into the chambers as if he were lord of the manor.

"I fear even God might not have been able to bar the door to them," Eleanor whispered back.

The cat jumped up on the table.

"It is not your fault," Eleanor continued.

Arthur crouched, crept slowly up to the bones, and sniffed with some interest.

Looking for your dinner after a good day's hunting, Eleanor thought with a smile. At least the cat had managed to improve her mood.

The praying pair had yet to notice that anyone had entered the room. As most people beyond supple youth were wont to do, Sister Ruth shifted back on her heels to give her knees some ease.

Suddenly Arthur gave the kneecap a mighty swat. The bone tumbled off the edge, right into Sister Ruth's lap.

"Praise the Lord!" the sub-prioress screamed, grabbing the relic and clutching it to her bosom. "It is a sign!"

Arthur scuttled off the table and disappeared into the safety of the priaress' private chamber.

Gytha ran from the room, her face scarlet with barely controlled laughter.

Eleanor prayed she could control her own.

Brother Matthew opened his eyes, looked at the ecstatic nun cradling the bone, then realized his prioress stood nearby. He raised his hands to heaven. "Without a doubt, Saint Skallagrim has signified that Tyndal must be home to his sacred relic. See how he has thrown himself on the mercy of our dear sister!"

"So it seems," Eleanor said.

The monk rose to his feet, his lanky body straightened to full height. "Seems?" He glared down at his tiny prioress.

"Seems, Brother Matthew. Seems. I have never heard of Saint Skallagrim. Perhaps you can enlighten me."

Brother Matthew did not hesitate. "A local saint. Not being of this place yourself, my lady, I suspect you would have no reason to know of him."

"Not yet canonized?" Eleanor was chary of these local saints. England was full of former but much beloved pagan spirits who had been converted, as it were, by their former worshippers to the true faith. Thus the deities' ancient and established powers would not be lost, nor their anger provoked by rejection. Eleanor preferred to wait for the Church to decide whether these spirits had been truly persuaded to change allegiance.

"It is just a matter of time. If we were wise enough to recognize his sanctity first, he would surely grace us with many miracles."

"And he was such a sweet boy," Sister Ruth cooed, still cuddling the bone.

"Boy?" Eleanor raised one questioning eyebrow as she stared at the bone. She stepped closer for a better look.

"Any man could tell it was the bone of a child, my lady. Look at its size."

"It is small, Brother." She stepped back and frowned. "Were you not raised at Norwich in a family noted for their skill as goldsmiths?"

Brother Matthew sniffed as if detecting a foul odor. "My rank in the world may not be the equivalent of yours, but I remind you that Robert of Arbrissel did not allow these distinctions within our Order. You and I must be accorded the same respect in our sacred vocation and our opinions given equal hearing."

"You do well to remind me of that. Wisdom and knowledge must always rule, not family status. In that I do agree." Eleanor smiled.

Brother Matthew bowed. He did not even try to hide the smirk twisting his mouth.

"Therefore, I will allow this bone to remain at Tyndal in the care of Sister Ruth…"

The nun looked at her prioress with a beatific glow that all but removed the deeply ingrained signs of her many bitter years on this earth.

"…until you can bring me the required proofs of authenticity as well as the man who is so willing to sell us this fine relic. Am I correct in remembering that both were available, Brother?"

Matthew blinked, then replied with indignation. "Of course, my lady. The holy man would have come himself with these sainted bones, but he feared he would not receive a welcome reception." He stared at Eleanor in silence, which was both meaningful and lengthy. "Fortunately, he trusted my, rather, *our* honesty at the priory and released this sacred item so your doubts might be destroyed with a revelation of its power and desire to rest at Tyndal."

All done by the grace of one orange cat, Eleanor thought with irreverence, but perhaps Saint Skallagrim had been fond of the furry creatures when he was on earth.

Brother Matthew glanced down at Sister Ruth with tender esteem. "A sign which our most modest and worthy sister has been granted and you have been honored to witness."

"Do arrange for a meeting, good brother, and we will greet your seller of relics with a reception proper to the significance of what he has brought us."

Satisfied with his victory in this matter, Brother Matthew gently raised Sister Ruth from her knees, and they turned to leave.

As the two monastics walked away, the nun following the lanky monk, Eleanor watched Sister Ruth holding the reliquary with so much love and awe. We should all savor those precious moments of pure happiness that God grants us, the prioress thought. When life turns cruel, their memory must comfort us.

Then, despite all that had happened that day, she caught herself chuckling with much merriment as she went into her private chambers. Arthur would have an especially fine piece of fowl for his midday dinner, she decided.

Chapter Thirty-seven

"Sir!"

Ralf opened one eye again, then the other. The brightly sweet glow of last night's ale had been transformed into a bitter foretaste of Hell. In this morning after, he understood too well why drunkenness and lechery were sins. His head hurt. His sex felt raw. Swearing he would never drink so much again and that he would find himself a wife, the crowner rolled off the bed and vomited sour liquid into the chamber pot.

"Sir?" Cuthbert stood, arms crossed in a determined pose at the entrance to the room above the inn.

"May your balls fry in Hell." Ralf wiped his mouth. At this precise moment, he understood why men like Thomas took the cowl.

"Indeed, sir, but you are called to Tyndal."

"You woke me with that news." Ralf dry retched. "You failed to tell me why."

"Prioress Eleanor sent word that someone has been beaten in the priory," Cuthbert replied.

"Why should I be so blessed?" Ralf muttered, his head spinning as he pushed himself to his knees.

"I knew you would immediately ask who had suffered the attack and the severity." Cuthbert waited while the naked crowner staggered to the basin of water near the bed.

"So give me the answers to those questions I have just asked," the crowner growled, pouring icy water over his head. When the freezing water hit his genitals, he winced, then grabbed his braies from the floor.

"Sister Christina. She was battered but will survive, and Sister Anne says the infirmarian is still a virgin."

Ralf drew his shirt over his head. It stank but there was no time for the nicety of a fresher one. "Pity," he spat.

"Sir!" Cuthbert's eyes widened in horror.

"Hush, man. That she remains an uncracked nut proves God's grace and confirms her saintliness. I only wish that someone more deserving, perhaps Brother Matthew, had been the victim, not the little nun."

Ralf reached for his sword, then sat heavily on his bed. Along with waves of dizziness, a memory began to flicker through his head. What was important about it? "Last night," he muttered, rubbing his eyes as if that would help give substance to the image. "Last night…"

"Sir?"

"Silence!" The crowner swatted as if grabbing at the memory, but it slipped through his grasp. Did it have to do with soft Signy?

He grimaced. She had joined him willingly enough for several couplings until he cried out Annie's name by mistake. Then the lass had jumped from the bed, grabbed her clothes, and cursed him. He shook his head, carefully. Nay, it was not that, although perhaps she did have something to do with…

Cuthbert cleared his throat. "The prioress is waiting…"

Like an angry dog Ralf growled, then rested his bristled chin in one hand. When he had arrived at the inn, Signy came to dally with him. The innkeeper had not been pleased and for good reason. With the storm last night, there had been a good crowd at the inn and that meant profits. A merry, attentive serving wench increased the willingness of men to part with their coin…

His head throbbed. The image he was chasing shimmered seductively at the edge of his memory. The crowd? Was it that? "It was large," he repeated. "The crowd…"

"Sir!"

It was gone. Ralf swore at the sergeant and grabbed his sword.

Cuthbert jumped back.

"To Tyndal, then, where I will hear all the details of last night," Ralf said, buckling the sword with shaking hands, "and you may entertain me with tales of your sheep hunt while we ride."

As the crowner walked past his sergeant, he saw Cuthbert shake his head with annoyance. His sour mood sweetened slightly. Cuthbert might be a good man, but he deserved some whipping about for daring to tell him what he should have asked had he not been busy tossing his guts into a chamber pot.

Chapter Thirty-eight

Although the daylight held too gray a cast to claim the sun had ever fully risen, the major force of the storm had passed. The wind was now soft, as if apologetic for its recent fury. Rainwater dripped from the roof with a moist, melodic tone, and drops tapped sporadically against the wooden shutters of the prioress' chamber.

Ralf and Thomas stared at each other.

"Now that you have heard what Brother Thomas has said about the attack on our infirmarian, what do you think?" Eleanor asked, breaking the silence.

"Someone is lying." The crowner belched.

"A reasonable conclusion, Ralf." Eleanor's mouth twitched upward despite the cautionary look she shot at Gytha. "Who is lying?"

"If you will forgive me for saying so, and I have no wish to cast doubt on Sister Christina's most admirable faith," Ralf said carefully, "but I do not believe her beating was done by Our Lord." He looked at Anne. "Not that I think she is lying…"

"Nor do we, although I pray she may one day be granted a true vision, one that is kinder than this she believes she has received." Eleanor turned to her maid. "Would you see if Sister Matilda has some fresh bread and ale for all? I fear some have not had time to break their fast." She glanced at the crowner.

After Gytha shut the door, she continued, "I thank you, Brother Thomas, for not describing the details of the attempted rape. There are some things a young girl should not hear."

Thomas bent his head.

"Now it seems we may have both a murderer and a rapist at Tyndal," Anne said.

Eleanor frowned. "Might they not be the same?"

"We know of no connection between Sister Christina and the dead soldier," Ralf replied. "Unless they are kin?"

"This man was a common soldier. Sister Christina's family is of much higher rank," Anne replied. "Nor was he a family servant. Our infirmarian did not recognize him."

"If I may speak further on this, my lady?"

"Your observations are always welcome, Brother."

"Although Brother Beorn confirmed that Sir Maurice has been a most peaceful patient, except for that one incident in the chapel, he seems the most likely suspect if we accept Sister Christina's description of the color of her attacker's face."

"What of the man Walter assumed was an attendant assigned to watch over his master?" Anne asked.

"That may be a lie…" Thomas started.

"Or the truth," Ralf finished.

"Why do you think it might be true, Ralf?" Eleanor looked thoughtful.

"As Brother Thomas noted, Sir Maurice has caused no trouble, and you have not found anyone who has ever seen his servant elsewhere than by his side. Aye, the knight lashed out in fear when I showed him the corpse, but his man had warned me and I failed to heed him." Ralf flushed with the memory. "I would also point out that his only violence was against other men. Can any of us imagine how a gentle nun could frighten him into beating her?" The crowner shrugged. "Sister Christina was making progress with the knight's sick soul. He has been quiet in her presence, according to his servant. Why would he suddenly try to rape her? I would look to someone else."

"Well argued, Ralf," Thomas replied.

Ralf gave the monk a weak smile. "You have confirmed that no one was assigned to watch Sir Maurice. There is, however, one now resting in your hospital whose face bears a reddish hue.

His dress is also much like that of a religious, especially in the dim light of nighttime."

Eleanor nodded, although her expression suggested some doubt. "You speak of our madman, someone you dismissed as a suspect in the soldier's murder?"

"Aye." Ralf scratched at his stubbled cheeks. "When I talked with him, he seemed too weak to have committed that crime but would not be incapable of rape against a meek woman. I was also convinced that he did suffer moments of madness. Might he not attempt rape during such a fit?" Ralf looked sheepish. "After what you overheard between the fellow and Brother Thomas, however, I fear my prior observations are sadly flawed."

"Do not dismiss your thoughts so readily, Ralf," the prioress replied. "I was wrong in my assumptions about the man for I hoped to frighten him into renouncing his false witness if he saw Brother Thomas and realized he had failed to cast blame on our innocent brother. Instead, we learned that the man had only told part of his tale, thus making it seem that our brother had more knowledge of the crime than he did."

Ralf's face was as gray as the sky outside. "I regret that I was not here to assist, my lady, but you were clever to take Brother Thomas down to the man's cell to see how he would react. You learned far more from him than I. Had I questioned him better, I would never have concluded that our brother..."

"A deduction that I stubbornly encouraged out of angry pride." Thomas folded his arms. "Nay, crowner, like you I thought him mad, yet not so. His speech is not that of an ordinary man, for cert, and he is either witless or else possessed of more wit than most. I still wonder. Whatever the truth there, the man's face does have a reddish cast, a color that might be seen as purple if the light is dim, the sight is poor, and the viewer is convinced she is seeing a vision."

"Sister Christina has also spent time in prayer with him," Anne added. "Sir Maurice was not her only concern."

"What motive would he have?" Eleanor asked. "We should not forget that Sir Maurice is deeply disturbed by the presence of women, and we do not know the reason for the unease."

"Yet he has shown no violence to any," Anne replied. "When I was with him, he ignored me. Sister Christina has assured me that she carefully heeded the servant's advice and was never with Sir Maurice when his man was not there."

"Which does leave us with the madman," Thomas said. "He was quite clever with his riddles, Ralf. I did wonder if he was hiding something, something to do with the murder."

"I doubted he had the might to do the deed, yet..." The crowner looked at Sister Anne.

The nun nodded. "The murderer did need great strength, but both lunatics and men possessed by demons could have that power, Ralf."

"I do wonder if the attack on our dear sister was meant to distract us from our hunt for the soldier's killer," Eleanor said softly as if talking to herself.

Thomas continued. "Walter has not kept his master's fear of women secret. This strange madman, who will not even give us a name, might have overheard the servant speak of that, for the fellow rests not far from the two men. Perhaps he wanted to cast suspicion on Sir Maurice when he saw that blame no longer rested on me?"

"Or he heard the lay brothers speak of it," Ralf said.

"Or heard Walter discuss it with Sister Christina when she came to pray," Anne continued.

"If so many were cognizant of this," Ralf said, "then the man might well have known it and taken action to divert suspicion on to Sir Maurice."

Eleanor shook her head, then rose, gesturing to Ralf and Thomas. "If this man ranks so high in your suspicions of one or both crimes, then we cannot delay further. Come. We must talk with this nameless man now. If he is innocent of both murder and the attack, he has nothing to fear from us, for we shall treat him and his ills most kindly. If he is guilty of either, we cannot let him freely roam our priory hospital any longer."

Thus the prioress, the crowner, and the monk all left for the hospital, but when they converged on the cell belonging to the madman, he had quite disappeared.

❦ ❦ ❦

"No one knows when or where he went," Sister Anne said, looking up at the stained glass window above the altar, its bright colors now dimmed with the diminished light of the season and the mold that had found new life in the corners.

"None of the patients or lay brothers saw him leave?" Ralf asked, his tone abrupt. "Have you questioned all the monks and nuns as well as lay brothers and sisters?"

"We have questioned almost everyone. Not one, so far, has seen anything," Thomas replied.

"Our knight and his man? What say they?" The crowner rubbed at his chin, his growing beard clearly annoying him.

Anne shook her head. "Thomas questioned Walter…"

"…who did not hear the man singing as he was wont to do. I did confirm that he knew what the fellow looked like. How could he forget the merry chase the man had led the lay brothers through the hospital was how he answered me."

"Your lady prioress will not be pleased with this," Ralf said.

"Nor am I." Thomas curled his hand into a fist. "The man will wear a fine mark from the blow I'll give him for fooling us so."

"A wish I hope will be confessed, Brother, but I concede there is some justice in your desire and that your anger is understandable. God may attend to the needs of simple sparrows, but He gave us the responsibility to look after our brethren. As imperfect creatures, we often render violence unto the violent."

The two men spun around in unison. "My lady!"

Eleanor stood just behind them, her hands neatly tucked into her woolen winter robe. "I assume the man we seek has not been found? This is not good news." She turned to Thomas. "Do I understand that you and Ralf now believe that our madman was less than mad?"

As Thomas looked into his prioress' eyes, dark as a North Sea winter storm, he shuddered. That look was not for him, he quickly reminded himself. After all, she had been most gentle since he had told her of his imprisonment. He nodded.

The crowner did as well.

"Does no one know the man's name or whence he came?"

Ralf looked at Thomas. Thomas shook his head.

"Nor I. None of the lay people have recognized him either," Anne added.

"Not a local man then." With a slight smile, Eleanor glanced over at Ralf. "I would not presume to direct you in your work outside Tyndal, Crowner, but I am curious what you may have found in the questioning of the villagers and anyone at the inn."

"Nothing has been discovered that we did not already know. Cuthbert has been talking with the villagers. I have just come from the inn." He bowed his head to hide his discomfort. Signy, of course, had refused to speak to him, saying that she would only answer questions from his sergeant. "Nor has anyone seen him since he disappeared."

"Our time is short," Eleanor replied, her lips white with anger. "We must find this man."

Chapter Thirty-nine

"As soon as I found him, my lady, I confirmed that he was dead, then came to you immediately. I bear the guilt, as your porter, for failing to keep Tyndal safe from violence."

Eleanor hoped he could not see her hands tremble and quickly hid them in her sleeves. "It is not you who is to blame, Brother Andrew. It is I. This is the second time our priory has suffered a violent death within its walls since I arrived."

"At least this body was not left in the cloister garth," Anne said from behind the monk, her voice a whisper.

"Nonetheless, my responsibility is to everyone inside the walls of Tyndal," Eleanor said, both frustration and anger evident in her tone. "My full attention has not been on the crimes…"

A knock at the door interrupted her. When Gytha opened it, the prioress gestured for Crowner Ralf and Brother Thomas to enter.

"Now that our crowner has arrived, Brother Andrew," she said, "please repeat to all what has transpired."

"Lord Maurice has been murdered. I found his body near the parish church."

The prioress nodded for the porter to continue.

"Stabbed in the back, he was, but I could find no weapon. We have not moved the body, but I believe we should do so before light. If others see what has happened, I fear panic will ensue."

"In that I concur. Crowner?"

"I will immediately examine the corpse, my lady."

"Since this occurred on priory grounds, Sister Anne and Brother Thomas will assist you. My first concern may be for the safety of this priory, but much else is at stake. If panic and fear drive the needy from our hospital, that would be a tragedy. We must capture the killer before the news spreads."

"I left two lay brothers to guard the body. Two," Andrew added, "whose silence I can depend upon."

The prioress nodded agreement. The porter had handled this situation to her liking, and her approval was apparent.

"Shall I shall fetch his servant?" Brother Andrew asked her. "I have not told him of this."

"Since Walter sleeps little, he may be searching for his missing master even now. Let us go to him quickly with the news, Brother Porter. He must have what comfort we can bring. In the meantime, Crowner Ralf, Sister Anne, and Brother Thomas will take torches and learn what they can from the dead man where he lies. Before we bring Walter to see the body of Sir Maurice, however, we must move the corpse to the chapel where none will question the presence of another body. Daylight will not wait for us."

⁂

Walter fell across the body, his legs losing any strength to hold him upright. As he put his arms around the shell of the man he had called *master*, he uttered a cry so poignant that tears rose in the eyes of any who overheard.

While Walter hugged the body of Sir Maurice like a father might his dead child, Eleanor gestured for Brother Andrew to join the others standing a respectful distance away. Although the man's grief seared her heart, Eleanor found herself studying Walter with a detached mind. This was not a servant mourning his master, no matter how devoted he might be. Of course, she had suspected early on that he had lied about his relationship to Sir Maurice as well as his own rank. Perhaps it was time to ask.

"Was he your son?" she whispered, bending close to the man.

Walter looked at her, tears streaming from one dark-rimmed eye while the other remained dry as if empty of emotion as well as sight. He shook his head. "He was my brother's son, my lady." Then he struck his heart. "But to this childless man he was near enough." Although he spoke, as did she, in a whisper, the sound was like the last rattling breath of a dying man.

"You wished no one learn of this?"

"He was my Absalom!" the man murmured, then threw his head back and wailed with an intensity that should have caused the very angels themselves to weep for his agony.

Eleanor rested one hand gently on the man's back, then turned her head. "Come, Brother Thomas. He needs a priest's comfort." She knew there was little she could say to ease this man's sorrow. Tomorrow, her reminders of God's promises might bring solace. Today, the pain was too raw for any woman's balm.

This man was answerable for much, she knew, but now was not the time for confrontations and accusations. There were many other questions to resolve first before she was certain that would be necessary. For now, she would let him grieve.

Chapter Forty

Thomas and Ralf stood in front of the second trestle table laid for the second corpse. By order of the prioress, the screen to the chapel had been closed, thus barring this sight from all. Eleanor remained apart in the shadows as if she did not want to intrude, or else wished to be alone with her thoughts.

Sister Anne bent over the body. With two fingers she raised some hair from the dead man's neck, then stroked his head once as if it had been that of a child or the hospital cat. Cuthbert pulled the cloth back over the still face.

"What think you, Annie?" Ralf said, his voice soft as if he feared the dead might be disturbed by his question.

"There is little more to see than when we first examined him by torch light. The only wound is the one that killed him, and it was a swift death. The murderer aimed for the heart and did not miss."

"No other blows?"

"None, Ralf. There are no bruises, cuts, or any signs of a struggle. The width of the stab wound would suggest a common knife. Since you found none nearby, I assume the killer took it with him."

"Not the same kind of murder as that one then." Ralf pointed to the overripe body of the soldier.

"There are no signs of rage in this deed. As these things go, it was a kind act. I might guess that the murderer slipped behind

Sir Maurice in silence, then stabbed him with one hard blow
to the heart."

Ralf nodded.

Anne continued. "The position of the knight was most
certainly interesting. Lying on his back with his hands crossed
over his chest? It was as if he had died in his bed with a priest
at his side. Someone took time to position him like a peaceful
corpse ready for burial. All that would suggest a certain reverence despite the killing."

"Could we have two killers then?" Ralf turned to Thomas.
"You have thoughts, Brother?"

"Although we should be grateful that this murder occurred
on the public grounds of our priory, that also means almost
anyone could have done it. From what Sister Anne says, the
method does not suggest the murderer was the same one who
killed…" Thomas waved at the first corpse without looking at
it. "We could have two killers abroad."

"I do believe we must find our madman and hear the riddles
he now chooses to tell." Eleanor's words came like a ghostly voice
from the shadows. "Perhaps they hold the key to all of this."

"Aye, my lady," Thomas said, glancing at the crowner.

"Has anyone disturbed the cell he occupied?" Ralf asked.

"It has been left almost untouched," Anne replied. "When I
saw a lay sister coming from it with the bed sheets, I asked that
no one touch anything else and that the cell remain unoccupied
until someone had searched it."

"You are ever wise, Annie." Ralf gazed at her tenderly, then
cleared his throat. "Has anyone done so?"

Thomas shook his head. "There were so many to question
at the hospital, we had no time for that."

"Then I shall now," the crowner said. "If I had searched
earlier, perhaps Sir Maurice would still be alive."

⁂

"Satan's tits! I am but human," the crowner muttered as he left
the chapel for the madman's former cell. He cursed himself for
his frailties. Instead of chasing down a murderer, he had gotten

drunk, bedded one woman as substitute for another, and suffered raddled wits ever since.

He spat. His mouth still tasted of sheep dung. "Get a wife?" he snorted as he approached the cubicle. Reeking of sweat and vomit, he was no Sir Lancelot. He rubbed his ear where Signy had hit him yesterday when he arrived at the inn to beg her pardon as well as question her on the madman. He could not blame her. He was a rough man.

Ralf kicked the screen aside and strode into the cell.

"It matters not. Once this crime is solved, I will avoid Tyndal Priory and never again care for any woman, wench or wife," he said with conviction born of despair. "Back to murder," he said and set his torch into a bracket in the wall. If he was going to feel miserable, he might as well concentrate on madness, death, and a vanished man.

In the weak light of the torch, he could see little, but there was little enough in this bare space. "My brother will not replace me for fornicating, but he will if I do not catch the man who killed the crusader," he growled, but when he kicked the strewn herbs on the ground, the only thing he unearthed was dust.

Whether or not his brother did choose someone else as crowner, Ralf still held the office, although he would be the first to say that any man who spent his time drinking and wenching in the middle of a murder investigation was unworthy of the position. Nevertheless, crowner he was, and at least his hangover had faded. Perhaps after all the mistakes he had made in this investigation, he was owed some good fortune.

"God should be so gracious," Ralf growled as he sat on the edge of the narrow bed. He began sifting through the straw with one hand. Was this madman capable of beating, then trying to rape the little nun? Might he be the murderer of the crusader? Could he be guilty of both crimes?

He had agreed with Prioress Eleanor when she first told him about releasing Thomas to see if the sight of the monk might leech truth from the fellow. The madman did seem guilty of something. Yet where did his guilt lie? Perhaps his crime was but a petty thing. Spending time on him and whatever minor transgression he had committed might be like stirring up muck in a clear stream. Perhaps it was wisest to ignore the man.

Something began to buzz in his head like a large bee going from flower to flower in the full heat of a summer's day. Had he seen the fellow before? Perhaps it had been on a market day when he and Cuthbert wandered about, watching for cutpurses? Brother Matthew had told Beorn that the fellow had been in the village for some days, had he not? Now that he thought on it, he realized that Cuthbert had never seen the madman while the fellow was in this hospital. Again he cursed himself. If he had brought his sergeant with him when he had questioned the man, Cuthbert might have recognized him.

Ralf struggled to focus. A vague image danced across his mind, then disappeared like a playful maid around a corner. He shook his head in frustration. When Cuthbert had awakened him with news of the attack on Sister Christina, Ralf had tried to remember something from the previous night. Had it to do with the madman? Murder? Or just Signy's hardened nipples under his fingers?

"S'blood! Why does ale make a man's mind so clear while he drinks but leave his wits so muddy afterward?"

The memory dallied with him again, then coyly hid once more. "Women and memories," he growled. "They tease men's souls like flax." With a grunt, he quickly tossed aside the effort to catch hold of the thing and began to dig farther into the straw, tossing large bits onto the floor.

This fellow was far too clever to be as mad as he purported. Ralf was troubled as well by the man's broken nose and especially the reddened skin, as if the sun had permanently marked him. Had the man been to the Holy Land? Was he one of those soldiers who bore few visible wounds but hid a mortal one in his soul? Did his wits perhaps come and go with a soldier's hellish vision, asleep or awake? Did he scream at the sight of flames or strike at anyone who came upon him unawares? Ralf had seen these things often enough. Maybe this fellow suffered like that, thus might have attacked the infirmarian given the right circumstances...

Ralf started. His hand had just touched an object buried deep into the straw. He pulled it out. It was a small leather pouch, much stained. The strings that would be used to tie it to the braies had been neatly cut. Since Anne insisted that each new patient be given fresh straw bedding, this had to belong to the missing man.

He put the purse on the ground, then began digging out great handfuls of straw. There was nothing more in the bed, so he got down on his knees to see under it. Something else was on the ground. Ralf flattened himself, reached out, and grabbed a handful of coarse sackcloth. He carried it carefully to the torchlight.

The thing was a sack. As he looked inside, he saw that the cloth was covered with a pale dust. He ran his finger through it. It was gritty, sharp. Then he peered at the residue on his hand. Suddenly, a host of memories, not just the one he had been chasing since yesterday, returned to him like children to a mother's loving arms. Ralf began to laugh.

"Cuthbert!" he yelled. "Come here! And bring Brother Thomas."

Chapter Forty-one

The following day, a weak sun had done its best to warm men's spirits before the next storm swept the coast. As that sun was setting, however, it must have grieved that its best efforts had failed so with Sister Ruth and Brother Matthew. Both were standing, heads bowed with dejection, in the prioress' chambers.

Prioress Eleanor's look was most grave as well, but Sister Anne did smile. As long as the twitching muscles at each corner of Brother Andrew's mouth were ignored, his expression might have suggested a neutral stance.

In front of these five stood Crowner Ralf, Brother Thomas, and the man heretofore known only as *mad*. The latter's hands were bound, but Cuthbert still gripped him firmly by the arm.

On a central table lay a bulging bag and a flat pouch. Next to these items was the thigh bone with kneecap attached that Sister Ruth had been protecting with most loving care.

"Repeat, knave," Ralf ordered, pointing to the bones. "I want everyone to hear this one more time so there will be no doubt."

The captive looked nervously around him, then cleared his throat. "Sheep. The bones are from a sheep." He coughed.

Brother Andrew's facial muscles twitched with more liveliness. Eleanor raised one hand to her mouth, but the expressions of Sister Anne, Sister Ruth, and Brother Matthew did not change.

"So the relic you wanted to sell Tyndal was a sheep's thigh bone and kneecap. And what is in that bag?" Ralf pointed to the round sack on the table.

The man remained silent.

The crowner walked over to the object and dumped out the contents. They slid and clattered across the table. "Sheep bones. Sheep blood in vials. Bits of wool," he said, sorting the things into uneven piles by type.

The prisoner was making a careful study of his naked feet.

"The latter to be transformed, no doubt, into many hairs of various aged saints. None, in fact, sacred." There was not even the hint of a question in Ralf's words.

"You wish me to confess to something, Crowner?" The fellow's voice did not tremble; yet he was quite pale, a color suggesting he might be a very frightened man.

"You may confirm what my men and I have found; however, your refusal to do so is unimportant."

"Shall you torture a lie from me, then?"

"No need. The facts are simple. A farmer reported one missing sheep. After determining that no wild creature had killed it, we set watch on his land, and Cuthbert saw you steal another beast, then slaughter it. My sergeant observed as you cleaned the bones, had a good feast of mutton, put these items in a bag, and hid all under a bush before disappearing into the storm. Fortunately, my sergeant decided to ask me, before he arrested you solely for stealing sheep, why I thought you might have saved the bits, then hidden the bag. His tale reminded me of something I had seen the other night at the inn."

The fellow shrugged. "Your sergeant has such good vision in a bad storm?"

"Cuthbert can see a seagull standing in a fog bank. From his description, I knew you were the same man who has been leading the lay brothers here a merry chase."

The captive twitched uncomfortably.

Ralf smiled with little humor. "According to the innkeeper today, you were seen talking with pilgrims who had some coin. The inn was a profitable place for you, was it not? When I told Cuthbert and Brother Thomas what I suspected, we decided you might return there with your newly created relics. Cuthbert went back to the hiding place, waited until you arrived, then followed you back to the inn where you met with a pilgrim for the purpose of selling him a vial of…Saint Poculum's blood, I believe?" Ralf looked over at Brother Thomas.

"Saint Poculum Butyri," the monk confirmed.

"Butter?" Brother Andrew sputtered, losing all semblance of solemnity. "A canonized cup of butter?" he repeated, then doubled over with laughter.

"Our relic seller, it seems, has both humor and some knowledge of Latin." Thomas grinned at the prisoner. "Were you a cleric once?"

The man refused to answer.

"The pilgrim may have been quite ignorant of Latin, but I am not, and our relic seller failed to recognize that the hooded traveler snoring so loudly nearby was I."

"Few would argue with my sergeant's testimony and none with Brother Thomas'. What use would torture be?" Ralf asked.

"Surely the man is innocent!" Brother Matthew looked up and glanced with pitiful hopefulness at the man with the broken nose.

The face of the captive lit up with some joy. "As you see, Crowner, this good brother is a man of faith. If you believed in the wonders of God, you would have no doubt that a sheep's knee could become a sacred thing. Saint Skallagrim…"

Ralf spat just in front of the bound man's toes.

"Saint Skallagrim never existed," Eleanor said. "So I have confirmed with Brother Beorn who grew up here. It is blasphemy to pretend that some falsity is sacred. You are a fraud and may not deny what both a man of God and the king's liegemen have seen."

"I gain all by silence, my lady."

"Little," she said. "Any countryman would know the difference between the thigh bone of a sheep and that of a man or child. Of course, the kneecap does look much the same as that belonging to someone of about ten summers; nonetheless, this thigh bone, the one you tried to sell us, is uniquely curved." She pointed to the rounded bone.

Brother Matthew opened his mouth but, upon seeing the expression on his prioress' face, shut it. Beside him, Sister Ruth's face had turned the color of shame.

"Clearly that of a sheep," Eleanor continued. "Since our hospital has had the sad task of preparing bodies of young children for transportation some distance to a family grave," she gestured toward Sister Anne, "we know that the same bone in a child would be straighter." She looked over at Brother Matthew. "Or, if curved for some other reason, quite differently so."

"As you heard me say, my lady, I now know the thigh bone and kneecap are those of a sheep, but I was defrauded myself when I was sold the bone." The bound man had developed a noticeable facial spasm.

"Sold?"

"I was sold this item, my lady." The man was sweating as he nodded at the Tyndal bones.

"You have, of course, the name and description of this person?"

"Name? He gave me none, but he had an honest look. As for description, he was of middle height with light brown hair and hazel eyes. One eye wandered…"

"And thus he describes half the men in England." Ralf gestured with contempt.

"And you bought these bones where?" Eleanor continued.

"In Norwich…"

"Near the farmer who is also missing two prime sheep," Ralf interrupted.

"Accidental. Purely accidental," Brother Matthew remarked, hope brightening his expression. "You have no witness to explain the disappearance of the first beast."

The prisoner's expression showed less enthusiasm.

"Nonetheless, this bag of bones most certainly contains those of sheep, and the blood you attempted to sell the pilgrim came from the one we watched you butcher and feast upon. There is no doubt who is responsible for these fraudulent relics."

"As you have had ample opportunity to notice, Crowner, my wits are often weak. This monk," he bent his head toward

Thomas, "can confirm that as well. When I am possessed, I might slaughter a beast, believing upon recovery that God has graciously gifted me with sacred items to sell at some small price. Thus I sustain my fragile body."

"Were you resting at Tyndal on your way to Saint William's shrine in Norwich to seek a miraculous cure for your madness?" Brother Andrew interjected.

"I would if you would so advise, good brother." The man's voice was both hesitant and meek.

"Nay. Rather I would seek your advice on the effectiveness of the cures for I have heard said that you have been there already." The lines around the monk's eyes crinkled with good humor.

The man did not reply.

"The registrar of miracles at the shrine has just informed us that a man with your exact facial features has been twice cured by the grace of the young saint. The third time, the registrar denounced this person in his records as a fraud." Brother Andrew turned to Brother Matthew. "We sent a messenger early this morning to the shrine and he has just returned. It seems the registrar has banned our prisoner from the presence of the saint, and, should he ever come again to the reliquary, he will be tossed out as an example to others."

The relic seller opened his mouth as if to argue.

Brother Andrew shook a cautionary finger at him. "The fellow's madness involved fits of dancing, quite strange and unknown by any at Norwich, until someone just back from the Holy Land recognized it as a dance done at wedding feasts amongst the infidels. He so informed the registrar of miracles."

"Were you once a soldier in the Holy Land?" Thomas asked.

A stream of sweat began to slide down the man's cheeks. "What if I had been? Many are these days." The man's sour stench wafted through room.

"There lies in our chapel a butchered crusader…" the monk continued.

"I had naught to do with any murder!"

"Did you not?" Ralf stepped closer to the relic seller.

"Liar! Anyone who said I had anything to do with that soldier is a liar."

"Do you not lie yourself? First you tried to sell bones to Tyndal, claiming they were relics of some local saint. Then you admitted they were sheep bones, but tried to say that the truly faithful could transform them into Saint Skallagrim's. When our prioress confirmed there had never been such a saint, you alleged you had been sold the bones and thus could not be blamed if their validity had been misrepresented. Finally, you now blame every act of fraud on your madness, fits that have been proven false at Saint William's shrine. Which of your many wondrous tales are we to believe? Methinks nothing you say is true," Thomas continued.

"You are trying to put the blame on me, monk. I saw you leave the road near the place the murdered man was found. Perhaps you killed him, and you are now trying to cast blame on me."

Thomas leapt at the man.

Ralf and Brother Andrew grabbed him, but not before the monk had bloodied the prisoner's already broken nose.

"I had some sympathy for you, knave, but I will not stand accused…"

"Brother Thomas, step back!" As the monk reluctantly did so, Eleanor turned to Ralf. "Perhaps you had best show all Cuthbert found when he was searching this man and his store of relics."

The crowner returned to the table and reached into the bottom of the bag, then pulled out a knife. The blade and hilt were curiously carved with a most graceful script.

"This is no English knife," Ralf said, waving it at the bound man. "Cuthbert discovered it with your purported relics. This is a Saracen thing, much like the one found in the corpse. Were you not in the Holy Land? Might the blade found in the corpse be a twin to this one?"

"Yes! No!" the man screamed as he squirmed to escape Cuthbert's firm grip.

"Truth, knave, truth!" the crowner yelled at him.

"Ralf! This is a house of peace and forgiveness," Eleanor said, then turned to the prisoner. "Nonetheless, we will not countenance your lies. You have tried to sell false relics to me. That I can forgive. Being a woman raised with sheep and other country beasts, I recognized the fraud the moment I saw the bone."

Brother Matthew's face turned quite scarlet in hue. Sister Ruth moved ever so slightly away from the angular monk.

"In the interest of justice and compassion, I might ask for mercy on your behalf..." She raised a hand as the prisoner opened his mouth. "Make no mistake, your guilt in selling false relics has been established beyond doubt by witnesses in good standing under secular and church authority. What I will not forgive is your attempt to dress one of my priests in the guise of a murderer. If you continue refusing to confess your part in that foul deed, I shall beg the courts to make you suffer severely for all your crimes."

The man turned as gray as death's shade. "I did not kill him, my lady," he whimpered, his voice hoarse with terror as Cuthbert allowed him to slide to his knees. "What will you do for me, my lady, if I speak true? Will you protect me?"

Eleanor glanced at Ralf. He hesitated, then nodded.

"I will guarantee a fair hearing and mercy," she said.

The man inclined his head in Thomas' direction. "He is innocent. I did see him, but he turned into the forest as I told him once before. I claimed otherwise just now only because the crowner bullied me." He glared at Ralf. "Surely I would have accused your monk earlier if I had been guilty of murder and wished to find another to bear the blame?" Sweat was now pouring into his eyes. He blinked from the stinging.

Eleanor reached over for a cloth from the table and gently wiped the man's eyes. "Continue," Eleanor said as the man hesitated. "As God's servants, we believe in compassion."

"I traveled behind your priest when he left the village. With me was the bag containing the sheep bones, which Brother Matthew had agreed to purchase from me as relics for the priory."

Brother Matthew winced.

"After your monk went into the forest, I rounded the road's bend only to discover three men in front of me. Two were arguing."

Thomas frowned. "I heard nothing, yet that bend is not far from where I left the road."

"Nor did I, Brother," the man explained. "With the rain and wind in the trees, the sounds must have been muffled until I made that turn."

Thomas nodded. "I accept your explanation."

"Go on," Ralf ordered.

"I hid myself in the brush. No one saunters past armed men in dispute. Madness I may suffer but rarely foolishness." He looked at Eleanor again. "You have promised me mercy in this?"

"As you speak true, so shall you be treated."

"Some wine, please, my lady?"

Brother Andrew stood closest to the pitcher. "Good priory ale, but it serves as well for dry throats." He poured a cup. Nodding at Cuthbert to help the prisoner rise, the monk gently assisted the man to drink.

The relic seller coughed, then continued. "Two were crusaders. The third was not. One was a common soldier who bore a crude red cross on his quilted buckram. The other, the one between the quarrelling men, was as well, although his dress suggested a higher rank. He rested his hand on the other soldier's chest as if to push him back."

"Two crusaders?" Ralf frowned as he considered this. "And the third?"

"The third man, standing with his back to me, looked like a leper with his long robe and the cloth wrapped around his head. Suddenly, he screamed, and the crusader in the middle spun around. The common soldier began to run. That third man darted around the crusader and gave chase."

"He killed him?" Thomas interrupted.

"He threw a rock, hitting the soldier on the back of the head. The man fell. As he did, the crusader grabbed the third and they struggled. The soldier was only dazed. He rose and began to laugh as he watched the other two. With the roar like that of a wild beast, the dark-robed man threw the crusader aside as if he were a stick and leapt at the soldier, lifting him into the air. I was terrified! No mortal could have that strength!"

"Unless the Evil One gives them the power." It was the first time Sister Ruth had spoken.

"Then the demonic one lowered the soldier, pulled out a knife, and thrust it into the man's belly, ripping it upward toward the heart. The man must have been alive when his guts fell out. I heard him scream. Once. I could not bear to look any longer." The prisoner retched.

No one said a word.

The man began to weep and slipped to his knees. "I was scared! I did not know what to do. What could I do against three men?"

"You are not to blame, for cert," Eleanor whispered.

The relic seller lowered his head. "Good people, I have been in battle and seen monstrous things, but they are done only when the soul sleeps and the blood burns hot. This killing was done as if the killer savored the act."

Ralf broke the silence. "The rest of the tale. There is more."

"I have told the truth!" the man howled. "God is my witness! I have told…"

Ralf grabbed the relic seller by his robe and yanked him upward. "Nay, not everything. By all that is holy I will hang you, then watch you slowly choke as you spin in the air…"

The man began to sob.

Ralf dropped him.

"There is little more. The demon started to weep as the corpse twitched. The other crusader rose, then walked to the body and pulled the dagger out." The prisoner gulped air. "He cleaned it in a puddle of water."

"The demon, as you call him, was…?" Thomas asked.

"He was squirming in the mud like a witless creature. The crusader pulled him up into his arms and held him 'til he calmed. Then he turned him around so he'd face away and drew a short dagger from under his robe." The man's eyes grew large. "I thought he was going to kill the demon!"

"But he did not." Eleanor spoke as if lost in thought.

"Instead, he stabbed the dead man in the chest, took off his own robe, and wrapped the corpse in it as if the man were but asleep and needed the warmth."

"You saw their faces?" Thomas asked.

The man nodded vigorously. "The man who gave up his cloak later called himself Walter. In the fray, the cloth hiding the demon's features fell away, and I recognized the man I later knew as Sir Maurice."

"And then?" Ralf asked.

"That is the story, Crowner. When I saw these men in the priory hospital, I kept silent out of fear."

Ralf shook his fist at the man. "Nay. Cuthbert, take the man away. He longs for the rope."

"No! I am innocent. Please!" The man struggled back to his knees. "I have done no murder and have been promised mercy over the matter of the sheep!"

"I think you killed the soldier for his fat purse," Ralf said.

"You have no proof!"

Ralf reached for the cut purse that rested on the table. "I found this hidden in your bedding."

The captive squealed like a pig. "I confess! I stole from a corpse who would have no further use for a mortal man's coin where he was going, but I did not kill him for it." He turned, stretching toward Eleanor. "I waited until the two men had left the glade. Then I took the purse from the dead soldier. It belonged to no one. I am a poor man, my lady. He had a fat purse filled with blinding bright coins. I was starving…"

"Silence, knave. You have eaten too many fat sheep," Ralf said. "Why should any of us believe you? You commit crimes against the innocent by selling false relics to earn your bread. You are a proven liar." He shrugged. "You believed Sir Maurice saw you kill the soldier and thus you killed him. In order to divert attention elsewhere, and thus give yourself time to escape, you attacked the infirmarian." He looked around at everyone assembled. "I think we have our killer."

Chapter Forty-two

"I did not murder any man, my lady!" The man tried to drag himself on his knees to Eleanor, but Cuthbert pulled him back. "Knave I may well be," he cried, "but never would I do such a thing as was done to that crusader!" He raised his wide eyes to the heavens and wailed. "By all that is holy, my lady, I have been a soldier myself!"

Ralf put his hand on his sword.

"Do not draw a weapon in this place, Crowner." The prioress looked down at the groveling man. In his terror, he had now pissed on himself and stank of both urine and sweat. "You cannot deny that you disappeared around the time Sister Christina was beaten and Sir Maurice was killed. Although Cuthbert saw you killing a sheep, you still could have committed the other two crimes. Have you a witness who can confirm that you were elsewhere at the time of either event?"

Brother Matthew cleared his throat. "My lady."

Eleanor looked at the monk with pleasant surprise. "You have something to say in this man's behalf?"

"He is innocent. I cannot speak to the murder of the soldier, but, on my hope of Heaven, he is blameless, both of the attack on our beloved infirmarian and the murder of Sir Maurice." Matthew spoke in a hoarse whisper.

"Please explain, Brother."

"I would prefer to do so in private." The monk briefly glanced at Brother Andrew, Brother Thomas, and Sister Anne, then settled his gaze on Sister Ruth. "If I speak in front of these, word will spread throughout the priory."

"Not from my lips, Brother," Andrew said.

"Nor mine," Thomas seconded.

Anne nodded concurrence.

Brother Matthew continued to gaze at Sister Ruth, his look quite sad.

She turned an angry red. "You, of all people, should know that I do not run about spreading gossip."

The monk bent his head.

"It is important that we have witnesses, Brother, but whatever you have to say shall remain within these walls, unless the protection of the innocent and justice require otherwise. So I do order." Eleanor looked at each person in the room. All nodded. "Should I find that this command has been disobeyed, my punishment will be swift and severe." Eleanor gestured for the monk to continue.

Brother Matthew sputtered as if longing to protest, then gave up and continued. "This man and I met the night Sister Christina was attacked." He stared at the prioress as if no one else was in the room. "When you hesitated about buying this purported relic for a pilgrimage shrine, I knew I must do something to make you see the merit in my decision..." He coughed. "...rather, my way of thinking."

Eleanor smiled. "And thus gain greater support in the coming election."

"Persuading you to make Tyndal a station on the pilgrimage route would have enhanced my standing amongst the monks." His eyes flashed with some indignation. "Yet I was, and am, convinced of the rightness of such a decision, my lady. My error was in the choice of the relic, not the premise."

"As I said at our last meeting, Brother, your idea had merit. Sadly, the bone you offered was that of a sheep, not a saint. Fraud is not unusual in the sale of relics; therefore, I felt caution was advisable."

Brother Matthew looked down at his long feet.

"Do continue with your tale," Eleanor said.

"I had arranged with this man to get the relic…" He spat out the word.

Eleanor nodded.

"…believing that you would change your mind in the presence of the sainted…"

"Indeed," Eleanor said.

"So I slipped out of the priory grounds and met him…" He shot a glance at the grim-faced Sister Ruth. "…at the local inn where we…"

"Do not fear for the reputation of the priory, my lady," the prisoner interrupted, his voice no longer trembling. "Brother Matthew was quite disguised. He borrowed a cloak left by one of the men building the stable and had put up the hood so his tonsure would not show…"

"Silence, fool!" the monk shouted. "I'm trying to save your filthy neck!"

"Do continue with your forthright tale, Brother," Eleanor suggested mildly. "God does so love the truth."

The monk flushed vividly. "We shared a jug of priory ale at the inn, which, I might add, was quite good. We are wise to sell it to…"

"Of that, we are well aware."

Brother Matthew walked over to the table and put his hand on the bones. "It was there that he gave me these for which he also had a most ancient box."

"When did you bring them back to the priory?" Thomas asked.

"After we shared much more ale," the relic seller added, "the pleasure of which was increased by the sight of the sweet serving wench."

"I protest, my lady! I am willing to provide this cur with an alibi, yet he insists on trying to defame me. Aye, I did drink more than one mug of ale. Surely you would agree that confirmation of quality is a prudent measure? I thought there might be improvements we could make in the flavor. Our only discussion of the serving wench, however, involved this impious crowner's lewd attentions to her that evening. Under no circumstances would I ever participate in…" he spat, "…lustful talk!"

"Would you not?" Sister Ruth asked under her breath.

Eleanor glanced with sympathy at her sub-prioress.

"When I left, our crowner had just disappeared up the stairs with the wench," Matthew continued. "He was quite drunk. Respectable men were seeking more honorable beds."

"Not as drunk as you hoped, Brother, although I did not recognize either of you when you arrived. Then I noticed how careful you both were not to let your hoods slip after you saw me. Were you just dishonest men, I wondered, or priory monks come to test your virtue in a place rumored to provide worldly pleasures? As I recall, Brother, you were especially entranced by the bouncing breasts of the lass on my lap."

"Impious dog!"

"Fie! I meant only to compliment you on your self-control. I admired your ability to hold your cowl with one hand so I could not see your face while, under the table, your other hand was so busy…"

"How dare you accuse me…"

"Which would you prefer? I could tell of your not-so-private pleasuring or I could charge you with corroboration in the murders. You may decide."

Brother Matthew stepped forward, but Brother Thomas grabbed his arm and pulled him back.

Ralf shook his head. "Fear not, monk. You may be guilty of lust like every other mortal man, but I know that you and your companion were still there, as you said, when I went upstairs with Signy. It was past the Night Office, for I heard the bell ring. By then, I understand that Walter had reported the attack on Sister Christina to Brother Thomas."

"Why did you not say any of this before, Ralf?" Anne asked, her question voiced with tenderness.

The crowner looked at her for a long time, his expression as grief-stricken as if he were biding her a final farewell. "I did drink deeply that night, and thus details of the earlier evening faded from memory until I searched the relic seller's hospital cot. As my mind cleared, I thought back on the two men at the inn. One was so tall I thought he was the monk I had seen standing near where our relic seller rested. At the time I had thought he resembled Brother Thomas whom I believed still to be in…"

"…protective custody, lest I be harmed by a most violent man for what I might have seen," Thomas finished.

"There was only one other monk at Tyndal with similar height, and thus I realized he was the same man at the inn who was engaged in eager…"

"May Satan fry your…" Matthew was writhing.

"Silence, Brother," Sister Ruth hissed.

"This tale clears you of the attack on Sister Christina," Eleanor said to the relic seller. "There is still the murder of Sir Maurice to resolve."

Matthew fell to his knees and raised his hands in supplication. "Please, my lady! I pray you to let me tell this in private!"

"Surely there is little else to relate that would cause you much more shame," Eleanor replied, "and this matter is so serious that we must have witnesses to all you have to say. The need for the crowner's presence is, of course, indisputable."

The monk gestured at Sister Ruth. "Must all stay?" he begged piteously.

The sub-prioress' expression now changed from disgust and sorrow to one of deep humiliation. She rose and bowed to Eleanor. "Others should remain as witnesses, but is it truly necessary that I do so? For the sake of modesty, will you excuse me, my lady?"

"Of course, Sister," Eleanor said gently.

The nun glared at the monk. "I thought you a better man than this, Brother. You have much for which to beg forgiveness."

He reached out a hand to her, then drew it back.

"I will pray for you," Sister Ruth said, then stormed out of the chambers.

After the door slammed, Ralf turned to the monk. "I will make your confession easier by telling it myself," he said.

"According to Brother Thomas, you met with our relic seller at the inn just after the pilgrim had left with his vial of blood. Perhaps you came with some payment for the bones, but, from what our good brother has described, I must ask you this: did you and the relic seller pray before or after sharing the bed of a village whore that night?"

Chapter Forty-three

Cuthbert had taken the relic seller into custody. Brother Matthew begged leave to find his confessor. Sister Anne and Brother Andrew returned to the sick and the watching of gates. Still seated in the chambers were Thomas, Ralf, and Eleanor. Before departing with her prioress' blessing, Gytha set out more ale and a fine creamy cheese on the table for the renewal of everyone's strength.

Strength was needed.

Thomas cut into the cheese and offered his prioress the slice. "In truth, I did hope at one time that he was the murderer," he said with evident discomfort.

"There was cause enough to wonder," Eleanor replied. "We had to establish his exact involvement, and we needed to know what he had seen."

Shaking his head, Thomas ran one finger around the rim of his pottery cup.

Ralf thumped the monk's shoulder. "I do not blame you for wishing so. At first, I doubted he could have done the killing. After he fooled me into believing you were involved, I grew angry, thus was blinded and thought to change my mind. His theft of the soldier's purse made more sense, although I confess I had little enough evidence of the thievery. The purse was in his bedding, but anyone might have placed it there. In fact, it might have belonged to any man, except for the bloodstains. Fortunately, he was so frightened that he spilled his tale."

"We were wise to keep secret the story of the attack on Sister Christina. Had our relic seller heard it, he might have fled the area entirely for fear that he would be the suspect," Eleanor said, then fell silent, noting that Ralf's usually fine appetite had abandoned him.

"You promised him mercy in exchange for the truth, my lady," the crowner said at last. "For a knave, he showed some honor and did serve justice today, thus I will gladly agree to whatever punishment you think is meet. The farmer, however, must be paid for his dead sheep."

With a brief smile, Eleanor nodded, but her look grew distracted.

Thomas watched his prioress with curiosity before speaking. "So Ralf has found his seller of false relics, and the death of the crusader has been solved. Sir Maurice killed him."

"Your brother will be satisfied." Eleanor studied the crowner.

Ralf started as if his thoughts had drifted elsewhere. "Aye."

Thomas frowned. "The murder of the knight and the attack on Sister Christina remain mysteries. Now, it seems, those crimes were separate."

For one long moment, the crowner seemed not to hear, then he scowled and picked up his mazer of ale.

"Have those who did the deeds escaped, then? Will they never be brought to justice?" Thomas asked, his voice sharp with anger.

Eleanor cradled her cup and gazed at Thomas. "Perhaps he will, Brother."

Ralf lowered his ale before the mazer even reached his mouth. "What do you mean, my lady?"

"We must question Walter."

"That we must surely do to confirm the details of the soldier's murder," the crowner said, his expression puzzled.

"He is not the servant he claimed to be," Eleanor said. "Sir Maurice was his nephew. He has much to explain, I fear."

Ralf slammed his fist on the table. "You are not suggesting that he murdered his own kin?"

"He lamented like a grieving father over the corpse. No man could weep so over someone he had just slain," Thomas said.

"I think we must hear the tale from him," Eleanor replied.

"If he did murder the man, he will surely be on a boat to Normandy by now."

"Ah, Crowner, is there no difference between *kill* and *murder* in the world of secular justice?" Eleanor's lips turned up with grim humor. "He has not fled."

Ralf shook his head. "Forgive me, my lady, but this is not a matter for philosophical dispute. A murderer does not seek the rope. He flees."

"Engaging in entertaining debate was not my intent. We should put the question directly to the test." Eleanor rose. "If you are correct, Ralf, then Walter has left Tyndal. If I am right, he waits for us to come for him."

The crowner stood up and bowed. "My lady, lead the way."

Chapter Forty-four

They found Walter kneeling at the altar in Tyndal's main chapel, his head bowed in prayer. When he heard their echoing footsteps behind him, he rose, turned, and drew his sword, placing it point down in front of him. Otherwise, he was unarmed.

"Peace, good sir," Eleanor said as the three halted just a few feet away.

"There is never peace on earth, my lady." He brought his other hand to rest on the hilt. "Only fools think there is."

Ralf reached for his own weapon.

Eleanor gently touched her palm to the crowner's hand. Ralf pushed his sword back into its scabbard and stepped back.

"There is peace in God's love," she said. "And in His mercy."

Walter's laugh rang out like a raven's cry.

"Do you doubt this, sir?"

"Doubt? Nay, I do not doubt that He forgives when it pleases Him, my lady, but God can be both wrathful and cruel. Women may believe He is merciful, even kind, but I have seen only God's vengeful face."

"In battle most certainly, but you stand on priory grounds, a place of compassion and absolution."

Walter shook his head sadly. "Yet you come to take me to my hanging. Is that not vengeance?"

"Justice," Ralf replied.

"Words that may have many meanings," Eleanor countered, looking only at the man with drawn sword. "You brought violence to my priory, sir. I would know why."

"That was not our intent, my lady. We came for healing."

"Maurice murdered a soldier outside these walls. Soon after, you killed your nephew with a blow to his heart. Where is the healing in this bloodshed?"

Walter's lips twisted into a bitter smile. "Ask your merciful God why He put that soldier and Maurice on the same path. As for my nephew's heart, He struck him there long before I did. If you knew what he had suffered, you might understand why I thought my deed was kind and one for which I willingly face the rope." He nodded at Thomas. "Did I not ask your priest to shrive him after Maurice thought he saw the angel of death? I may be angry with God for the cruelty he has shown my nephew, but He has promised forgiveness to those who confess. Surely, He will forgive whatever sins were forgotten because my nephew's wits were gone." The last was said with a sob.

Thomas turned pale. "I never would have agreed had I known confession would allow this uncle to become an angel of death himself and thus..."

"Brother, I saw the future no more than you did and believed the knight's soul would regain peace when shriven. The only one here who bears any guilt in failing to prevent this death is I. The signs were plain, but I allowed other things to distract me from seeing them with clarity." Eleanor turned to Walter. "As for your nephew, sir, you did send him to God with a cleansed soul."

Walter's grief had etched deep lines into his face. "What company he has in Heaven, my lady! He must have longed to meet his wife there. Instead, she burns in Hell, while he sits, until the Day of Judgement, with the man who butchered her. Is that God's mercy as well?"

Eleanor gestured in supplication. "Sir, how can I answer when I know nothing of you or your nephew?"

"I will bring some brevity to the tale. Will you hear it?"

"We must," Eleanor replied.

"My beloved nephew might never have come to Acre and gone mad had it not been for me. For that, good people, I bear full blame. To understand why, you must first know that I am a younger son with neither wife nor child and went to Outremer as a mercenary for gold as well as the good of my soul. Then an arrow took out this eye, and the Hospitallers saved my life. By then I was most weary of both the world and war. I approached the Order to enter their number and end my days in service to the wounded. They were willing enough, but before I could take vows, Maurice arrived from England."

"A man you loved as much as King David did his son, Absalom." Eleanor's tone was gentle.

"From birth." Walter's good eye seemed to be staring at something in the vast distance, then he smiled. "Nor could he have loved me more had I been his sire."

"His father had died?" Thomas asked.

Walter shook his head. "My brother is not unkind but had little time to show love to any child, even his son. His lands lie near the northern border and, although he husbands them with competence, his yield is determined more by the raids he suffers than the weather. Thus he was rarely at home, and I became the father he could not be."

"Until you went on crusade," Ralf said.

"When Maurice took the cross, my brother blamed me. Had I not gone to Acre, he said, his son would have remained by his side in England. Thus it was my responsibility, he said, to watch over his only son and bring him safely home. I chose to delay my vows."

"Your nephew was severely wounded. His scar was terrible," Eleanor added.

"When his men came back without him, I grieved so deeply that I could not even send word of his death to his father. Then Maurice was found alive, and I rejoiced." Walter laughed but it had a bitter sound. "I praised God's grace too soon for he had brought with him the woman, a Saracen. Soon after, he married her."

"An infidel?" Ralf shook his head. "How could…"

"At first I assumed she was just his whore. It was not until we were in Sicily that he explained how she had saved his life. When she converted, he had married her."

"You said a man butchered her. Was her death the cause of his sickened soul? When did madness fall upon him?" Eleanor asked.

"In Acre." In the wavering light of the candles near the altar, even his good eye looked black in its deep socket. "He loved the Saracen beyond reason!" As if speaking to himself, he muttered, "Surely his wits were disturbed when he married the infidel."

"She converted," Eleanor reminded him.

"My lady, forgive me, but you are ignorant of the world. Her kin had slaughtered ours. Converted or not, she was the enemy's spawn," Walter snapped. "Maurice knew his soldiers would consider this marriage a traitorous and sinful act. As would his father. As would I, had he but told me! Thus he hid the deed and sent her to live with the other captured women."

Eleanor said nothing for a moment, then abruptly nodded once.

Tears flowed from the man's one eye. "Soon after, a soldier from my nephew's company went to the Saracen women's quarters and happened upon Maurice's wife. After satisfying his lust with her, the crusader mocked her with lewd jests. When he saw my nephew arrive, he assumed he had come to bed a whore as well and claimed this one had not fully satisfied him. Not knowing who she was, he skewered her like a pig with his sword as punishment. Maurice went mad."

"And thus his secret was revealed?" Thomas asked, a tear slipping down his cheek as well.

"Only his love for her. That he screamed to Heaven, frothing and howling like a mad dog. The men who dragged him back to me said they knew little more than that his whore had died. I stripped him of his weapons and armor, tied him like a wild animal until he calmed, then carried him onto a ship for England."

"Where he killed a crusader on the road outside this priory. Why?" Ralf asked.

"It was that man who had murdered his wife."

"'S blood," Ralf hissed. "I believed the man was one of God's brave soldiers!" His eyes narrowed with fury. "Why did you do nothing to prevent this? Surely, you must have known…"

"I did not know who the man was until Maurice charged after him that day, screaming that the crusader had killed his wife. I tried to separate them but failed."

"We heard the tale," Thomas added. "Was it true or was the soldier an innocent man that your nephew mistook for the other?"

"When we boarded the ship, the man was there amongst the crowds. He was the only other crusader returning home, but I thought nothing of it at the time nor did Maurice say anything to me. Not long out of port, however, my nephew tried to throw himself into the sea. As you must understand, I cared nothing then about some common soldier. I could only pray that we would reach Sicily where I could take my nephew off the ship before he succeeded in killing himself."

"And thus the man traveled on while you rested in Sicily. What strange fortune that you should happen to meet again on the road to Tyndal," Ralf said, disbelief evident in his voice.

Walter shook his head. "Patience, Crowner. Let me finish with the monk's question. During their struggles on the road, the soldier bragged about his deed in Acre. He mocked my nephew for caring what happened to a whore. Maurice did not kill an innocent man."

"God may have forgiven this crusader his past wickedness," Eleanor said, "but no one who so flaunts His benevolence will be free of His wrath. Have some comfort, therefore, in knowing that this crusader suffers a special torment in Hell."

Walter looked at her in thoughtful silence.

"For the soldier's cruelty, I most sincerely pray that you are correct about his punishment, my lady," Ralf said. "Nonetheless, I find the accident of this meeting to be most remarkable."

"With all my soul, Crowner, I wish it had not happened, nor can I explain why it did. The meeting between the two was like a miracle without grace. Perhaps the man went on by land while we took another ship from Sicily when my nephew had regained some clarity of mind. Perhaps the crusader's ship was delayed by storms while we had clear sailing. Maybe the meeting was God's joke." He turned to Eleanor. "Or an example of His mercy?"

Ralf stepped forward. "Then it may remain one of God's mysteries, but you have confessed to murder…"

"Wait, Ralf, there is more to this tale," Eleanor said. "You and your nephew are from the west of England, yet you came here, begging for your nephew's cure. Why?"

"Because I was given hope, my lady. Although most avoided Maurice after his wife's murder, there was one who was kind, a man you should know."

Eleanor's hand went to her heart.

"Your brother told me that you had written him of Tyndal's hospital. Someone here, he told me, might be able to treat a man's broken soul." Then he quickly added, "Lord Hugh was well when we left, my lady."

"Yet you said nothing about this to Prioress Eleanor when you arrived?" Ralf asked. "I find that odd."

"Tell me, Crowner, what you would do if your nephew had just killed the man who had slaughtered his wife? Might you decide it was a just, albeit regrettable, death or would you give your brother's only son up for hanging?" Walter watched Ralf's expression. "Aye, I thought so," he said, then continued. "I knew the death would be discovered quickly, thus chose to cloak the deed with a semblance of truth, stabbing the corpse with a knife I had brought from Acre and wrapping the body in my crusader cloak. A sheriff might conclude that an infidel had done the murder or that another crusader was involved. Meanwhile, Maurice and I became a knight and his servant, two simple pilgrims seeking healing shrines."

"In misdirecting the search you succeeded," Ralf said. "Still, you need not have stayed here. As soon as the rain lessened, you could have left Tyndal and made your escape."

"You forget how much I loved my nephew." He turned to Eleanor. "His face glowed, and he grew quiet when Sister Christina came to pray. I was regaining hope that I might yet return a whole son to his father."

"What changed?" Thomas asked.

"The night your nun was attacked, I had gone to the latrine, but Maurice was missing when I returned. I searched for him, heard a noise in the chapel, and found him there. Your nun was unconscious from his blows and, forgive me, my lady…"

"Speak plainly, sir."

"He was trying to mount her." He ran one hand over his mouth. "On my honor, I swear he did not know what he was doing, nor could he have broken her maidenhead. His manhood was limp." Walter's voice cracked. "When I pulled him away, he wept and asked why his wife had come back to him in a religious guise. Then he begged me to tell her he had meant only to close her eyes, not to hurt her. He fell into my arms like a child. I covered his nakedness, pulled him back to his bed, and gave him a potion to make him sleep. After that, I sought you out, Brother."

"And left Sister Christina lying exposed so any crude man might stare. What kindness was in that?" Thomas asked.

"I wanted there to be no question that the attack was a violent act and hoped you would believe there might be a connection to the foul murder of the soldier, or even some random deed. Surely, I thought, no one would conclude that my mad, helpless, and weak nephew could have done either. As you all did, you looked elsewhere."

"Why did you kill your nephew?" Ralf's hand moved toward his sword hilt.

"That night I knew with certainty that Maurice was beyond all prayer and would remain forever mad. Not only had my brother lost his heir, but I also feared my nephew might harm others as well as himself. The kindest act would be to send him as gently as I could to God's justice. For shriving him when you did, Brother, I am most grateful."

"And you?" Eleanor asked. "Why did you stay when you could have escaped?"

"I am guilty of my nephew's death. Perhaps he came to Acre of his own volition and not to follow me, but I am to blame for his madness. I failed him. Of course I would have argued against his ill-advised marriage had he come to me before he committed such an outrageous act. Nonetheless, if he had at least told me of it afterward, I could have found a better solution than to send the woman off to a place where she would surely meet with violence. I was like a father to him, yet I must have given him reason to think my heart was too hard..." Walter stopped, speech failing him. "I have no reason to live," he whispered. "I wished only to tell God that I knew my place in Hell was ready. Had you not come for me when you did, I would have sought you out and confessed the deed, my lady."

Eleanor looked over at Ralf, her head bent as if asking a question. He frowned, then shrugged with uncertainty.

"I have one favor to beg of you on my nephew's behalf before your crowner takes me to the hangman," Walter continued. "Will you grant it, my lady?"

"If it is a just one."

"Send word to my brother that his son died of honorable wounds. Indeed, that is no lie. Having seen his face and witnessed his terrible agony, you would surely agree he never recovered from his sufferings in Outremer. Then, Crowner, you may hang me for the murder of the man on the road. One murder is as good as another, and my nephew may be kept innocent of it."

"As you wish, I shall tell your brother that his son died from the wounds of war, as he most certainly did," she said. "Hanging you for killing the man on the road, however, is to punish you for an act you did not commit and one you did everything in your power to prevent. What reason can you give for this murder if you do not want your brother ever to learn what happened to his son in Outremer?"

"Yet his request is fair, my lady. The sheriff..." the crowner began.

"To accept it does not serve justice, Ralf. The murder of the soldier has been avenged. The man who killed him is dead. If your brother hears that the soldier's killer was found but that he died soon after as the result of unspecified wounds, do you think the sheriff will care what happened to the body of the soldier's killer, or even ask his name?"

"Any satisfactory tale will content him as long as his position in the shire remains secure. Nonetheless, do we not still face a murderer, my lady?"

"Murderer? Did you never turn your back on the battle-field when one comrade eased another out of misery when he screamed with unendurable wounds?"

Ralf nodded.

Eleanor turned to Walter. "You, sir, are a soldier. You understand what bravery is, even when mixed with fear or pain. Why do you then ask for cowardly death when the more courageous deed would be to live?"

"After killing my nephew, how can living be..." Walter suddenly fell silent.

"I think you see my meaning," she replied. "You most certainly owe a very painful penance for your deeds. Return to Outremer as a Hospitaller monk, dedicate the rest of your life to the wounded, and pray daily for the soul of your nephew's abused wife. Do you not owe this little to the woman who saved Maurice's life, a soul who showed more understanding of God's commandments than most mortals? Hell will wait for you, but, by living with the horror of your crimes while doing good for whatever time on earth God grants you, you may find He will grant some forgiveness."

"Why should God listen to my prayers for her any more than He did for those on my nephew's behalf?"

Eleanor closed her eyes, then took a deep breath. "You asked about His mercy. Do you not wonder why your nephew and the soldier left Acre at the same time? Do you not ask why your nephew found the man alone on a normally well-traveled road? Might you not ask whether God answered your prayers in His own way by letting your nephew avenge his wife's slaughter? You question God's mercy, only because you fail to see it."

Walter turned pale, then silently raised his sword.

Ralf reached out to pull Eleanor to safety.

The man turned the weapon slowly around until the hilt pointed toward the trio. "I surrender my sword and myself to you, my lady, and request sanctuary at Tyndal's altar. May I ask, however, that your monk accept this? My sword should be given to a man of God if I am to leave the world to serve Him."

Chapter Forty-five

Winter had now come to Tyndal. Despite the sharp air that rushed to attack when Eleanor opened the wooden shutters in her private chambers, she stood her ground and looked out on the white morning. The night had left a light dusting of snow over the earth, and, for just this moment, the world looked as unblemished as Eden.

Although she shivered, she silently watched the black shapes of two birds darting against the gray sky. Then conceding victory to the pervasive chill, she closed the shutters and turned back to the blazing fire that brought cheer to her room.

Arthur, lord of kitchens, had curled himself into a tight circle near enough to the fire, one orange paw covering his eyes. Eleanor reached down and picked him up, settled herself into a chair, and lowered him gently onto her lap. He circled once, gave a great yawn, and went back to sleep.

"Do cats ever suffer heartache?" She shook her head. "Nay, I suspect God was more merciful to your kind than He was to mine." As the fire crackled, she gently ran her fingers through his thick fur and laughed. "Indeed, good sir, I doubt you have ever been rejected in your courting. Tyndal is most blessed with your progeny."

Leaning back into her chair, she pressed one hand against her eyes. The headaches she had suffered over the last two days were finally receding. Now she knew she should have listened to Sister Anne's advice months ago and begun the regimen of feverfew for relief. This time the herb had reduced her suffering by at least a day. Would that the pain in her heart could be so easily lessened.

In the days after the murders were solved she had slept but little, spending the dark hours on her knees, begging God for respite and wisdom. Finally, she had struck her fists against the prie-dieu and shouted at Him, demanding that He give her understanding if He would not grant her peace. Must she wait for both, she asked, until her allotted years on earth were done?

It was the next night that she had finally fallen, exhausted, into such deep sleep that she had failed to awaken for the Night Offices. When she opened her eyes and looked with confusion at the weak light of morning, she wondered why no one had come for her. Sister Anne later explained that she had but could not rouse her. Since the sub-infirmarian had detected no malignant reason for this, she had left the prioress to her dreams, deciding that it was God's will.

So it must have been, for although Eleanor could no longer remember the details of her dreams, she had felt a strange relief upon rising, as if one prayer had at last been answered. As she knelt at her prie-dieu that morning, to give thanks for another day of service, she knew with certainty that sending Thomas from Tyndal would be wrong. She must not sacrifice his peace for her sin, and she bowed her head in gratitude to God for keeping her from committing that selfish act. Of course, she had whispered, it should be she who suffered for her lust, not an innocent man, and she prayed that God, in His infinite mercy, would forgive her for even considering it. The ache in her woman's heart might remain undiminished, but the soul of a prioress was at peace with God's will.

Brother Matthew, however, had left. When the monastics learned that the relic he tried to buy was fake and tales spread from the inn about his lapse into carnal pleasures, he begged to go to another house. Although she disliked the man, Eleanor acknowledged that few would have so willingly saved an innocent man from unjust punishment at the cost of advancement and reputation. For that, Eleanor granted his plea and sent him to the abbess in Anjou. In her letter requesting his admission there, she praised his virtues but failed to mention his failures. Just the other day, she had heard a rumor that he had abandoned the Fontevrauldine Order for the Cistercian, asking specifically to be sent to a monastery without women.

Brother Andrew had been elected prior at Tyndal, a decision that greatly pleased her. Although she expected they would have their differences, she knew him to be a sensible man and one with whom she could work. After all, there was always ground for compromise amongst the reasonable when disagreements arose.

Would that all the world were as prudent as Brother Andrew, she sighed. No matter how hard mortals might try to emulate God's wisdom, man's imperfections could so easily taint judgement, turning innocence into guilt and guilty men into innocent ones. "We can never equal God's most perfect justice," she said aloud to the bright flames. "Yet we must always strive to do so."

Even now she wondered if she had erred last autumn when she argued for Walter's life and allowed this confessed murderer to live, making service and prayer his penance. How many times had she asked herself whether she had exceeded the bounds of mortal judgement and thus honored evil more than just mercy by granting him asylum? Had she sinned as well in suggesting that the killing of the soldier near her priory gates might even be God's will?

Yet the crowner had concurred, albeit silently as he turned and left the man in the sanctuary. Although Walter was allowed forty days in the church at Tyndal, the crowner had sent a message the next day that trusted men could take him on a boat to the south where he could board a ship bound for Outremer. Knowing Ralf to be an honorable man, she had no reason to doubt him when he sent word that Walter was safely on his way. Daily thereafter, Eleanor had prayed that the man's ship would survive the seasonal storms.

Had she sinned? In truth, she did not know. She believed Walter to be a good man, one who would keep his word to return to Outremer as he had promised. The hospitaller Order of Saint John would find him a most dedicated and humble monk, she thought, and surely God would smile on his constant prayers for the soul of his nephew's wife. In truth, she would never forget the woman in her own.

As Walter had said, Eleanor did believe in a merciful God, although she had no doubt that His anger could be terrible. In her heart, she believed that He must have snatched the poor woman's soul from the fires of Hell, if in truth it was ever there, and later returned her to the company of her husband, a man guilty only of love and human frailty before he fell into madness.

"Surely God would be merciful to a woman who showed mercy to one of His own," she said aloud to the sleeping cat on her lap. "Surely."

As for Sir Maurice, his father had eventually come to take his son's bones, quickly stripped of flesh for preservation, back home for burial. There had been relief as well as tears in the man's eyes. Perhaps he himself had feared that his son would return, mutilated in body or in soul. A dead son, martyred in the crusading cause, could be mourned with honor and without guilt. When told of his brother's return to Outremer as a monk, he had simply nodded.

And the relic seller? She smiled as she thought of him. There was a knave, but not an evil man or unworthy of mercy. In exchange for his honest telling of what he had seen that rainy day on the road to Tyndal, she and Brother Andrew had told him that another visit to the shrine of Saint William in Norwich might be arranged. If the relic seller would agree to end his days with repentant deeds, they would assure the registrar of miracles that the fellow would most certainly be cured this time of his inclination toward strange dancing, not to mention sheep theft and the making of false relics.

Not being a fool, the former relic seller had agreed and thus became a lay brother in service to the saint who had cured him, a wise choice since a monastery meant decent food, a dry bed, and honorable labor. Eleanor thought that the young William of Norwich might understand since fakery and contrition must surely have existed in his day as well.

In all of this, Ralf had been most cooperative, yet subdued. Although she knew he loved justice more than he did either the law or those who most often administered it, she realized he had been very angry over the murder of the soldier and hated those who sold fake relics. Nonetheless, he had done all as she had wished it, then quickly left Tyndal. He had not come back since, even to congratulate Brother Andrew or to jest with Brother Thomas.

Eleanor understood at least one reason why the crowner had not returned to the priory. Knowing the grief of an impossible love, she wished she could comfort him in his pain, even if she could not comfort herself.

As for the sheriff, not one word had ever been heard from him on the matter of the crusader's murder.

Arthur muttered deep in feline dreams. Eleanor caressed him, soothing her soft companion into gentler imaginings. As the exhaustion she often felt after her headaches began to lull her into a doze as well, she last remembered saying to the cat, "Ah, sweet sir, it is times like these that I do most miss my aunt at Amesbury."

Author's Notes

Although we live history in the brightness of the moment, we learn it by looking backward at its shadow.

Without hindsight, of course, we could never see the clear route history was taking at any given period. Yet by removing the unessential details, minimizing the seemingly promising paths that actually went nowhere, and deeming irrelevant all those daily things that got in the way of our ancestors seeing exactly where history might be taking them, we lose a tactile sense of the time. Perhaps that is one reason we fail to learn from their mistakes—or at least realize how difficult it was to make those right choices when the passions of the moment pointed in other directions.

Failure to clearly see where historical events are leading can be quite devastating, although ignorance can be benign as well in the short term. For England in 1271, the immediate future turned out to be relatively calm. Nevertheless, the coming years would not only bring a king who imposed much needed order on a lax legal system, but also one who brought tragedy to the Jews and the Welsh, and wars on all borders.

Those living in 1271 must have felt some unease about the future. We may know that Edward returned to England safely and reigned with a firmness much lacking under his father, and that there would be no more civil war. They did not. Simon de Montfort had not been forgotten either, and the range of his followers from peasant to prince suggests that issues raised by him could not be set aside without serious social consequences.

One indication of this was the attempt to canonize de Montfort, although he had been twice excommunicated before his death. The number of miracles claimed by people from all classes at the burial site of his mutilated remains was significant. As Henry II discovered after the murder of Thomas Becket, not even kings may ignore the meaning behind such movements with impunity. Edward I wisely learned from his ancestor's mistakes.

A change in kingship was clearly imminent. In late 1271, some believed that the current king was senile, and all should have suspected that his remaining time on earth would be short. At the time this book takes place, King Henry III had approximately one more year to live.

Like Queen Victoria, King Henry III enjoyed a long reign. He came to power in 1216 as a nine-year-old boy after the death of his father, King John. Fortunately, he had both capable and honorable men to rule for him. Thus he remained alive and king, despite a long minority and the de Montfort rebellion, until he died in 1272. Whatever opinion his subjects had of Henry, most had known no other monarch.

History has been unkind to Henry III. Even Dante placed him in Purgatory for having been too preoccupied with religiosity to pay adequate attention to governing his subjects. He has been condemned as a pale man, incompetent, and lacking in a certain vigor. Compared to his colorful grandfather (Henry II), his notorious father (John), and his more bellicose son (Edward I), he does rather fade from view. Perhaps that is unfortunate because his reign was not entirely lacking in merit; however, the complex political problems that have led historians to conclude he was less than successful as a monarch would, and have, required some lengthy books. For an understanding of those issues, I recommend those excellent studies.

On the other hand, we should not assume that Henry did not have his supporters at the time as well as his detractors. Few have ever accused him of being a cruel or vicious monarch. Even in his later years, unlike other rulers who suffered mental deterioration, Henry slipped only into gentleness. Thus it might not hurt to point out some personal things about the man in order to add some flesh and color to the figure on the coffin lid—while acknowledging that these do not, in any way, give the whole picture.

Henry was a most uxorious man. Unlike his father, a lusty fellow by any definition, Henry produced no known illegitimate issue, although having them was not always considered a bad thing for kings. Part of the reason for this marital fidelity was Henry's strong religious bent. Another equally important reason was his wife. Eleanor of Provence, one of four remarkably intelligent and beautiful sisters of an equally well-endowed mother, married him when she was twelve and he was twenty-eight. Despite the standard ups and downs of the union, they both seemed to have considered it a very happy marriage.

At sixteen, she bore their first child. They had at least five known children and probably other unrecorded stillbirths and miscarriages. Despite the assumption that upper class parents didn't have much to do with their offspring, there is strong evidence that Henry and Eleanor adored theirs. When their son, Edward, fell ill at a Cistercian abbey, Eleanor refused to leave him, despite the Order's prohibition against women staying within their precincts. Henry made sure she was allowed to stay. When their deaf and mute little Katherine died at age four, both parents fell seriously ill from the strain of deep grieving.

Henry, despite his hot temper (a very Angevin trait), was also a rather merciful man. Unlike at least one of his ancestors, he seemed to have reconsidered his words and acts when he stopped chewing the rushes and cooled down. He was outraged, for example, when his sister, Eleanor, secretly married Simon de Montfort, but Henry soon welcomed them back to court when other kings might have imprisoned or even executed the offending pair. Some might say that Henry's more compassionate act was not the wisest decision since his brother-in-law later paid him back with rebellion, but I'll leave that interesting discussion to others for resolution.

The king also had a reputation for some leniency toward criminals. He was known to commute the sentences of those who illegally hunted the king's deer. He did not seem awfully fond of putting people to death for relatively minor offences, and he gave substantial alms to prisoners as well as the poor in general. Matthew Paris wrote scathingly about his legal "laxity", but not all would have agreed that it was worthy of so much contempt. As is true today, people have always had various opinions on what constitutes justice.

Henry was also known for his love of the arts, although his methods for getting the money to pay for his projects were often less than admirable. His dedication to the rebuilding of Westminster Abbey ranks as his most splendid achievement. An example of one of his more minor ones includes the remnant of a tiled pavement from Eleanor's apartments, now in the British Museum.

Whatever his flaws as a king, he seems to have been a kind man who tried to practice some of the basic tenets of his faith. When he died, there was a brief flurry of miracle allegations at his tomb. His widow encouraged the stories. His son, Edward I, quickly put a stop to any such claims.

The Middle Ages had a plethora of alleged miracles, yet the medievals had a healthy skepticism about cures and relics. This did not mean they lacked faith, but they were as cognizant as we that clever scam artists are often just waiting to take in the innocent and gullible. They also shared our outrage when this happened.

Pilgrimage sites were staffed with people required to log in all alleged cures and determine their validity at the time claimed. Those who traveled from place to place to gain attention by dramatic cures were a known problem, and the more notorious were chased away whenever recognized.

The medievals were also aware that the newness of something had a special power to it, although they did not use our psychological language to explain why. Each site had records showing that the efficacy of cures diminished with some predictable regularity after the relic first arrived. To correct this trend, the religious knew that doing something dramatic helped to recover that power. A ceremonial moving of the relic was one such method. Over time, however, there was no question that cures declined, and recorded ones involved increasingly local populations. Thus income from the site dropped as well.

The other problem with having a relic was the need to guard it. Relic thieves were quite inventive in their ways of stealing bits of the enshrined saint. Yes, they did take bites of the holy object, filched molars, and even sucked dust into their mouths, all of which could later be sold as legitimate parts thereof. When whole saints were stolen, the thieves, usually from a place that wanted to become a shrine, often argued that the saint had wanted to move and thus their act was justified. (Ellis Peters dealt with a similar issue in *A Morbid Taste for Bones*.)

In addition to acceptably documented relics, there was an impressive number of body parts (including many of the same type from the same body), uncountable slivers of the True Cross, and gallons of blood from just about anyone of sacred note. The honest faithful passionately hated the fraudulence, but it was prevalent and many did find humor in this fakery. For the latter, I refer readers to Chaucer's *Canterbury Tales*.

Illness in the Middle Ages was frightening. Some of the cures were even more so, and presumed causes of sickness may seem quite ignorant today. Swallowing crushed gemstones or chowing down on sheep lice no longer has wide appeal. The belief that a leper caught the disease because he had committed some especially horrible sin, like having sex with his wife during her menstruation, would seem bizarre to most today. The assumption that a child born with red hair was conceived during a woman's monthly bleeding does, however, show an interesting logic.

On the other hand, what we accept as good medical practice in 2006 may turn out to be quite primitive by standards seven hundred years from now. Nor may we ignore that the medical breakthroughs we enjoy today evolved from discoveries made by those in the distant past. Despite resistance to new methods and ideas from the medical professions, religious leaders, and the general public, there have always been observant, thoughtful, and curious people who persisted until their insights became conventional wisdom.

Not all medieval theories about good health or the cause of illness were completely outlandish. Physicians regularly prescribed exercise and moderation in both eating and drinking to stay healthy, understanding that good health once lost was very difficult to recover. As a cause of illness, the effect of "bad air" was a major concern. Although most blithely tossed their nightly slops into the public street, they also wanted good drainage or at least an adequate number of pigs to clean it all up. The medievals might not have known about germs, but they knew there was some relationship between the smell of sewage and getting sick.

Hospitals were also rather advanced even though they were primarily intended for the poor. Although whole families (plus valuable animals) of the least affluent often lived in one room and shared sleeping accommodations, the sick in the larger hospitals were not only given a single bed but also regularly washed sheets. (The Savoy Hospital, during the reign of Henry VII, not only offered sheets and blankets but also a tapestry coverlet monogrammed with the Tudor rose.) A light but nourishing diet was provided for free, as well as night-lights and staff to help patients should they need to visit the latrines.

Much like today, medical care funding depended upon the priorities of the powerful. While Henry VII founded and supported some of the first hospitals for the temporarily ill poor, his son, Henry VIII, confiscated any hospital land if he fancied the location for personal use. Saint James' Palace, for example, sits on land once dedicated to the cure of the sick.

Since dissection was discouraged by the Church (although autopsies were allowed in cases of violent death), Christian physicians and surgeons learned most about anatomy, technique, and viable treatments during wars. At the time covered by the first mysteries in this series, a crusade was being fought in the Holy Land; thus these doctors not only got their practical experience but were also exposed to the superior medical knowledge of the Muslim world.

Despite gaining much scientific, culinary, and philosophical enlightenment from people they called "infidels", the Western world considered these wars less than successful because Jerusalem remained in Muslim hands. When Prince Edward arrived in Tunis full of fervor for the fray, he was horrified to discover that a treaty between the two archenemies had actually been signed. Despite his determination to fight on and ignore an act he considered almost blasphemous, he himself eventually offered a truce and left the Holy Land, unsuccessful, much impoverished, and barely alive. His Western contemporaries considered him a hero.

Although we obviously lack the vivid photos of a Matthew Brady for the crusades, the handwritten accounts are quite graphic. The memoirs of Anna Comnena (First Crusade), Villehardouin (Fourth Crusade), and Joinville (the life of Saint Louis up to his death in 1270) are some of the most famous from the Western perspective. Books from the Muslim point of view are harder to find for the general Western reader, although a few compilations and Ibn Al-Qalanisi's account of the First Crusade are reasonably available. Of course, all these books contain descriptions, often idealized, of heroics. Nonetheless, the medievals did not sugarcoat the grimness or the atrocities, acts that we ourselves have utterly failed to eliminate despite four Geneva Conventions from 1864 through the current 1949 codification.

As for the mental and physical effects of any war on men, women and children, combatants or noncombatants, it is probably best to let those who went through the experience speak for themselves. There are a large number of firsthand accounts available, beginning at least with the ancient Greeks and most likely others of whom I am sadly ignorant. One very succinct summary, however, was given in 1880 during a speech at Columbus, Ohio, by William Tecumseh Sherman: "There is many a boy here today who looks on war as all glory, but, boys, it is all hell."

Bibliography

I would like to give special thanks to Dr. Juricek of Pinole Pet Hospital, who kindly explained some very crucial details about sheep anatomy to me.

For those interested in reading more about some of the subjects touched on in this book, the following are sources I consulted while writing this mystery. None of these authors should be blamed for any of my errors of interpretation or for any of the twists of imagination I took. Where I have exercised just a bit too much imagination, I take full blame.

David Carpenter, *The Struggle for Mastery: Britain 1066-1284*, Oxford University Press, 2003

Anna Comnena, *The Alexiad*, trans. E. R. A. Sewter, Penguin, 1969

Jean Dunbabin, *Captivity and Imprisonment in Medieval Europe 1000-1300*, Palgrave Macmillan, 2002

Francesco Gabrieli, *Arab Historians of the Crusades*, trans. E. J. Costello, University of California Press, 1969

Joinville & Villehardouin, *Chronicles of the Crusades*, trans. Margaret R. B. Shaw, Penguin, 1963

Ronald C. Finucane, *Miracles and Pilgrims: Popular Beliefs in Medieval England*, St. Martin's Press, 1995

Patrick J. Geary, *Furta Sacra: Thefts of Relics in the Central Middle Ages*, Princeton University Press, 1990

Nicholas Orme and Margaret Webster, *The English Hospital: 1070-1570*, Yale University Press, 1995

Ralph B. Pugh, *Imprisonment in Medieval England*, Cambridge University Press, 1968